NO MORE HEROES

MICHELLE KAN

No More Heroes

First published on June 27, 2015
Second edition published February 2017
Fish & Swallow Publications

Cover illustration by Michelle Kan

Michelle Kan asserts the moral right to be identified as the author of this work.

Michelle Kan
Fish & Swallow Publications
http://nomoreheroesnovel.com

Ordering Information:
No More Heroes is available to order direct from the author at the address above.
Signed copies also available on request.

This is a work of fiction. Names, characters, businesses, places, events and incidents are either the products of the author's imagination or used in a fictitious manner. All stunts and actions depicted are included for entertainment purposes only and should not be attempted without supervision or prior experience.

Printed in the United States of America

iii, 266 p., lc22.8 cm.
ISBN 978- 1503294301

Second Edition
First Issue

Michelle Kan can be found at
http://fishandswallowproductions.com
http://facebook.com/fishandswallow

CONTENTS

PROLOGUE

Equilibrium was uneasy.

It was not always a simple job, being a Vigilante. Your work was cut out for you and you got to make your own rules, sure. You got a lot of fresh air and exercise and met some cool people from time to time, that was for certain. But sometimes the small-time crooks you apprehended refused to give in, or plans didn't go the way you wanted them to. Sometimes you didn't always get along with your partner, which could be difficult if you were in a real bind.

Equilibrium couldn't say that he always saw eye to eye with his partner, Shooting Star, but he'd be damned if they didn't try, and they got along well enough when it was a good day.

But today was not a good day. He and his partner had argued (over a small, ultimately insignificant thing, really) and the latter had left in a huff, saying that she needed some air. He had waited for her to return, but she did not.

That was three hours ago.

He left to go look for her after his text messages met no response and his calls went unanswered. It wasn't like Shooting Star to ignore him, even if they were having a disagreement. He searched the streets and tried all her usual haunts, but his attempts were met with nothing but disappointment, and a steadily growing sense of dread.

Perhaps a better vantage point was what he needed. Equilibrium hopped up onto a drainpipe, bolted to the wall of a nearby building, and began the climb up to the top. Once he was there, he quickly surveyed the surrounding buildings and found what he was looking for.

Stretched between his current location and a taller complex across the street was a steel cable, three centimetres wide – a single thread of the enormous wire web weaving the city together, from office block to apartment complex, to embassy mansion and telegraph pole. The cable hung over the street six storeys below, the precipitous drop inviting vertigo to anyone who might chance to look at it.

But vertigo was something that didn't bother him. Equilibrium moved to the edge of the building and, without hesitation, vaulted over the parapet and onto the cable. The steel below his feet swung a little under his weight, but he, unfazed, stayed perfectly upright. He crouched down, took the cable in both hands, and began to move.

With unbelievable deftness and an inhuman steadiness he scaled the cable, using his hands and feet, as easy as if he were a monkey, and began to make his way over to the opposite rooftop. Any other person would have surely fallen to their death long before now, but Equilibrium was not just any other person. After all, what were heights or drops or narrow pathways to a person who had the Ability of perfect balance?

He came to the end of the cable and reached up, grabbing the edge of the concrete and hauling himself up onto the top of the building. Settling on the rooftop he examined his improved view of the city, scanning the streets beneath. Scouring the alleyways and backstreets to the south side of the building, he suddenly noticed a figure down below, clad in familiar shades of reds and browns; inert and unmoving, slumped prone at the foot of the wall.

His breath caught in his chest.

Equilibrium hauled himself over the edge of the building and seized the drainpipe, quickly sliding down, jumping from the pipe over to a windowsill, letting himself drop to another sill below and leaping back to the drainpipe again. When he was mere metres off the ground he let go, hitting the ground and sprawling clumsily over all fours on his landing. He looked up and scrambled towards the still form, dropping heavily to his knees beside it.

"Hey. Hey!" he called. "Shooting Star!"
He grabbed her by the shoulders and shook her urgently. "Wake up!"

No response.

Equilibrium uttered an oath, took firm hold, then turned her over. Almost immediately he clasped both hands over his mouth and gave a shocked cry. Shooting Star's hair had fallen away from her face to reveal blank, wide, dead eyes and an open, gaping mouth. There was dried blood streaked from her nose and mouth and her face was drawn a terrible expression of surprise and fear. Her hoodie was damaged with knife slashes, there were burn marks on her hands and the soles of her shoes, and the knees of her jeans were torn and bloody.

Equilibrium fell back onto his elbows. He could feel his gorge rising. At once he felt hot and cold, his breathing coming quick and ragged.

"Oh God," he said. "Halley."

He turned and dry heaved into the gutter. Breathed hard and fast through his nose. Took a moment to try calm down. He glanced back at the dead body of his partner and wondered what kind of a monster had been able to wreak this kind of damage to a Vigilante as capable as Shooting Star had been.

"She put up a good last fight," a voice said. "If that gives you any peace of mind."

Equilibrium whipped his head around. A little distance behind him stood a figure clothed in black, taller than him, hands in the pockets of their jeans and their face obscured by the shadow of their hooded winter coat. Equilibrium got to his feet.

"You did this?" he demanded. The hooded figure shrugged a shoulder. Nonchalant.

"In a manner of speaking."

A dozen different impulses ran through Equilibrium at that moment. He wanted to demand of the figure why they had done what they did; he wanted to rush at them and destroy them for what they had done. A million different questions were fighting to be answered and a million different vengeances were waiting to be waged on this person who had so pitilessly killed his partner in such a brutal fight.

But other thoughts raced through his mind as well. Shooting Star, who could jump so easily to great heights without difficulty, had been a much better fighter than he had ever been. If she hadn't been able to win this fight, then there was no way that he would ever be able to.

So he turned and ran.

Equilibrium ran through the streets, away from the hooded figure and Shooting Star's dead body, trying to put as much distance
as he could between himself and his enemy. As he turned a corner
he suddenly saw ahead of him another figure dressed in black, hood
obscuring their face, a coil of something long and silvery at their
side. He skidded to a halt and turned to change direction – suddenly he felt something seize him around his ankle and a fierce
electric shock ran through his body.

He gave a strangled, gargling yell of agony, the sensation seeming to go on forever, every single muscle in his body feeling afire.
Abruptly as it had begun it ceased, and he fell clumsily to the
ground, the soles of his shoes hissing and smoking. Scrambling back
to his feet, his vision hazy, his mind foggy, he sought out the near-
est drainpipe and ran for it, grabbing on and climbing fast. His
hands were shaking but he kept his balance, clambering for the top
of the building and tumbling over the parapet and onto the rooftop.
He saw the steel cable connected to the next building and stumbled towards it when out of the shadows, a huge black dog lunged
towards him, hackles raised, snarling, and clamped down on his leg
with powerful jaws.

Equilibrium screamed and toppled hard onto the concrete. The
air was knocked from his lungs and he gasped for breath, heavily
winded.

The black dog let go of his bloodied leg; from the darkness it had
seemingly come from, two figures stepped out onto the dimly lit
rooftop to join them. They were the same two that Equilibrium
had seen – the tall, slim one in the winter coat and the one with

the coiled length of chain, both dressed in black from head to toe.

The tall one strode up to Equilibrium and grabbed him by the wrist. A feeling like a static shock ran through the Vigilante and he realised it might be fear. He tried to shove the hooded figure away but only earned a slap across the face for his troubles.

The figure grabbed Equilibrium by the collar of his sweat-shirt and hauled him up and over to the edge of the building, dangling him just above the ledge. Equilibrium scrabbled for purchase on the concrete but his toes were just far enough off the ground that he barely scuffed the surface.

"Nice try," the hooded figure said. "You get an A for effort."

The figure let go and stepped backwards. Equilibrium dropped onto the parapet. He gave a howl as the weight came back onto his injured leg. Then he felt something that he hadn't felt in a long time. It was a sort of dizziness, a light-headedness; a feeling like he was going to faint.

He was off balance.

For a moment everything seemed as if in slow motion. Equilibrium looked towards the hooded figure, dark surprise and a horrified realisation dawning on his face. The figure waved at him.

He pitched backwards. Wind rushed past his ears, the city lights shot by in a blur. As he fell, the words *so that's how* echoed blankly through his mind; two – no, three figures clothed in black stood watching him from the rooftop; the last and only thing he could think of as he fell was Shooting Star –

The ground rushed up to meet him.

CHAPTER ONE

THE NIGHT

The City at night could be a pretty thing.

Take this night, for instance. The way the lights from street-lamps, traffic lights and shop windows shone in the blackness gave a soft, gentle glow to the dark, a colourful reflection of the stars in the night sky above. The streets, wet from the evening rain, glittered like slick black crystal, and a veil of fog blanketed the ground, a faint white shroud against the severe grey concrete.

But it could also be a dangerous thing.

For while the lights provided a touch of tranquillity to the scenery, they could not brighten the end of each and every street, and as sure as the fog gave one the impression of walking through a cloud in the sky, it also provided convenient cover for those looking to cause trouble then make a quick getaway.

Tonight was one such case. Larceny was not an uncommon occurrence on a night like this, especially when weather conditions gave such an easy opportunity for thieves and other petty criminals to get away unseen. Someone was up to mischief in the City tonight, in the form of a small-time crook called Jan, who wore a beaten leather jacket and a backpack full of stolen goods on his back. Jan dashed through the streets, fog swirling in his wake, laughing as the sounds of a shop alarm echoed after him. All he had to do was get home safely and then he would be a richer and happier man.

He rounded the corner into a shopping street and continued running, when the most peculiar thing happened before him.

At first he thought he was dreaming – or perhaps it was the fog, playing tricks on his mind.

For before him, out of the reflection of a shop front window, a figure phased through the pane of glass, sneakers first, to swing himself onto the street, as easy and elegantly as if he were only passing through an open doorway. Jan stopped in his tracks, surprised. It was a Samoan boy, no older than eighteen at most, with untidy brown hair and blue eyes. As he landed on the concrete and straightened he pulled a cellphone out of the pocket of his white and grey hoodie. He held it up to his ear and stared straight at Jan. Jan stared back.

"I got him," the boy said. There was a hint of a smile on his face. Another voice, indistinct, replied. Jan couldn't hear. He didn't care to stay and listen either.

He turned and ran in the opposite direction. He heard shouts but he ignored them. He rounded another corner, running at full tilt through the mist when another utterly impossible thing happened right before his eyes.

Surely this time it had to be his eyes playing tricks on him – literally from out of the fog, whirling into existence to stand before him, came an olive-skinned girl with chestnut brown hair and dark green eyes. The hood of her indigo anorak was up, but she seemed the same age as the young man before; she carried in one hand a battered-looking softball bat and there was a cheeky grin on her face. She raised the bat to rest on her shoulder and gestured to Jan.

"Come on then!" she said.

Jan, utterly bewildered, turned and ran in yet another direction. First the young man and now this? What was going on? Was it the fog playing tricks on his mind? People didn't just phase through windows or materialise into existence from out of nowhere. That kind of thing just didn't happen – it was plain impossible.

The word rattled through his mind as he continued to run pell-mell down the street and towards an intersection. Impossible. Impossible. Impossible!

"Impossible!" Jan blurted out loud, as another girl stepped out from around the corner and swung a tyre iron into his solar plexus.

The effect would have been almost comical if it hadn't been so brutal. Jan flipped over from the force of the blow, crashing spread-eagled onto his back into the remains of the evening rain long since stopped. The goods in his backpack drove upwards, driving the rest of the air from his lungs. If the hit from the tyre iron hadn't already winded him, then the impact when he hit the ground made certain of that. Jan, wide-eyed and absolutely confounded, wheezed for air as he lay on the street and tried very hard not to move.

"Impossible," he croaked in disbelief. The girl stood over him and cast the tyre iron away nonchalantly. She was very tall, with a long brown ponytail and hazel eyes, the sleeves of a khaki me-chanic's jumpsuit tied around her waist.

"What was that?" the girl asked. "I couldn't hear you." Jan noticed a weathered crowbar held loosely in the girl's other hand and thought it might be best not to answer. Not that he had sufficient air in his lungs to do otherwise.

The girl rested the end of her crowbar on her shoulder.

"Just calm down," she said, seemingly nonplussed by Jan's distress. "Take big, slow breaths. Relax your muscles. You'll be alright in a minute."

Jan tried to relax. There was a faint sound, a kind of *whoosh*, and the tall girl looked up. Jan turned his head slightly and his eyes widened even more. Once more, out of the fog, the girl with the chestnut hair appeared out of nowhere to join them, and from the surface of a rain puddle, glittering with the reflections of the street lights above, came the untidy-haired boy, climbing out onto the concrete to join them. Despite having seemingly risen from the surface of a body of water, he was completely dry.

"Well that was successful," the chestnut-haired girl said, looking down at Jan. He could only stare bug-eyed back at the three youths, still wheezing for breath.

The one with the ponytail grunted. "Only because I was here."

"Here, Mallory." The boy stooped to pick up the discarded tyre iron.

The ponytailed one, Mallory, held up a hand. The boy tossed the tyre iron lightly towards her and suddenly it was in her hand, fast as lightning. It happened so fast, Jan thought, that it was almost as if it had been drawn to her like she was a magnet.

Jan began to make a high-pitched whining noise. He wasn't sure he could take that many more impossible things in one night. The three youths grimaced at the sound.

"What do we do with him now?" the boy said.

"Well that's a no-brainer," the chestnut-haired girl replied. "Help me with this guy."

She crouched down and began to grab Jan by one of his arms. Mallory lowered her crowbar.

"We'll take him to the station and give back the stuff he stole. It'll be a nice little present for whoever's on duty tonight."

Clare, Linus and Mallory stepped back out into the city streets and breathed in the cool night air.

"I'd say this was a pretty productive evening," Clare said cheerfully. She pulled her hood back off her head and rested the length of her softball bat across the back of her neck.

"If by productive you mean 'we sat around for ages and waited for the sound of alarms', then yes, it was rather productive," Mallory said drily. She slid her crowbar into the belt loop of her jumpsuit and tucked her tyre iron under her arm. "We should really find a better way to figure out what's happening around town without having to sit out in the cold for hours."

Linus laughed. "But isn't that like our thing? Kick our heels and wait for the action to come to us?"

"Maybe it's your thing, but my hands get all antsy when they've been still for too long. Don't you know what they say about idle hands?"

"Idle hands do light work?"

"I think you're mixing up your proverbs there, champ."

"Aw, come on, Mallory," Clare said easily. She strolled slightly ahead of her friends. "Things aren't that bad! Any night that we come out is productive by default. If we didn't come out regularly like this then we'd never get you out of the garage."

Mallory made a sound that might have been laughter.

"Besides," Clare continued. "You know the nights we decide to call it quits early are always the ones where something good happens right after we up and leave."

"Alright," Mallory replied, a wry smile on her face. "Point taken. So can we get back home now? I've got a garage that needs tending to."

Clare opened her mouth to reply when the sound of shattering glass pierced the night. The three of them turned sharply towards the direction of the noise. Clare and Linus glanced at Mallory.

"You were saying?"

Mallory sighed and rolled her eyes.

"Okay, fine," she said, pulling her crowbar from her hip. "We'll have a look."

As they turned and began to make their way towards the source of the noise, Clare pulled her hood back up and dashed into the fog – with a whirl of the hem of her anorak she vanished into the mist, as if she had been a part of it all along. Linus ran towards the glass doors of an office building and dove hands-first into it, disappearing into the reflective surface like a ghost passing through walls.

"Hey!" Mallory shouted after them. She cursed, then picked up her pace and started running. She hated when they took off ahead of her when they knew she couldn't follow.

Following the noise took the three into a long-abandoned industrial district of the City. Clare and Linus arrived first, Clare travelling with and out of the fog and Linus alighting from an apartment window. They stared, open-mouthed and taken aback, by the sight before them.

Blood and bruises and injuries all that kind of thing, those were sights that they could handle. That kind of thing happened all the time, especially if you played sports. Linus had taken more than his fair share of high-speed tumbles running track in high school, and Clare could recall a couple of accidents and some minor concussions on the softball pitch when she and Mallory used to play for the school team. But big steel-and-glass warehouses caught on fire – that was not something they were used to seeing.

The fire didn't seem to have been going for very long, but even from the distance they were at, they could already feel the heat of the flames on their skin. Some of the windows were shattered; whether this was from the heat or if they had already been broken, they couldn't tell.

"Clare," Linus began, doubtful. "I don't know if we're equipped for this kind of thing."

Clare thought for a moment. True, there wouldn't be any fog in there, so she wouldn't be able to do much, and judging from the gradually decreasing number of windows, Linus wouldn't be able to either.

Mallory joined them then, out of breath from running. She grabbed Linus' arm and tried to regain her composure.

"You two are awful," she panted. "I hate when you take off without me."

A crash and a sudden cry suddenly split through the growing roar of flames; a distinct shout of pain from somewhere within the burning wreckage of the building. Clare, Linus and Mallory looked at each other in surprise and dismay. Mallory glanced at Clare. She was getting that look on her face, the one that usually preceded a thoughtful pause and the declaration of a new plan. Mallory knew that look all too well. So did Linus.

"You'd be useless in there," Mallory said plainly. Clare broke from deep thought and smiled at her friend.

"Maybe," she replied. "Or maybe not." She swung her softball bat up to her shoulder. "People do this kind of thing all the time without having special powers, right?"

Mallory sighed. She eyed the steel structure of the burning warehouse and made a quick decision.

"Here. Hold this." She thrust her tyre iron and crowbar into Linus' arms and began walking fast towards the warehouse, untying her jumpsuit from around her waist and pulling her arms through the sleeves.

"What are you doing?" Linus called after her, alarmed.

"Stay here!" Mallory shouted back over her shoulder. "I mean it! And call the fire brigade!"

She marched towards the burning warehouse with quick, determined strides, pulling her ponytail up into a tight knot, the set expression on her face belying the unease she felt in her gut. She was older than both Clare and Linus by almost a year and had known them both long enough to understand that they would have gone in unprepared if she hadn't been there. She couldn't tell if it was selflessness or stupidity but either way, without a plan their noble (or foolish) intentions would have gotten them into even worse trouble.

Mallory was fully capable of taking charge but preferred to quietly follow; nonetheless, even though she was fine with Clare being their de facto leader, she wasn't averse to giving them both firm orders if she felt she was in a better position to lead than her friend. And in this case, she was best equipped of them all.

Mallory drew close to the warehouse, approaching the front side that was not yet in flames, ducking back as another window exploded into pieces. She ran towards the doorway, kicking it in with two sharp strikes of her boot, and charged into the building, covering her mouth with the crook of her arm; the immediate heat wave was almost overwhelming and the roar of the flames was frightening but she choked down her anxiety and began searching the building, running down the length of the floor.

"Hello!" she yelled over the cacophony. "Is anybody here?"

A creaking from above her – she looked up just in time to see part of the steel framing collapse and drop down towards her. Mallory threw up her hands and with an exclamation almost like a battle cry, moved her arms as if to shove the falling debris aside in midair. As like two south poles of a magnet coming close together, the falling steel suddenly changed direction, following the motion of Mallory's throw to land with a crash against a heap of scrap metal near a wall.

A flash of movement out of the corner of her eye – Mallory whirled around to see a dark figure escape through a doorway to her left.

"Hey!" she called after them. She made to follow but then –

"Is someone there?!" a voice shouted. Mallory turned back around, searching for the source of the call. She saw then, at the far end of the room, a form pinned under a mass of debris. Immediately she ran towards them, jumping over collapsed rubble and deflecting falling debris as she could.

She finally reached the figure at the end of the room to see a young man lying on the ground, face-down, his legs trapped under a pile of debris and the same steel framing that had almost fallen on top of Mallory just moments earlier. She grimaced – she would have to move the mass and there was no real subtle way to do it.

"Don't move!" she said. "Lie back down."

Despite his predicament the young man gave a laugh. "Not like I really have a choice here!"

Mallory ignored him and planted her feet firmly on the concrete growing steadily hotter beneath her feet. She made a powerful sweeping gesture with her arms; the steel was shifted up off the young man and thrown across the floor to the opposite side of the room. Mallory ran forwards and began to push the rest of the debris away. The young man looked back over his shoulder in surprise to see that which had pinioned him to the ground was no longer there. Now that he was no longer pinned down, Mallory could properly see his face.

"Did you do that?" he asked her, astonishment clear on his face.

He was Polynesian, Māori perhaps, with dark hair and dark eyes, older and bigger than she was. Sweat had slicked his hair into rough spikes and his t-shirt was torn and burned in places, a rip in his left sleeve revealing a swirling dark green koru tattoo on the shoulder beneath.

Mallory waved off his questions, quickly examining him.

"Are you hurt?" she asked. "Can you walk?" She began to help him up.

The young man jerked his head towards the removed debris. "Apart from that mess, I'm fine. Now get me out of here before this place comes down."

Outside the burning warehouse, Clare and Linus stood watching the inferno spread and grow to engulf more and more of the building in its fiery maw. Linus still cradled Mallory's tyre iron and crowbar in his arms and Clare's softball bat dangled loosely from her left hand. The fire brigade, supposedly, was still five minutes away. Some civilians had started to gather some way behind them, gaping and gasping at the sheer size of the blaze.

"Are you sure we should have let her go in there by herself?"

Clare shrugged a shoulder in a noncommittal way, but she had an uncertain look on her face.

"You know how Mallory gets when she puts on that voice."

They fell into silence, but for the roar of the flames. There was another explosion of breaking glass.

Clare and Linus looked at each other, nodded stoutly, then ran towards the building. The heat was intense and for a moment they were beaten back by the severity of it, but they continued on towards and through the doorway they had seen their friend disappear into, shouting her name. Flames and debris were everywhere and they could barely see a thing, but they made their way into the next area of the warehouse, coughing from the smoke, tears in their eyes.

"Mallory! Mal!" The sound of movement behind them. "Mallory?"

Clare and Linus turned; someone moved out onto the floor before them but it was not their friend. Instead, a figure with short black hair and piercing brown eyes beat through a flurry of flames to stand before them, a large blue scarf covering the bottom half of their face and obscuring their identity. They were smaller than Clare, but not by much; a drawstring bag with a blue and brown strap was slung around their shoulder, white sweatbands adorned their wrists, and they wore a simple black singlet and grey marle sweatpants.

The figure saw Clare and Linus and their eyes widened.

"What the hell are you doing here?" they demanded, their voice muffled by the scarf over their mouth. "Get out of here before this place collapses!"

"But our friend–" Clare began, pointing down the length of the building.

The figure uttered a curse under their breath and began to run towards where Clare was pointing.

"Hell's teeth – if anyone in here snuffs it, I swear to God–"

A sudden rumble shook the building from head to toe and there came a terrible screeching groan from above their heads. The masked figure glanced up at the ceiling and swore, running back towards Clare and Linus.

"Get out of here!" they shouted. Clare and Linus were too slow to react but the figure was fast, almost too fast – they grabbed Linus by his collar and the back of his jeans; Linus saw where this was going and began to protest ("Wait, *wait*!!") but the figure abruptly lifted him off his feet with much, much more strength than their stature would have suggested, and hurled him bodily through a wall of flames and out of the space where there was once a window. Linus hit the concrete outside with a heavy *thump* and *oomph!* and rolled clumsily across the ground, broken glass crunching beneath him, the tyre iron and the crowbar skittering ahead of him, coughing the smoke from his lungs. Clare came after, hitting the ground in a similar ungraceful fashion, her softball bat following her with a series of *clang*s and rolling away.

The two of them pushed themselves up onto their elbows and looked back at the building in time to see part of the roofing collapse where they had just been.

Mallory and the young man were just about to exit through one of the rolling steel doors at the front side of the building, warped from the heat of the inferno surrounding them, when a pile of rubble crashed down just in front of them, blocking off their safe exit. The young man shouted a warning but she had been too slow to react; some of the rubble struck him on the head, turning him into a massive deadweight and bringing them both to the floor.

Mallory wasn't usually one to panic but she was starting to panic now – the growing flames behind them meant that they couldn't go back, her powers only worked on metals, and she didn't know if they could safely navigate the rubble the way that they were, with the young man out cold. She hoped Clare and Linus had called the fire brigade, and that they were coming soon.

A voice suddenly rose out of the smoke and flames behind her.

"Hey! Stop where you are!"

Mallory turned awkwardly to see a slight, black haired figure run up towards her, a bandanna covering their nose and mouth.

Before Mallory could even think, the figure rushed past, grabbed one of the chunks of fallen concrete, then heaved it to the side with a roar. Mallory stared, mouth agape, as the figure continued to shove the rubble aside, piece by piece, with more strength that she could have possibly imagined from a person of their size. The figure seized one final piece of rubble and hurled it towards the warped steel door and it ripped through with a horrible sound of tearing metal.

The figure turned and ran back towards Mallory, grabbing the young man from her and pulling his arm over his own shoulder.

"Go!" they yelled to Mallory, over the sound of flames. Mallory nodded dumbly and staggered to her feet, still stunned from the display of strength she had just seen. She ran for the makeshift doorway – outside she could see the flashing red lights of fire trucks, the blotted outlines of a gathered crowd, and the silhouettes of Clare and Linus, running towards her. The figure followed a little distance behind, pulling the unconscious young man with her.

No sooner had Mallory exited the warehouse than an explosion tore through it – a shockwave, hot and violent, threw her off her feet and sent her sprawling and skittering, painfully, across the asphalt.

The explosion knocked Clare and Linus backwards as well, but they were far enough away that they weren't sent tumbling across the ground. Still, they felt the wave of heat on their skin, and they raised their arms to shield their faces.

Firefighters ran past them dressed in full gear, dragging heavy hoses behind them, shouting and relaying orders to each other. They positioned themselves around the blazing wreckage of the warehouse, aiming powerful jets of water at the flames.

Clare and Linus clambered back to their feet and ran towards Mallory. A few people had rushed to her aid as she was sent flying and one of them was helping her to her feet, holding her hand and supporting her as she stood.

"Mallory!" Clare called.

The girl looked up at the sound of her name, the call seeming to break her out of her daze, and began to jog towards Clare and Linus, thanking the people who had helped her with a wave.

Clare and Linus pulled Mallory into a tight, fierce hug, which the taller girl received without complaint.

"God, I was so worried!" Clare exclaimed, squeezing Mallory tighter. "Don't do that again!"

"Hey, next time you feel the need to march into an inferno by yourself – please don't." Linus' tone was an attempt to be cool and calm but the worry underneath was evident.

Mallory tried to smile. "Yeah," she said. "Sorry."

"Well that was stupid," an annoyed voice cut in. Clare, Linus and Mallory broke from their group hug to see the masked, black-haired figure approach them, the unconscious young man still draped around their shoulders.

Mallory stepped towards them.

"You really saved my hide in there," she said, grateful. "Thanks. I mean it."

"Same here," Clare added. "Thank you."

The figure grunted and set the young man down onto the ground gently.

"Don't mention it," they said. "Just don't make a habit of it, alright?"

"Who are you anyway?" Linus asked. It was a question they all wanted to know the answer to.

"Me?" The figure straightened up and dusted off the knees of their sweatpants. They pulled the blue scarf away from their mouth to reveal the face of a girl – Asian, maybe Chinese – probably not that much older than the young man lying at her feet.

The girl stepped towards them and held out a soot-streaked hand.

"My name's Resonance," she said. "I'm a Vigilante."

CHAPTER TWO

REPERCUSSIONS

The fire was continuing to rage on, but the firefighters were starting to win the battle. After paramedics had checked them for smoke inhalation and declared them all okay, Clare, Linus, Mallory and Resonance sat in the back of the ambulance. The young man Mallory had helped rescue lay on a gurney, still unconscious, an oxygen mask over his face and bandages over the burns on his arms.

Despite having only recently emerged from a blazing inferno, Resonance seemed perfectly calm, as if narrowly escaping exploding buildings was something that she did on a regular basis. Clare, Linus and Mallory were still a little shaken, having realised only afterwards that things could have gone a lot worse than they had. Mallory personally couldn't wait to get back home to her garage and her tools and take a moment to sit down at her workbench and regain her composure, but she was just as curious as Clare and Linus to find out more about this mysterious stranger who had come to them at exactly the right moment.

"I didn't realise there were many in the City with powers like us." Linus spoke first, saying the words that they were all thinking.

"Powers? You mean Abilities?"

"'Abilities'?"

"Yeah, that's what they're called." Resonance settled herself at the end of the unconscious young man's gurney. "'Abilities' keeps it nice and neutral-sounding. Whether what you've got in a pain in the ass or the greatest thing in the world, that term just about covers it. And of course there are others," she laughed. "A couple hundred thousand people in the City alone and you think you're the only ones with Abilities?"

"Well, we know we're not the only ones," Clare cut in, a bit miffed at the older girl's laughter. "I mean, we know about Fisticuffs."

"I think anyone who's anyone knows about Fisticuffs," Resonance replied. "Fisticuffs is an army of one. But no, I get what you're saying. There are plenty of us around, we just keep on the down low. If you look a little harder you might be able to spot us."

"You said you were a vigilante?"

"Vigilante. With a capital 'V'." She held up two fingers to indicate. "And yeah, that's what we call ourselves. You haven't been in the business long, have you?"

"Business?"

"Night patrols. Hunting down bad guys, rescuing kittens, all that jazz."

"Oh. No. Just a few months. Half a year at most."

"After you got your Abilities, right?"

"I – well, yeah, I guess so."

"Yeah, I thought so." Resonance leaned forwards, resting her elbows on her knees, and studied them all carefully.

"Your Ability," she finally said. "It feels like having a ton of extra energy that you don't know how to handle, right? Especially at night. No matter what ungodly early hour you get up in the morning or how much you do during the day, you never feel worn out by the end of it. Sometimes it's hard to get to sleep, or your hands get all jittery, or you feel like running a mile for the hell of it. So you think hey, if I can't go to bed at night then I might as well do something with all this extra mileage. Do some good with my Ability. Fight crime or something. Am I right?"

Clare, Linus and Mallory were stunned. In just a few seconds, Resonance had described exactly a situation that they themselves had found hard to fully grasp. The Vigilante smiled at them.

"Right on point, aren't I? It's the same with almost everyone who has an Ability. There's a couple dozen of us in the City alone, and there's even more over in other places. Those of us that take to the streets at night, we call ourselves Vigilantes. We give ourselves new names. We make our own rules, we try to make good with what we got. We meet other people like us. Not everyone is going to use their Ability in the same way, sure, and you'll get a few bad apples, but it's not that bad of a deal. You wear yourself out enough to be able to get some sleep, anyway."

"So 'Resonance' is your alias?"

"You betcha."

"And you've been around for a while, I take it," Linus said.

Resonance nodded. "Yeah," she replied. "I was seventeen when I got my Ability and I'm twenty-two now, so you do the math. I used to live in the City Over and do my rounds there."

"Sorry," Mallory broke in. "I don't mean to interrupt. But your Ability... what is it?"

The Vigilante gave an impish grin.

"Have a guess."

Clare, Linus and Mallory glanced at each other. They had each seen definite displays of incredible strength, from being flung bodily out of a window to chucking massive blocks of rubble aside as if they were nothing. But Clare and Linus were equally sure they had seen Resonance move very fast across the floor of the warehouse before the roof came down on top of them.

"Strength and speed?" Clare suggested. Resonance shook her head.

"Not quite. Want to try again?"

Mallory thought for a second and realised something. When the explosion had happened, the force of it had sent her flying across the ground; any distance closer and she might have been hurt even worse. But hadn't Resonance been behind her, carrying extra weight no less?

"When the building exploded," Mallory began slowly. "The shockwave knocked me off my feet. But you were only just behind me and you weren't hurt."

Resonance winked at Mallory. "You got it," she said. "Shockwaves, kinetic energy, all that kind of thing. I can absorb that energy and store it for later if I want to. Comes in handy when there's earthquakes or exploding things."

"So that explosion before…"

"Yeah. All in here now." She flexed her arms, which were impressively fit. "If I knew the first thing about physics I could probably understand how it worked a lot better, but you get the idea. Anyway."

Resonance stood up and reached over, taking the oxygen mask

off the young man's face.

"Woah, hey," Clare was alarmed. "What are you doing?"

The Vigilante pulled the young man up into sitting position and slung him over her shoulders.

"Oh, don't mind me," she said. "I'm just going to take this guy home. He'll be fine, I'm sure."

"I don't think the paramedics are going to like that," Linus replied, troubled. Resonance laughed openly.

"They never do," she said. "Paramedics, fire brigades, the police… they're all the same. They don't like us and we're not crazy about them. 'Wrong place at the wrong time' isn't really a defensible position when it's the third time around and you've got some guy's blood on your knuckles all three times."

Clare, Linus and Mallory all glanced awkwardly at one another.

"They know about us?" Clare asked. "About Vigilantes?"

"Well, not exactly." Resonance shrugged a shoulder. "Like I said, we try and keep on the down low, but sometimes things just get out of hand. As far as the police are concerned we're just a bunch of troublemakers, so the more you can avoid them, the better, really. Anyway," she straightened up. "I should go before questions start being asked. And so should you, for that matter." She eyed the three youths sternly. "Go home and get some rest. I know I'm going to go and have a nice long sleep. You three should as well."

She stepped out of the ambulance, the young man draped around her shoulders as if he weighed nothing, and offered a smile.

"Maybe I'll see you guys again some time," she said. "'Til then, don't get into too much trouble. Rest up. Keep safe. There's not always going to be someone available to come and save your butts. And also," she twisted back mid-turn. "A word of advice. If you're thinking about continuing to do this kind of thing seriously, it's a good idea to figure out an Alias."

She waved, and then – before any of them could respond – was gone. Clare ducked her head around the side of the ambulance to see a strange and misshapen looking silhouette disappearing into the shadow of the streets heading back towards the city centre.

"Well," Clare said. She turned back to face her friends and shrugged. "I guess I am pretty knackered. What say we go home?"

It was quiet.

In the darkness, a young man, Māori, dark hair and dark eyes, opened his eyes. His vision was foggy. His head hurt, his hands felt raw – heck, everything about him ached.

He vaguely remembered a dream where he had been in hell and everything was on fire. No, wait, that hadn't been a dream – there really had been a fire, somewhere, and it had been all around him, but now it was cool and dark and quiet. Maybe that meant he was safe. Or dead. He couldn't really remember what had happened, and it was hard to tell.

"You feeling alright?" A voice from out of the dark.

He turned his head. At the other end of the room, a shadow rose from a chair and crossed the floor, leaning over and turning on a lamp beside his head. He squinted in the sudden light, raising a hand to his eyes, peering blearily at the figure above him. His eyes focused and he let his arm drop back down to his side.

"Oh," he said. "It's you."

Resonance scoffed. "Sorry to get your hopes up, buddy."

"I didn't mean it that way." He pushed himself up onto his elbows and reached over, turning the bedside lamp back off. Resonance turned it back on; he grimaced. She took his head in her hands and peered at his eyes.

"What are you doing?" he said irritably, trying to bat her away.

"Checking for concussion."

"I'm fine."

"How many fingers am I holding up?"

"*Aue*, Res, I'm fine!"

"Then how many fingers, dangit."

"Three! It's three."

"Good."

Resonance let go, sitting down on the bed by the young man's side. He shifted backwards cautiously to rest against the wall and examined the bandages on his arms.

"You had me worried for a minute there, you know," Resonance said. There was a look of genuine concern on her face. "If those kids hadn't been there I might not have found you in time."

The young man suddenly remembered something. "There was a girl who was with me in the fire."

"Yeah," Resonance replied. "You owe her a thanks next time you see her. Her and her friends have Abilities too, but I don't think they're very experienced at using them yet. Don't change the subject though." She tapped him on the back of his hand. "Next time you get into that kind of mess on your own, I might not be around to bail you out."

"*Aroha mai.* Sorry. Things just kind of… happened."

"What did happen?"

The young man looked at his bandaged arm. He flexed his fingers, slowly. A pained expression crossed his features.

"I'm not really sure," he replied. "But whatever it was… I don't think you should get hurt for a while."

Resonance looked at the young man's hand then back up to his eyes. A look of slow realisation dawned on her face, followed by alarm.

"Yeah," he said in a low voice, watching her reaction.

Resonance covered her mouth with her hand. She was silent for a long while. When she lowered her hand, the young man could see her mouth was drawn into a taut white line.

"He's not going to like this," Resonance said grimly.

"Are you guys thinking about what Resonance said?"

Linus looked away from the television and Mallory glanced up from her workbench. Their encounter with the Vigilante had been the previous night and while the events were still clearly imprinted into their minds, the details of who had said what was beginning to get a little hazy when compared to the memory of the exploding warehouse.

"…Which part?" Linus asked eventually, uncertain. "The part about not getting into trouble any more?"

"No, no. Not that part." Clare hopped down from her perch on top of the washing machine and crossed the garage floor, jumping onto the sofa beside Linus and throwing an arm around him.

"You know how she was saying every Vigilante chooses an Alias? We should do that." There was a grin on her face. "It'd be cool."

Mallory looked back to her workbench and picked her ratchet screwdriver, fitting the end into the screws on the contraption in front of her. "I think Aliases serve for a bigger purpose than just being cool, Clare. Like protecting their identities, perhaps."

"So it'd be cool and practical. What better! I know how you like practical."

"I also like the bit where she suggested we stay out of trouble for a while. Relaxing and staying alive! What a winning combination. I like staying alive."

"Okay, so the whole fire thing was a little intense. But you saved a guy's life, didn't you? Alright, new plan." Clare got to her feet. She put a hand to her chin like she was thinking, then smacked her fist down into the palm of her other hand. "I got it. Okay."

She sat herself back down, pulled her laptop into her lap, and started tapping away.

"There!" she turned the machine around, showing Linus and Mallory the screen. Linus craned his neck to look.

"'Cavall Robinson'?" he read out loud. Clare nodded.

"Yeah, he's this electronica guy on tour. He's going to be playing at The Niterie tomorrow night. That's staying out of trouble, right?"

"Isn't The Niterie a club?" Mallory put in. "Neither of you drink. How are you planning to get in without ID?"

"Ah, but that's where you're wrong. It's impossible to be a live music fan in this town without an ID, so Linus and I got our 18+

cards especially to go to gigs."

Mallory laughed. "I should have known."

"I'm down," Linus said. "You should come with, Mallory. You have ID, don't you?"

"Even better, I have my license. You two should get onto that as well. It's a bit more useful than an ID solely for gigs."

"Why would I need to drive a car when I can do this?" Linus stuck his arm into the screen of Clare's laptop. Across the room, a hand came out of the surface of the window and waved. Mallory made a face.

"Don't do that."

"But for real, Mal. Come along, it'll be fun." Clare smiled sweetly at Mallory. The taller girl shook her head.

"Thanks, but I'll pass. I'll hold down the fort while you two go. Enjoy yourselves."

"Alright then. If you change your mind, the offer still stands. Anyway," Clare closed her laptop shut and stretched her arms. "I might go for a walk. Anyone want to come with?"

"Sounds good to me."

"Mallory?"

"Next time. I think I'm getting somewhere with this thing." Mallory gestured to the contraption on the workbench.

"Okay then. Good luck! Call us if anything comes up."

"Will do."

Mallory listened as Clare and Linus left and waited for the closing of the door. She turned her gaze back to her workbench.

A small stack of metal plates sat piled at the corner of the tabletop, useful for all kinds of situations. Mallory hesitated, then held out her hand towards them. She concentrated hard and prayed that this would work.

Nothing happened.

Mallory lowered her hand, then tried again. Reached her hand out for the plates. Willed them to come into her hand, like they always did.

Still nothing.

The stack of metal plates stayed as they were, neither attracted to nor repelled by her. Mallory lowered her arm and stared at her hands numbly. A feeling of anxiety crept into her chest and made her suddenly feel cold. She had suspected something had changed about her since returning home after their adventure the previous night, but now she was sure.

Somewhere, somehow, Mallory had lost her Ability.

CHAPTER THREE

CRACK THE EARTH

Under cover of night, a lone Vigilante ran through the streets of the City, keeping to the shadows of the buildings and avoiding the glow of the streetlamps above. He was soundless and stealthy, drawing no attention to himself as he carried on through the city centre. He was swathed in shades of greys and navies, a scarf covering his nose and mouth and obscuring his identity. Had anyone noticed him, they would have been in awe at the style with which he carried himself – he cut through the night fog with long, fast strides, strong and steady, and his footfalls were soft and silent.

The way he moved through the City and navigated the obstacles it presented to him in its designs could only have been described as *flow*, a fluent and seemingly effortless grace that carried him around sharp corners, over walls and down flights of steps, as easy as if he were only the night air circulating through the channels between buildings.

He ran out of the suburbs, through the sleeping central business district and into the more nocturnal domains of the City only just awoken, going unnoticed by those who were now flocking to the thumping rhythm of clubs and bars, brightly lit to signal the unfolding of a night just begun. These three areas were usually the most common for trouble (and thus, perfect areas for the enacting of Vigilante action), but he was not interested in what the City's nightlife had to offer this evening, be it music or dancing or even petty crime. He had a destination in mind.

His run carried him to the derelict industrial sector of the city and he finally slowed down and came to a halt. There it was – the abandoned warehouse, burned half down in a massive fire only two nights ago. Lines of yellow caution tape declaring '*DANGER*' and '*KEEP OUT*' cordoned off the building, which was charred black as coal. Parts of the roof were collapsed and shards of broken glass still littered the concrete around the outside.

The Vigilante took this all in with a searching eye and walked towards the wreckage. Ducking under the caution tape he approached the building, making a short run up to a wall and pulling himself up and into the inside through a space where a window used to be.

Two nights ago this place had been a roaring inferno, but now it was eerily quiet. Ash and debris covered the floor and he could see the twinkling constellations in the sky above through the gaping holes in the ceiling. He wasn't here to stargaze though – he was here for a much more important purpose.

He cased the interior of the warehouse, slowly, methodically. There wasn't much to be found, but he did notice some things. On some of the walls still standing were marks that looked like gouges from a bladed weapon, and several of the concrete pillars that were left bore signs of having had small chunks taken out them. A door near the back of one of the rooms in the back seemed as if it had been caved in with something bearing the force of a sledgehammer.

He paused in his search to survey the area at large, deep in contemplation. All these marks could be nothing, left over from a time long before the fire even began. Or they could be something. Signs of a fight that had ended in arson and attempted murder.

He was so lost in thought that he didn't notice the sound of creaking that had begun to emanate from the ceiling above him. A screech of buckling metal broke him from his deliberations and he looked up in alarm, too late to move – a discordant crash and the rest of the concrete and steel framing of the broken roofing above came down upon him, sending a thick grey cloud of dust and ash into the air.

The Niterie was a modestly sized nightclub on the edges of the nightlife district, particularly popular with fans of live electronic music for its excellent stage setup, and well-known for its hosting of acts of both local and international acclaim. As such, on the evening that Clare and Linus decided to attend the performance of Cavall Robinson, The Niterie was already full of people dressed up and ready to have a roaring good time, long before the main act had even arrived.

Clare and Linus weren't much of the clubbing or partying sort, but they had a go at dressing up anyway, with Clare wearing a nice dress and Linus in his favourite t-shirt and best jeans. There was a line at the door when they arrived, with a massive, burly looking man with bleach-blond spikes asking patrons for ID in a heavy Russian accent as they came in.

Inside they could see the stage had already been set up for Robinson's performance, which seemed as if it was going to be as much a light show as it was a musical act. A technician was tending to some of the gear, an earpiece in her ear, occasionally speaking a few words into the microphone at the end of her headset. Loud dance music was pumping through the speakers, shaking the ground in rhythmic heartbeats, and the youths already on the dance floor were whooping loudly.

"This is nice," Clare said cheerfully. She had to raise her voice to be heard. "I haven't come out to see any gigs in a while."

"Is it usually this loud?" Linus asked, a slight frown creasing his forehead.

"Oh yeah, this is your first time to a club gig, huh? Aw, poor baby," Clare nudged Linus, grinning playfully at him. "Too much for your ears already?"

"Your old lady ears may be messed up already but I like to keep mine intact."

"Hey, you watch your mouth, young whippersnapper! We're the same age now."

They settled themselves down at two stools by the bar and a well-dressed bartender approached them, cleaning a glass.

"Hey, guys. What'll it be?" She smiled dazzlingly at them.

Clare fished her wallet from her bag. "I'll have an orange juice, thanks. Linus?"

"Oh, yeah. I'll have the same."

"You got it." The bartender winked at them and went to get their drinks.

"Do you think choosing an Alias would be like choosing a name for a band?" Clare said suddenly. Linus laughed.

"Are you still thinking about that?"

"Damn straight, I am! Now that I know it's an actual thing we should totally do it."

"Clare, aren't we supposed to be having a night off from getting into trouble? Or like, thinking about it?"

"Oh pshaw, trouble is my middle name," Clare waved a hand in a mock *away-with-you* gesture. "But I see your point. Okay. For the rest of the night, no more thinking about Aliases or Vigilantes. Nada. Zipped it."

The bartender returned and set two glasses down in front of them. There was a brief lull in conversation as they sipped at their straws.

"Actually, you know what would be really cool," Clare turned to look at Linus, a mischievous glint in her eye. "Imagine if you were famous *and* a Vigilante!"

"Clare!"

Loud cheering suddenly broke out over at the dance floor and they turned to see a handsome, dark-haired youth walk out onto the stage, wearing a short-sleeved denim shirt buttoned to the neck and grey jeans. He raised his arms, the crowd went wild, and the music began.

Mallory, first and foremost, was a mechanic.

Machines and engines and all those kinds of goods, things that worked because of a lot of smaller things inside them – that was the kind of stuff that she liked. Poring carefully over contraptions, taking them apart and putting them back together, fixing things...

that was what she considered to be her true calling. Her Ability to attract and repel metal objects at will, like a magnet, was a very useful power all things considered, but it wasn't something that she relied on too often. She could summon a wrench into her hand from across the room, sure, but she preferred to walk over and get it herself when she could.

Still though, the recent loss of her Ability disconcerted her, and made her start thinking hard about the kind of changes this would bring. She paced the garage floor, deep in thought. If an Ability was like a surge of extra energy that enabled you to stay active throughout the dead hours, then wouldn't losing it automatically mean that she would revert to the way she was before all of this happened? She looked at her watch – it was barely eleven o'clock, but already she was feeling tired. She reckoned she'd be in bed long before Clare and Linus returned. Assuming this kept up, she wouldn't be able to accompany her friends on night patrols anymore – without her Ability she wouldn't be able to keep up with them. But if she let them go unchecked for too long, who knows what kind of mischief they'd get into?

Mallory stopped pacing and whirled around to face her workbench. Well, if she were no longer useful then she would *make* herself be useful. It was time to take action. She stalked over to the workbench, plonking herself down in her chair, and drummed her fingers on the wood. A thought had occurred to her. Ideas raced through her mind. Her previous weariness was gone and had been replaced by an electric wakefulness.

Mallory thought about her strengths. She'd had a pretty good grasp of her Ability, definitely, but her real talent lay with working with her hands. Making things, knowing how they worked. And she definitely knew how magnets worked.

She caught sight of the stack of metal plates on the corner of her workbench and her eyes lit up. She leaned over, grabbed some of the plates, and reached for a box of rivets. If she couldn't have her Ability anymore, then she would make something to emulate it instead.

Linus' ears were ringing from the sound of the music long after it had stopped. Robinson had been incredible, a wizard working his magic on his Launchpad and his keys, the light show dazzling and bewitching. He had thrown himself into his music, dancing with the beats, swaying trancelike with the sounds, pouring his heart and soul into the melodies of his songs when he played. After he had done his bows and an encore and left the stage, Linus turned back around on his barstool and looked at Clare with wide, excited eyes. Clare nodded back at him enthusiastically.

"Right?" she exclaimed, over the crowd's shouts for another encore. "There literally is nothing else quite like watching electronica live."

"Forget being a superhero," Linus replied, still in awe. "I want to do what that guy does."

"It takes a lot of work," a voice said. Linus turned to his left to see a well-dressed man leaning on the bar counter next to him. He was Indian, with the fine, chiselled features of a male model; tall and slim with short black hair and bright eyes, wearing a well-fitted dark waistcoat over a shirt and black jeans. His sleeves were rolled up to his elbows, revealing an intricately designed henna tattoo on his right arm, going from the tips of his two forefingers up the back of his wrist and wrapping around his arm to disappear into the neatly folded cuffs of his shirt. He smiled charmingly at Linus and Linus felt his heart almost skip a beat. A stone could have been charmed by that smile.

"Thinking about getting into the business?" the man asked. Linus laughed awkwardly, a little flustered.

"I did when I was about fifteen," he answered, honestly. "But then I realised I wasn't any good at it."

"That's a lie," Clare chipped in. She leaned over so she could see the man more clearly and pointed at Linus. "He was pretty good, actually. Used to write us songs as presents sometimes."

"Now that's cool," the man said, and he seemed completely earnest. He clapped Linus on the shoulder. Linus felt a flush creep across his cheeks.

"Everybody starts somewhere, kid. If you think about getting back into it, as long as you keep at it and work hard enough then anything's possible."

He held out a hand and Linus shook it. It was a strong, firm handshake.

"Shaan Mehra," he said, leaning in so they could hear him. "I'm Cavall's manager."

"Oh my gosh, hi!" Clare was over the moon. "I'm Clare and this is Linus. It's really cool to meet you."

"Great to meet you as well. Did you enjoy the show?"

"Yeah, it was amazing," Linus replied. "Really fantastic."

"Excellent," Shaan grinned. "I'll let Cavall know."

"I really like your tattoo by the way," Clare commented, pointing at Shaan's arm.

"Oh, thank you," Shaan looked towards the design. He seemed pleased at the compliment. "Faye did it for me. She's pretty good with that kind of thing." He gestured towards left stage to the technician they had seen earlier, a Southeast Asian girl with a long ponytail and dangly silver earrings.

"Here's your drink, hun." The bartender placed a glass of coke in front of Shaan.

"Cheers, barkeep."

"Anytime."

There was a lull in conversation as Shaan sipped at his drink. He looked back towards the stage and seemed to frown slightly.

"Hm," he murmured, half to himself. "I thought he was going to do another encore."

He paused to take another sip, seemingly in thought, then glanced back at Clare and Linus and flashed them another smile.

"Well, I suppose I better see how Cavall's doing," he said. "It's been a long day. You know how it is. It was good meeting you though. You guys have a good one."

"Yeah, you too!"

Shaan raised his glass to Clare and Linus in a half salute, half toast, before turning and disappearing back into the crowds of people. Linus watched him go, then turned back to Clare.

"Okay, forget being a superhero *or* a live musician," he said quietly.

"I want to be like that guy."

In the ruins of the now-collapsed warehouse, all was very still. It had been a long time before the majority of the dust and ash cloud had fully settled back down again and after that all had been silence.

Until now.

Somewhere in the wreckage, something was moving. A chunk of broken concrete rolled clumsily off a mountain of debris, followed by two, three more after it. Something shifted underneath the pile.

For a second there was no further movement, but suddenly the pile split apart, rubble tumbling away to rest in other areas of the wreckage. A figure emerged from the middle of the pile with a gasp of air, covered in fine grey powder from head to toe. It was the lone Vigilante. He pulled the scarf away from his mouth, took in deep, shaky gulps of air, then carefully navigated out of the rubble and stumbled his way back out into the night.

He checked his arms. Fine. He inspected his legs. Also fine. If he had been any other person he might have broken some limbs or worse, but he was not any other person. He was a Vigilante, and he may not have been able to move before the collapse, but he had activated the fundamental aspect of his Ability just in time, and that had been enough to save his life.

He lowered himself down onto the ground and made a mental note to himself to be more aware of his surroundings next time. It was a few minutes before he got back up again. He was unharmed, but he decided it'd be best if he took his time returning home regardless. He had a lot to think about on the way, anyhow.

The next night brought surprises all around.

"You don't want to go on patrol?" Clare stared at Mallory with an exaggerated expression of flabbergasted dismay. "But you *never* turn down going on patrol. You complain about it heaps but you always come along just so we 'don't end up doing something stupid'. You said so yourself!"

Mallory tried to smile in an apologetic fashion. "Sorry," she said. "I would, but I am literally in the middle of making a breakthrough with this thing and I don't want to stop in the middle of it." She gestured to an item on her workbench that looked rather like a bulky, oversized gauntlet.

"Ahh," Clare held up her hands in surrender. "The infamous Inventor's Breakthrough! Say no more then. I will leave you to your work and we will go on patrol another time."

"I get the feeling you said the exact same thing the other night with something else," Linus remarked.

"Yeah well, it's breakthroughs happening all around at the moment." Mallory shrugged. "Who knows, I might actually be moving up on the mechanics' ranking board."

"You'll be a class S inventor-mechanic one of these days," Clare said, clapping Mallory on the back. "On that day, I hope you'll remember us, your two very best friends, when we are poor and destitute and in desperate need of money."

"See, I was with you right up until the 'poor and destitute' thing."

"So should we still go on patrol then?" Linus asked.

"I dunno... we might get into some serious trouble without Mal around to keep us on the straight and narrow. We're straight and she's narrow, by the way."

Linus began hooting with laughter.

"Very funny," Mallory said, suppressing a grin. "Did you come up with that one yourself?"

"You betcha." Clare winked at her.

"Alright, well for that terrible joke, I'm afraid I'm going to have to sentence you two to patrol without me. Knock yourselves out."

"You sure, Mallory?" Linus wiped a tear from his eye. "It won't be the same without you."

"Yeah well I was on the verge of a breakthrough here but now I think I'll just have to stay to recover from the agony of Clare's warped sense of humour."

"Ah, stop kidding yourself already. My sense of humour is the best."

"Right. Just don't run into any burning buildings this time, okay?"

"Last time I checked, I'm pretty sure it was *you* that was running into a burning building."

"Yeah, and I get the distinct feeling that you two idiots tried to do exactly the same thing after I specifically told you to stay put. Just keep out of any serious danger, alright? And come back soon."

"So what do you think 'come back soon' means, anyway?" Linus asked a few hours later, as he and Clare walked across the rooftop of a small apartment block.

"That's a good question," Clare replied. She crossed her arms, her softball bat dangling at her side, and pretended to be in deep, philosophical consideration. "Well, I guess it depends on your definition of 'time' and our perception thereof – for instance, do you consider 'time' to be an escort mission where 'soon' is counted in real time, or is it an open-world dealio where you can take as many side quests as you want in the middle of the main story without any negative impact on the–"

"Get down!" Linus hissed suddenly, pulling Clare down onto the roof.

"What is it?"

Linus pointed excitedly at the street below. "Look who it is!" he exclaimed in hushed tones.

Clare squinted down at where Linus was pointing, peering into the veil of mist. Her eyes widened when she registered the sight.

"Is that…!"

Linus nodded fervently. "*Fisticuffs!!*"

Anyone who was anyone knew about Fisticuffs. She was famous, in a roundabout sort of way – or perhaps, infamous was a more apt word. It wasn't that she used her Ability to wreak havoc, since she *seemed* to fight the good fight. It was the way she went about it that earned her her notoriety.

Fisticuffs was something of an urban legend – everyone had heard of her, but few had actually laid eyes on her in action. If she were the protagonist of her own piece of fiction then she definitely would have been considered the antihero; standoffish, devil-may-care and solitary, rumour had it that she fought for the thrill of it and that crime just happened to be standing in her way of a good time. She was fiercely independent to the point that she actively shunned the company of others; there was an aggressive air about her that suggested an inclination to jump headlong into a brawl without thinking, but she was just as well known for her efficiency and her tendency to thoroughly do her research on a situation.

One didn't boast the high crime takedown rate that Fisticuffs supposedly did without doing their homework, after all.

She was instantly recognisable through her long braid and her looking like she was ready to go off and fight some great battle at any moment. Clare could see her now, standing in the middle of the road below – a girl, tall and sturdy, well-built, wearing her long brown hair back into a loose plait. She wore a tough charcoal jacket with straps around the collar and cuffs, matching dark trousers and heavy combat boots. A canvas waist bag with brown leather straps had been slung around her hips and sat behind her, and fingerless leather gloves protected her hands.

Just the kind of getup that a Vigilante with her name would need.

She looked tough as nails. Clare was in awe, but she definitely wouldn't have wanted to get into a scrap with her.

She noticed something at the opposite end of the road from Fisticuffs.

"Look." She pointed and Linus turned his head to follow. "There's someone else."

Sure enough, emerging from a swirl of fog came another figure to stand in the middle of the road.

"Oh man," Linus whispered.

If Fisticuffs was tall, this figure was a mountain. If she was strong, then this figure looked even stronger. They looked massive, imposing, with broad shoulders and huge arms. They wore dark clothes, a hooded leather jacket and heavy jeans, all black. They wore heavy boots on their feet and leather gloves on their hands also. The hood of their jacket was drawn over their head, making it impossible to see their face; at this distance, it was difficult to tell if they were female or just a male with very large pectoral muscles.

Fisticuffs spoke. Neither Clare nor Linus could hear what she was saying from so far away, but they didn't have time to ruminate before Fisticuffs ran forwards and threw the first punch. The hooded opponent blocked the punch with a forearm then swung their own fist at Fisticuffs – Clare gasped – Fisticuffs ducked backwards, avoiding the blow with cat-like reflexes, and continued the movement, swinging up her right leg in a powerful roundhouse kick which caught her adversary on the side of the head and threw them over sideways.

Linus pumped his fist in a silent cheer as they watched. The hooded opponent fell into a roll then came back up on their feet, lunging back at Fisticuffs, who pre-emptively ducked to avoid their outstretched fist, but it was a feint – they twisted around and delivered a low, sweeping backwards kick to Fisticuffs' legs, and the Vigilante's feet were knocked out from under her, sending her crashing backwards with a shout.

Fisticuffs pushed herself back, narrowly escaping a boot stomp, then launched herself onto her feet with a kip-up, throwing herself at her opponent, who caught her fist in one hand, then the other in their other. The two grappled, Fisticuffs glaring with a fiery intensity into the shadow of her combatant's hood, scowling at a face that only she could properly see. She said another few short words that they could not hear, but could probably guess the tone of.

So engrossed were they in watching the fight that they didn't even notice another figure on the rooftops, only ten metres or so away from them. It was a glimmer of light that gave them away, a glint of sudden silver that Clare caught in the corner of her eye. She looked up abruptly, surprised, and saw them – on the edge of the rooftop of the building directly next to theirs crouched another hooded figure, much slighter than the one having it out with Fisticuffs down on the road. Like Fisticuffs' opponent, they were all in black with their hood drawn up over their face.

In their right hand, glistening, sharp and deadly in the night lights, was a gleaming stiletto knife.

"Hey!" Clare shouted suddenly. Linus' head jerked up, startled, and so did that of the hooded figure. They saw Clare and immediately leapt to their feet, beginning to sprint across the rooftop.

"Come on!!" Clare scrambled to her feet and Linus followed, giving chase and jumping over the parapets dividing the two buildings.

The hooded figure reached the edge of the rooftop and disappeared over the edge; Linus glanced around the area around them as they ran and yelled "Skylight!" – Clare grabbed his outstretched hand and they ran towards the window set into the concrete, leaping feet-first into it. They were ejected out onto the footpath at the foot of the apartment building via a ground floor window. The hooded figure was ahead of them, sprinting down the pavement on long legs. Clare and Linus followed and watched as they ducked around the corner of an intersection towards a maze of dead-end streets, vanishing into the nighttime mist.

"Fog!" Clare called, and this time Linus grabbed her outstretched hand – with a whirl and the sound of a sudden breeze, they disappeared into the whiteness and reappeared some distance away, approximately where the hooded figure had disappeared to. They rounded the corner, out of the fog, and into a loading alley.

The figure wasn't there though.

The alleyway was empty, with the only exit being the way that they had come in. To either side to the wide lane were the large corrugated iron doors indicating loading zones. At the end of the alley was a high wall, but it was much too high for anyone to have climbed in the short space of time it'd taken for them to reach the area. Or was it? After realising that there were, in fact, a fair amount of others with Abilities in the City, it wasn't that hard to imagine a Vigilante with the power to jump great heights, for example.

"I guess we lost 'em," Linus said, trying to catch his breath. Clare was put out.

"This was much easier when we thought we were the only few people with Abilities in the City," she commented.

"How does that even make sense?"

"Oh, you know. It's like the thing where you notice something one time and then suddenly you start seeing them everywhere. Like silver trumpets."

"Okay, well," Linus straightened. "I'm going to pretend I understood what you just said. Can we go back now?"

Clare *hmm*'d thoughtfully to herself.

"I guess so," she said. "There's no way to tell where they went. Okay. Let's go then."

They turned back around and that was when they saw it.

A huge black dog, almost blending in with the shadows of the building on either side of them, save for a pair of amber eyes glaring out at them from the darkness. It had its hackles raised, teeth bared, and saliva dripped from its jaws. It growled at them, low and threateningly, and Clare and Linus stepped back instinctively.

"Good dog..." Clare gave an awkward, faltering laugh. "Where did you come from?"

A soft tinkling sound came from behind them and they spun back around again. Standing at the end of the alley was another hooded figure clothed in black, smaller and slighter than the one they had been chasing before. There was a coil of something long and silvery at their side.

"Isn't there a saying for this kind of situation?" Linus whispered to Clare. "Between a rock and the deep blue sea?"

"Close, but not quite," Clare replied, keeping her eyes on the figure at the end of the alley. She gripped her softball bat in both hands and held it as if ready to swing.

The black dog behind them barked suddenly, viciously, and Clare and Linus jumped and turned. The same jangling sound again from behind them, a flash of something silver in the air shooting towards them – Clare yelled "Get back!!" and shoved Linus, sending him stumbling backwards to the ground. Something flew past Clare's face with a sharp whistling sound and the fizzing of something electric and she ducked backwards, dropping her softball bat, losing her balance and falling onto her behind.

The black dog lunged forwards at Linus, who rolled away as it jumped over him and skittered past. Linus scrambled to his feet, ran, and ducked out of the way as it turned back and lunged at him again, barely avoiding it as it sailed past, its amber eyes glittering with menace.

The hooded figure yanked backwards on the length of fine chain which had almost taken off Clare's nose – they recalled it to them with their right hand, the rest of the coil in their left, and wrapped it around their shoulders, their waist, then their forearm as they ran forwards – they swung the length of the chain and then suddenly it was shooting towards Clare again, who twisted away in a panic, narrowly missing the sharp metal dart fastened to the end of the chain.

"Clare!" Linus yelled.

"I know!" Clare called back, fearful. She grabbed her softball bat and leapt up, holding it up as if it were a sword. The metal chain flew towards her again – it wrapped itself around the bat and suddenly a brief but painful electric shock ran through it, the jolt running through Clare's arms. She gave a cry and dropped the bat, falling back onto the ground again. Linus threw himself towards her.

"Are you okay?" he asked urgently. Clare nodded but she looked noticeably uncomfortable.

Now they were well and truly trapped. The hooded figure with the chain and the black dog stood at the mouth of the loading alley, blocking off their exit, while Clare and Linus shrank back at the foot of the wall to the back. There was no fog, no windows nearby, nothing by which they could escape.

"We should've listened to Mallory," Clare muttered.

The figure and the black dog started towards them again.

"*Hey!*"

Suddenly there was the sound of a voice from above them. Clare and Linus looked up in surprise to see someone else at the top of the wall above their heads – a hooded someone with a scarf over their face. They launched themselves off the wall with incredible power then landed hard on the ground between Clare and Linus and their assailants.

At once there was a great and sudden rumble – the concrete beneath the newcomer's black canvas sneakers cracked with a thunderous noise as if they had landed with the force of a truck, and everyone felt the ground shift beneath them from the ripple effect. The hooded figure and the black dog skidded to an abrupt halt. The newcomer ran at them; the hooded figure pitched their chain dart towards them but they kicked themselves off the ground, towards the wall, pushing themselves off and hurling themselves with incredible force at the figure, who was knocked off their feet and thrown across the asphalt.

The newcomer landed on their hands and continued in a smooth roll, coming up to meet the black dog as it dove at them – they threw their arms forward in a two-fisted punch, catching the dog in the middle of its chest and sending it flying backwards with a yelp.

The hooded figure on the ground pushed themselves up on their elbows and spun their chain above their head, launching it towards the newcomer again. "Watch out!" Clare yelled – the newcomer turned at the warning and ducked back as the dart came towards their head; it caught them across the face, cutting them across the cheek and pulling their scarf away. The newcomer grabbed the end of the chain and *pulled*, wrapping more of its length around his leg and yanking it towards him with a hard, backwards roundhouse that caught the black dog as it tried to dive at him again and which ripped the rest of the coil of chain from the hooded figure's hands.

The newcomer dropped the chain to the ground then turned their attention back to the dog, launching themselves at it with a powerful moonkick which cracked the ground as they landed; the dog leapt away just in time then ran for the mouth of the alley. The hooded figure had gotten back to their feet and had scooped up their coil of chain from the ground.

The newcomer turned and stared at them, wordless. The hooded figure and the black dog stared back. The black dog barked at the newcomer, and then the two of them retreated out of the alley and back into the cover of night.

The newcomer watched them go. They didn't move for a moment. When they did, it was to pick up their fallen scarf from the ground and inspect it. There was a small tear in it now. They sighed, pulled off their hood, then turned back towards the end of the alley.

Clare and Linus had gotten back up and were now cautiously making their way towards the person who had saved them. Resonance had told them before that this kind of thing wouldn't happen again, and that there wouldn't always be a more experienced or powerful Vigilante around to save their hides, but somehow it *had* happened again, and they weren't about to complain.

The newcomer walked towards them. Now that they were no longer a scarfed blur in the middle of battle, Clare and Linus could see him better.

He was a little taller than Linus, with a thick shock of wavy brown hair and sober but alert brown eyes. His skin was fair but his face and hands were flecked with countless freckles from years spent outside in the sun. He wore a grey and blue hoodie and dark navy sweatpants; the now-torn scarf in his hands was green and matched the colour of his t-shirt. He seemed older than they were, but there was something young about his face too, despite his serious demeanour.

"You two okay?" he asked them as he approached. They nodded.

"Yeah," Linus replied. "Thanks. We were really in a bind."

"No kidding," the newcomer replied. He folded his scarf and tied it around his arm. "What were you even doing out here? It's late. Not really a safe time of night to go for a walk."

"Oh. We're… Vigilantes." Clare said. The sound of the word felt strange on her tongue. "We were on night patrol."

"Night patrol, huh?" the newcomer said. He studied them both carefully. "You both have Abilities?"

"Yeah."

"Hm." He crossed his arms. He seemed to be considering something. Clare and Linus looked at each other worriedly.

Eventually the newcomer dropped his arms. He held out a hand.

"The name's Shockwave," he said. "I think you two better come with me."

CHAPTER FOUR

BASE FOUNDATIONS

The Base was a large concrete cellar set mostly underneath the ground floor of what, at first glance, appeared to be a single-storey flat. This was not the case, of course – if one looked closer, they could see two windows on level with the ground, set on each side of the walls alongside the steps to the front door. It was the kind of setup that was less obvious if it was dark, but on this night a soft glow lit up the windows of the basement, a warm and familiar beacon of home to those who lived there. You couldn't see much of the interior from the outside unless you hunkered right down in front of the windows to peer in, at which point your ear would be on the ground and your backside up in the air.

The entrance to the Base was much like that of a storm shelter and was set towards the left of the flat, down a narrow pathway squeezed between the wall and the fence dividing the property from that of the neighbour's. It was not accessible exclusively through this means, but this was the route that Shockwave took Clare and Linus by as he led them back to the house.

The inside of the Base looked huge, but maybe that was just because of the way the sparse scattering of furniture was set out (large table in the centre, everything else around the edges of the room), and despite being entirely constructed of concrete there was something homely about it too. It was not, however, perfectly pristine – on one of the walls was a small crater at approximately chest height, about the diameter of that of a basketball, and the lighting was little more than naked lightbulbs suspended from wires in the ceiling.

"Nice place," Clare commented. "Spacious."

Shockwave gestured vaguely. "Living space is upstairs," he replied. "This is just where business happens."

"Sounds like us and the garage," Linus murmured to Clare.

Shockwave cleared a pile of paper off a chair and gestured at the table.

"Sit down," he said. "I'll be with you in a sec."

He crossed to a desk at the corner of the basement and dropped the papers on top. At that moment there was the sound of an opening door from above, towards the living area. A light clicked on in the stairwell.

"Shock, is that you?" a voice called.

Shockwave glanced at Clare and Linus at the table.

"Yeah," he answered. "Come on down. I was just about to come get you."

Footsteps clattered down the stairs and a familiar face appeared in the basement. Clare and Linus stared open-mouthed at the new arrival.

"It's you!" they exclaimed in unison.

Resonance stared wide-eyed back at them.

"Well this was unexpected," she remarked.

"You three already know each other?" Shockwave glanced over at them as he shrugged off his hoodie and tossed it onto a chair.

"Yeah," Resonance replied. She turned off the light in the stairway. "You know the fire the other night?"

"Oh, so these are ones?"

"Yeah. Two of them anyway."

She looked different from the last time they saw her. She wasn't wearing her Vigilante getup anymore, but instead a loose t-shirt tucked into a red woolen skirt and black tights. Her Vigilante gear had been casual already, but she seemed more relaxed now somehow. Something about her demeanour had changed completely from the slightly brusque personality from the other night. Even her voice seemed slightly different; higher, clearer. She smiled at Clare and Linus in a friendly way.

"How are things, you two?"

"Resonance. It's nice to see you again." Clare greeted the Vigilante. She flapped a hand at them impatiently as she approached the table.

"Please," she said. "Out there when I'm in my getup, I'm Resonance. In here or any other time I'm just Fang."

"'Fang'?"

"I promise that's actually my real name. Don't expect him to follow that same code though," Resonance jerked her head over at Shockwave. "He's Mr. Shockwave almost every day of the week."

Shockwave grunted in response. It was hard to tell if it was a laugh or a scoff.

"So what's the haps?" Resonance – Fang – asked, ignoring him.

"Why has Shock brought you home to our little hovel?"

"Just bailed them out of some trouble."

"Again? What'd I tell you kids about staying out of danger?"

"In our defence, we didn't actually know we were actually running into any," Linus said sheepishly. "Clare saw this guy with a knife, and we–"

"What guy? What knife? What?" Fang looked at Shockwave. "Is that what this is about? You punched out a guy with a knife for them? I think they could have handled that one on their own."

"Hang on," Shockwave said, holding up his hands. "Just listen to the whole story, okay? Start from the beginning."

Fang held up her own hands in a gesture of surrender and sat down at the table. Shockwave leaned back against the edge of his desk and folded his arms.

"Well," Clare started, uncertain how to begin. "We were on night patrol and we saw Fisticuffs–"

"You saw Fisticuffs?" Fang interrupted.

"Fang," Shockwave began, a pained look on his face.

"Sorry. Continue."

"Yeah. Well... we saw Fisticuffs having it out on the street with some big guy in a leather jacket. And then there was someone else on the roof with us, with a knife. So we ran after them but we lost them, and then there was a really big black dog and some other shady figure swinging a chain? And then he – Shockwave – came and saved us."

"A black dog?" Fang asked abruptly. She glanced over at Shockwave, who nodded shortly, then back to Clare. "These guys with the knife and the chain. They had their hoods up?"

"Well... yeah, they did."

"All in black?"

"Yeah."

Fang looked at Shockwave again and sat back in her chair.

"Well, I guess that's it then," she muttered. She rubbed at her brow with one hand, her mouth pressed into a tight line.

"They seemed pretty determined," Shockwave replied. "I didn't beat them, they ran off after a couple minutes. They'll be back though, no question about that."

"Yeah, that's what I was afraid of."

"Hang on," Linus interrupted. "What's this all about? Why are we even here?"

Fang glanced over at her teammate and threw him a look that neither Clare nor Linus could discern. Fang jerked her head towards them.

"It's your mission," she said to Shockwave. "You do it."

Shockwave unfolded his arms and exhaled through his nose. Approaching the table, he leaned forwards and placed his hands on its surface.

"You'd better listen," he said. "Because I'm not telling you this twice."

"Okay?" Clare suddenly felt uneasy.

Fang folded her arms. Shockwave drummed his fingers on the table before he spoke again.

"For the last six or seven months," he finally began. "There's been this rash of incidences all over the place. Vigilantes seem to be getting picked off one by one. Most of them just seem to have dropped off the radar, but the ones that have turned up... they're dressed up like accidents, but it's too careless of the Vigilantes we know of for it to be remotely possible. We don't know who, or why, or how," he said, as Clare opened her mouth to ask. "We only know that Vigilantes, particularly the ones with Abilities, are the ones being targeted. Unfortunately for us there hasn't been anyone lucky enough to be able to testify as to what's going on, but rumour is the ones responsible are a bunch of guys all in hoods with a black dog."

"So, the people that we saw..." Linus trailed off. Shockwave nodded.

"Right," he said. "I'm fairly certain that those are the same guys."

"Why hasn't anyone stopped them before now?"

"Didn't you just hear what I said? Nobody knows who they are. Anyone who gets close enough to see their faces probably ends up dead."

"What about the police?" Clare asked. "They haven't solved it or anything?"

"The police?" Shockwave scoffed. "The police couldn't solve anything like this. To them this is probably just all runaways or youths making trouble for themselves. As far as they know we don't even exist."

"I think I already told you this, but we don't do encounters with the police. Look at us," Fang gestured to each of occupants of the Base. "We're kids with weird abilities going out and enacting vigilante justice. Everything about that screams police disapproval. Besides, how effective could they be against an enemy like this?"

"These guys are no amateurs," Shockwave put in. "They know what they're doing. The Vigilantes they go after are both newbies and experienced fighters, but it doesn't seem to matter to them. Regardless of whether they've only been Vigilantes a short while, like you two, or if they've been in the business for years, like–" he stopped suddenly in the middle of his sentence. Clamped his mouth shut and looked away. Clare looked questioningly at him, then at Fang. Fang glanced at Shockwave and hesitated briefly.

"We had friends," she eventually said. "In the Next City. Vigilantes, really experienced ones–"

"Equilibrium and Shooting Star," Shockwave broke in. His expression was stony. "Equilibrium's Ability was perfect balance. Shooting Star could jump as high as she wanted to, no problem. They were Vigilantes for five years and a team for almost four. Literally went straight into it after they finished high school."

"Shooting Star was still in her last year when she started," Fang corrected. She seemed quietly sad all of a sudden. "She was going to move away at the end of the year. Travel the world."

"What does it matter?" Shockwave muttered. "They're both dead now anyway."

Mallory supposed she should have given a proper indication as to what 'come back soon' actually entailed. Several hours later, Clare and Linus had still not come back and Mallory was beginning to grow concerned. By the time she had noticed what hour it was though, she had finished the final touches of her invention and got it working.

Declining to go on patrol because she was on the verge of a

breakthrough was not, strictly speaking, a lie – it's true that she hated to leave a project in the middle of it, and she was nearing completion of the mechanics, so that much was honesty. But she had also refused because she was worried that a situation would occur in which she was expected to be able to use her Ability, and she no longer had an Ability to use. This was a fact that she had not confessed to her friends, and she did not intend to confess any time soon. Whatever had happened was her own problem and she would deal with it on her own terms.

The contraption on the table before her resembled a modern-ised medieval gauntlet with five small circular discs at the pads at the base of the fingers and thumb. It was made of moulded steel plates riveted and interlocked together – the design was plain, but Mallory was fine with plain.

She slid the gauntlet onto her right hand. It fit close – it had been bulky and oversized at first, but once Mallory had discarded some of the more superfluous elements of the design it got more streamlined and now fit snug on her arm.

Mallory got up from her seat and picked up her tyre iron lying on the floor. She placed it on her chair and stood back from her workbench, flexing her fingers and opening and closing her palm. This was the final test.

She held out her gauntlet towards the tyre iron.

There was a faint hum. The tyre iron vibrated for a second then shot towards her – Mallory caught it perfectly in her hand and pumped her fist in the air in triumph. It was flawless.

Mallory no longer had her Ability but now she had something to emulate it, and it was better than nothing. She checked the time.

It was late. Maybe it was time to check up on Clare and Linus. She pulled her goggles down around her neck and picked up her phone from the table but suddenly remembered she was out of credit.

Mallory groaned. She'd have to go about this the long way. She slid her arms out of the sleeves of her jumpsuit, tied them around her waist, grabbed her jacket, and began to head for the door.

"So is this what you're doing? Investigating?" Clare looked to Fang but she shook her head.

"Not me," she said. She nodded towards Shockwave. "*He* is."

Clare and Linus glanced to Shockwave in surprise and he nodded.

"You're not doing it together?" Clare asked, puzzled, glancing between the two of them. "Aren't you... you're not partners?"

Shockwave gave the faintest chuff of laughter and Fang smiled wryly.

"We're not a team in the same way that you guys are," she replied. "Or in the same way most Vigilante teams seem to be. I'm not touching this one – this one's his."

"The way it works..." Shockwave sat down at the table. "Vigilantes are a secretive bunch. There's no 'secret society' where we all get together and get to know one another. We have friends, sure. If we meet during an incident or end up working together on a big mission, fine. But not everyone is going to want to put themselves out there. We keep low profiles for a reason. As made apparent by recent events, not everyone with an Ability is going to use it for good intentions."

"That's what you said too," Clare said, looking at Fang. She nodded.

"Yeah," she said in a low voice. "From what little we do know, whoever they are, they've been travelling from place to place. They don't stick around for long. I'd suspected as much after the fire the other night, but now it seems we know for sure that they're here in the City."

"And I would strongly suggest that now *you* know," Shockwave cut in. "You do your best to stay out of trouble. Don't go on patrols. Stay home and keep your noses clean."

Fang looked pointedly at Shockwave.

"I still think you should stay off it too," she said. "Now they know you're around they might try looking for you. You should keep a low profile for a while."

"What good will I be if I'm out of action?" Shockwave responded curtly.

Fang sighed. She stood from her chair and looked at Clare and Linus.

"It's getting late," she said. "I'll take you two back home."

Clare and Linus glanced at each other then rose from their seats.

"What should we do if we encounter them again?" Clare asked.

"If you stay out of trouble then this shouldn't be an issue," Shockwave responded. "But if you do see them again, don't engage under any circumstances. Come straight to one of us."

The streets were quiet. In hindsight, Mallory realised that it may have been a foolish thing to go wandering around by herself with only a tyre iron as protection – she wasn't on patrol and she didn't have her team, so as far as the general public would have been concerned she would just look like a weirdo who forgotten where she'd parked her car.

Mallory was a little lost, true, but it wasn't a car she was having trouble finding. She'd hunted high and low for Clare and Linus, searching in all the spots they'd usually wander around when going on patrol, but she could see neither hide nor hair of them. She hoped they were all right and that they hadn't gotten into any serious danger.

Mallory paused in the middle of the road and heaved a great sigh. Well, there was nothing else she could really do. She might as well just go back to the house and hope her friends returned in one piece.

"Hey, you," came a voice from behind her.

She turned.

Clare wasn't one to be concerned about things. That was Mallory's job. Clare was an 'act first, ask questions later' type person, which wasn't necessarily a bad thing, but it meant she didn't always stop to process if there would be a better course of action before jumping straight into things. Mallory was the one who would say things like "*Well, hold on. Let's just stop and think for a moment*," and that balanced the whole team dynamic out – Clare would be first to suggest an initial course of action, Linus would chip in with an elaboration, and then Mallory would sit them all down and suggest a full plan. That was what made them work.

But Mallory wasn't here. She hadn't been at home when they had returned the previous night, nor had she made an appearance all day. Her bed was unslept in and her phone, jacket and keys were gone. They tried texting and calling her, but neither form of communication was met with a response.

"You don't suppose she went out looking for us, do you?" Linus asked. There was a note of worry in his voice. Clare tried to swallow back her own anxiety.

"Maybe," she replied. "Her tyre iron's missing though, see? So even if she did she should be fine, right?"

There was a pause. Clare and Linus looked at each other.

"You're thinking about what Shockwave and Fang said, aren't you?"

"Yeah. You?"

"Yeah."

Another pause.

"Maybe we should go look for her," Clare finally said, rising from her chair. She reached for her softball bat. Linus glanced at her.

"But what about the thing where we were meant to lay low?"

Clare tapped her bat on her shoulder thoughtfully.

"Well," she began. We're not strictly speaking going on patrol. We're just going to look for a friend, right?" Linus eyed her softball bat and pointed it at with a raised eyebrow.

"But then what about the bat?"

"Oh, you know. It's good to be prepared." Clare flashed him a grin. "Come on. We can go look for her together."

Linus looked uncertain, but rose from his seat on the couch.

"Okay," he said. "But let's leave her a note just in case she comes back."

The City, when they eventually wandered outside, seemed especially deserted tonight, the night fog lying thick and low; although as they walked around the edges of the central business district they could hear the faint, distant thumping of electronic music and the sounds of muffled cheering from far away. Another Cavall Robinson show, it sounded like. Linus wished he could go back to see it a second time.

They hunted high and low for Mallory, searching in all the spots they'd usually wander around when going on patrol, but they could see neither hide nor hair of her. Clare hoped she was alright and that she hadn't gotten into any serious danger.

As they were walking through a shopping street, Clare suddenly flung out her arm before Linus and he stopped abruptly.

"What is it?" he began. Clare put a finger over her lips and pointed down the street ahead.

At the end of the street, standing facing out into an intersection, stood two dark figures shrouded in the fog. It was hard to make out details from this distance, and they had their backs towards them, but this much was unmistakeable – both figures were dressed in black, had hoods pulled up over their heads, and the one on the left had a coil of something, long and silvery, dangling at their side.

Linus grabbed Clare's wrist.

"We should go back," he warned in hushed tones. "We should go back now."

"We should," Clare agreed. But her eyes were still trained on the figures ahead. Linus saw the look on her face and tugged at Clare's arm.

"Don't you dare," he hissed. "Don't you – Clare, we won't be lucky a third time."

"Maybe, maybe not," Clare replied, "But look around us." She gestured to the thick fog surrounding them, grinned, and pulled up the hood of her anorak. "I'm right in my turf."

Suddenly Linus was grasping at nothing but thin air.

Clare's Ability lay with the fog that blanketed the City at night. At will, she could disappear into it and use it as a passage through which to travel, alighting wherever else she wanted in the blink of an eye. As long as this fog was present she could go wherever she liked, and the thicker it lay the easier it was for her to vanish and reappear. It fuelled her Ability, made her powerful. She could not, however, summon the fog at will. Although she could merge with it, she could not create it on her own; the fog was its own entity, and the use of her Ability did not affect it in the slightest.

Despite this, Clare had figured out ways to use the mechanics of her Ability to her own advantage, experimenting with its limits when it came to factors such as speed, displacement, and momentum. And on one such occasion she had discovered that any motion she began prior to vanishing would be completed wherever she reappeared again.

And so it was with this knowledge that Clare raised her softball bat, ran forwards and began to swing in hard, as if striking a fastball, before jumping and vanishing into the fog.

She reappeared again at the end of the street, directly behind the two figures, and finished her hit hard into the chain-wielding figure's upper back, the momentum propelling her target forward.

A shocked, pained cry burst from the figure's mouth as they were thrown forward and onto the ground and Clare was surprised to hear that it was a female's voice as she skidded past onto the road ahead. The other figure's head snapped around at the sound and saw Clare; Clare twisted back into the fog again just in time as a stiletto knife flew through the air where she had just been. The one with the chain pushed themselves to their knees and the other figure grabbed them and pulled them to their feet. Clare whirled into existence again and disappeared almost immediately as another stiletto knife shot towards her.

The two hooded figures started running but Clare wasn't about to let them off that easy. She ran after them, ignoring Linus down the street behind her, shouting for her to come back. The fog was still heavy on this street and she could see the two figures up ahead – so long as they were still in her territory, she had the upper hand. She was strong. She was invincible.

Clare dove forwards, hands outstretched, and vanished into the mist – she rematerialised again and fell straight against the knife-wielding hooded figure's back, eliciting an *oof!* from them, both of them tumbling to the ground. Clare rolled clumsily away and glanced back towards the figure's hands, looking for the knife they might have, preparing herself to disappear back into the cover of fog if necessary.

Her eyes widened.

There was no knife to be seen in the figure's right hand, but something else even more startling was there. Something that Clare had seen the likes of only two nights ago.

Going from the tips of their two forefingers up the back of the wrist to disappear into the cuffs of the figure's black coat was an intricately designed henna tattoo.

Clare looked up, her mouth open in astonishment. In the collision that had occurred, the knife-wielding figure's hood had come away from their head and for the first time she could see the identity of the somebody they had chased over the rooftops and through the streets of the City the previous night.

Black hair and bright eyes.

Shaan Mehra grinned back at her.

Clare was too surprised to move. The chain-wielding figure grabbed Shaan, hauled him to his feet with an unmistakeably feminine voice urging *"Come on!"* – for a split second as they ducked down Clare could see *their* identity also and was even more taken aback to see another familiar face; that of a Southeast Asian girl with a long ponytail and dangly silver earrings. The two of them bolted away down the street, disappearing from view into the swirling mists, and Clare could do nothing else but watch them as they left.

"Clare? Clare!" The sound of running footsteps. Linus ran onto the street and dropped to Clare's side. He seized her by the shoulders, his voice agitated. "Cripes, I was so worried, that was such a stupid thing to do! Are you okay??"

Clare looked up at Linus, her eyes shining. She grabbed Linus' wrist.

"We need to go back to the Base," she blurted excitedly. "We need to go see Resonance and Shockwave *now*."

"What? Why?"

Her voice dropped to a fervent whisper.

"*I know who's behind the Vigilante attacks!*"

CHAPTER FIVE

PARADIGM SHIFTS

Far away from the sprawl of the City, a young man in a red hoodie pulled a ringing cellphone from his pocket and held it up to his ear.

"*Kia ora.*"

"*Hey. It's me.*"

He smiled to himself at the sound of the caller's voice.

"Hey," he replied. "How's the mission going?"

"*Fine.*"

"Really?"

"*No.*"

He chuckled sympathetically.

"*Kia kaha.* You'll get there."

"*Thanks. I just thought I'd check in with you. Where are you now?*"

The young man looked at the buildings around him. They were similar to the surroundings he was used to, but at the same time entirely foreign to him.

"I'm inbetween places at the moment," he said into the phone. "I'm on my way east. I thought it'd be worth a try."

"*Any luck so far?*"

"*Aroha mai.* Nothing yet."

The voice on the other end of the call sighed, sending a wave of distorted white noise down the line. There was a beat before they spoke again.

"*Hey,*" they said. "*So how are you holding up?*"

The young man thought about the bandages still fixed on his arms and legs. He thought about last few days and the physical pain that had visited him, coming and going in waves, and the fact that he hadn't experienced such a prolonged and sustained period of discomfort in a long time. It was not a feeling he was used to.

"Fine," he said aloud.

"*Really?*"

"No."

Another chuff of distortion as his correspondent laughed or sighed.

"I'll be fine," the young man continued, reassuring. "Things are different, but I'll be fine. Just focus on your mission, alright? Don't get in too much trouble."

"*I'll try. Hey, I gotta go now, but I'll keep you posted if anything comes up.*"

"*Kia ora.*"

"*And, Rehua?*"

"*Āe?*"

"*Stay safe out there, alright? I need you back in one piece.*"

Rehua smiled.

"You got it."

"I thought we told you to lay low for a while." Fang sounded exasperated. Clare hadn't had time to think about it before now, but now she felt a little guilty.

"I know," she replied, a little sheepishly. "Sorry. We weren't on patrol or anything, we were just–"

Fang held up a hand.

"Save it," she said. "We've already given you fair warning, but you're your own responsibility when all's said and done. Just exercise more caution in future. What did you want to talk about?"

They sat down at the table in the middle of the Base. Fang, still in her Vigilante getup from night patrol, brought out a first-aid kit from a shelf to fetch a bandage for a graze that Clare didn't even realise she'd gotten. No amount of surprise scrapes and bruises could put a damper on her excitement, however.

"I know who's behind the Vigilante attacks," Clare said, cutting straight to the chase. Fang looked up abruptly, looking at once shocked and dismayed.

"You *saw* them?" she asked sharply, her voice suddenly slipping into the lower, rougher tones of Resonance. "Up close? After Shockwave told you specifically not to engage under any circumstance?"

"It wasn't really – I mean, it wasn't like it was a *fight* or anything–"

"We saw them at the end of the street," Linus put in. "And Clare went and tackled them from behind."

It was Fang who had picked up the first-aid, but it was Resonance who now put it down.

"Hell's teeth, Clare, could you think of a stupider thing to do?"

"That's what I said too."

"They were right in my turf," Clare objected. "There was fog everywhere, I had it covered. Anyway, these two, Vigilante killers, they–"

"Woah, hang on a second," Resonance held up her hands and shook her head. "Don't say a word. I don't know and I don't want to know, alright?"

There was a moment of surprised, taken aback silence.

"But I saw who it was!" Clare exclaimed. "We know who it is! If you knew then you would have a one up on them – doesn't that make any kind of difference?"

Resonance smiled grimly and took out a bandage from the kit, handing it to Clare.

"Sorry," she replied. "Not how it works. I'm out of this one and I'm staying that way. The less I'm involved in this mess, the better. There's nothing to be gained from it but trouble and more trouble."

Clare had been stunned into speechlessness, but Linus was quick to respond.

"Can you at least pass it on to Shockwave?" he asked, half-pleading. "Please. It's important, and it could help him with his mission."

"Why don't you tell him yourself?"

"Well, do you know where he is, or when he'll be back?"

Resonance paused, thought for a long moment, then narrowed her eyes at Linus.

"You're putting me in jeopardy by telling me this," she said, almost frosty in her tone. "I hope you know that."

"I know. We're sorry."

"Skip it. Just tell me who you saw."

Linus elbowed Clare in the side and she snapped her mouth shut and sat up quickly, shooting Linus a grateful look.

"How many people did you say were behind the attacks?"

"Three, supposedly. And a black dog."

"Okay." Clare took a breath and collected her thoughts. "So, there's this electronica guy in town at the moment, on tour, right? Linus and I went to see him the other night at the Niterie and we met his manager while we were there, this guy named Shaan Mehra. And the guy I tackled tonight, his hood came off and it was the same guy! And the one who was with him was this girl that we saw at the show as well, the technician, what was it…"

"Faye," Linus prompted. "He said her name was Faye."
"Faye, right."

"A musician's manager?" Resonance repeated. "And his technician?"

"Yeah."

The older Vigilante rubbed at her brow, still cross but contemplative.

"If they were using their employer's tour as a pretence to be able to travel from city to city…"

"That's what I'm thinking," Clare said, trying not to sound too eager. "I think that Shaan and the technician, Faye, they're both using the tour as a way of being able to scope out Vigilantes with Abilities. It's the perfect cover."

"Okay, but what about this third person? There are three of them."

"Oh, yeah." Clare suddenly felt deflated. A silence fell over the room. She tried to think – she wasn't wrong, her theory so far was solid. But the third figure...

"Any celebrity needs security, right?" Linus broke in. Clare and Resonance looked up at him. He looked suddenly embarrassed at having the entirety of the room's attention focused on him, but didn't falter.

"That fight we saw the other night," he said to Clare. "That big guy who was battling Fisticuffs in the middle of the street. Maybe that's the third guy. Maybe that's why Shaan was on the rooftop too, to help him out and take out Fisticuffs when she wasn't paying attention."

"Sure," Clare replied, but she sounded uncertain. "Maybe. But who are they? I don't remember seeing any security personnel near–"

"Wasn't there a security guy at the door?"

Clare stopped mid-sentence. She tried to think back to the night of the concert, when they had arrived at The Niterie.

"The one with the Russian accent?" Linus shrugged a shoulder.

"He was a pretty big dude," he replied. "He might well be the same guy that was fighting Fisticuffs. If he was in Cavall's team as security or something..."

"Okay, great, so now you have an idea as to who's behind this," Resonance cut in. "But the question still remains – why? Why go to all this trouble to kill off Vigilantes? What are their goals, or their Abilities even?"

"I don't know if Shaan even *has* an Ability," Clare responded, doubtful. "I mean, he hasn't shown any sign of it from what we've seen – I was right up close and he didn't even do anything."

"That was probably because you took him by surprise," Linus commented. Clare waved a hand.

"Not my fault if he was unprepared," she retorted. "The other ones though…"

"If one of them was able to keep up with Fisticuffs then it's highly likely his Ability has something to do with strength." Resonance stated plainly. She stood up from her chair and went to replace the first-aid kit. "You said one of them had a knife?"

"Yeah. Shaan did. Several, actually. Stilettos, I think they're called? Faye, she had this chain with a thing on the end…"

"A rope dart." Resonance turned around and leaned back against the shelf. "Shock said it was a rope dart. Old Chinese soft weapon, good for mid-to-long range. Can be made of rope or chain. You anchor it in your left hand and shoot it with your right. Dart on the end gives it an extra edge. Not sure if it being made of chain changes the name though."

"Right. A rope dart." Clare was slightly overwhelmed by the sudden information. "Or chain dart. Anyway… she did this thing where she used it to grab my bat, but then it felt like I got shocked. She almost took off my nose with it at one point and it sounded like it was… buzzing. Like electricity."

"Electricity, huh." Resonance folded her arms. She was quiet for a while, thinking. Neither Clare nor Linus spoke, watching her for a reaction. When she looked up there was a look in her eye that was somehow both resigned and yet focused. She came back to the table and sat down at her chair.

"So, to sum up," she began. "We have a little bit of an idea of who's responsible for all these Vigilante deaths. First we have this guy, Shaan. No obvious Ability. Uses knives, stilettos. Then we have this girl Faye. Seems to be able to control electricity in some capacity. And then…" she waved her hand vaguely. "Some big guy with a Russian accent and a strength Ability, maybe. And then the black dog."

"Is the black dog significant?"

"It'll be significant as far as it's related to the people responsible for these incidences. Animals aren't affected by whatever fairy dust it is that allows us to have Abilities and I haven't heard of it happening otherwise. I wouldn't worry about it."

"What about Fisticuffs?" Linus asked suddenly. Resonance looked up at him.

"What about Fisticuffs?" she echoed.

"Well, I mean… she was up close and personal with the big guy the other night. Maybe she knows a bit more about it. Maybe she'll even help out." Linus shrugged a shoulder half-heartedly. Resonance gave a chuff of laughter.

"Up until the other night I didn't even know Fisticuffs wasn't just an urban legend. I've been here almost three years now and haven't seen her once. She's infamous for working alone; what makes you think she'll even want to help? Besides, without having been there you can't even say whether she won that fight at all. You can't rely on someone you can't find. Or who doesn't want to be found."

Clare and Linus looked at each other uncomfortably. Resonance caught the look between them and frowned.

"What?"

Clare bit her lip and looked back at Resonance.

"It's… Mallory," she replied, reluctant. "She wasn't home when we got back last night and we haven't seen her all day. She's not answering our calls or texts either. It could be nothing, but…"

A strange look came over Resonance's face and she leaned back in her seat and ran her fingers through her hair.

"That's not good," she muttered. "That's not good at all."

"Please," Clare urged. "I know you said this wasn't your fight. But we brought you information, didn't we? Surely with your experience, and with that kind of advantage…"

"Look, you've asked me to pass on a message and that's all I'm going to do," Resonance said curtly. "I already know way more than I'd like to. Don't make me say it again. I don't like Shock going and getting himself involved either – with his attitude and his methods he's going to wreck himself before he knows it."

"You mentioned before…" Linus began. "You said that you're not like other Vigilante teams in that you don't do patrols together. Why is that?"

Resonance offered a faint smile, the first they'd seen since they'd arrived.

"Call it being too set in our ways," she replied. "We do go on patrols together sometimes, but not often. We'll work together on big missions that require collaboration, but we've each got our own agenda and way of going about things. I was a Vigilante long before I teamed up with him and I'd already figured out a routine that was comfortable for me. Same with him."

Clare and Linus glanced at each other.

"Does that surprise you?" Resonance asked. They nodded. Resonance chuckled.

"It's not as if we don't get along," she said. "We make a great team when need be. Maybe you'll get to see us in action some time. You might want to keep your distance though." She rose from the table. "He's not called Shockwave for nothing."

Afterwards, when Resonance had dismissed them to go home, Clare and Linus made their way through the silent and softly lit streets in apprehensive silence. Clare walked with a distant look on her face, staring into nothingness and lost in her own thoughts. Linus listened closely to the quiet of the night, every now and then uneasily surveying their surroundings, wary now of the danger present in their city.

A dark shape moving against the soft glow of the night sky caught the corner of his eye and he froze in his tracks, looking up quickly, his shoulders tensing. Along the rooftops of the buildings beside them, a silhouette ran stealthily, soundlessly across their edges towards them. As they drew closer, there was a turn of a shadowy head and the silhouette stopped and seemed to stare down at him through the hazy glow of a streetlamp.

A dark blue hood drawn over a familiar head of tousled brown hair; a green scarf hanging loosely around his neck. A backpack was slung over one of his shoulders and the clothes were different, more civilian, but the figure beneath them was the same. Shockwave gazed down at Linus with an inscrutable expression on his sober face, his shoulders gently rising and falling as he sought to catch his breath from running.

After a pause, Linus slowly raised a hand in silent greeting to the Vigilante. Above, Shockwave didn't budge, looking back down at Linus for a few seconds more before moving his own hand to the scarf hanging around his neck. He pulled the fabric up over his nose, gave a solemn nod, then hitched his backpack higher up onto his shoulder, leaning into a run back towards the direction of the Base.

Linus watched him disappear over the rooftops and thought, for all his solemnity, Shockwave might well be one of the most lethal Vigilantes in the City.

That is, if the newly arrived threats to their city weren't even stronger.

One of the most important unspoken rules of being a Vigilante could be summed up in one word: compartmentalisation.

Everyone who took their Abilities to the night knew about compartmentalisation, and anybody who didn't would soon learn about it for themselves. Compartmentalisation: the act of separating your true self from your Vigilante self; keeping apart your person during the day from your façade during the night. It was the reason that Aliases were so important to an active Vigilante. They weren't just a tool to hide your identity from others, but also a handle to which you could fix your Vigilante persona, to regulate the time which you spent in the hellraiser corners of your mind, be able to pick up and pack away during the day and put on again come the night.

Compartmentalisation was vital to any Vigilante. It wasn't just a matter of discipline, but also a way to deal with all the things that came with having an Ability and spending your nights fighting for justice. It wasn't just about being able to protect yourself from others, but also about being able to protect you from yourself. And most importantly, it allowed everyone with an Ability to play at something that they would never truly be able to do again – and that was to resume a normal life.

Compartmentalisation, Shockwave knew, came easily for Fang. Switching personas came as naturally to her as putting on clothes, and that was apparent both in the shift between her identities as Fang and Resonance as well as in her daily life. Her Alias aside, Shockwave frequently found himself interacting with the many different faces of his teammate from week to week or even day to day. From the reserved, coolly confident and more masculine personality, to the good-natured and unapologetically frank more feminine self, to the even-tempered, easygoing and genderless persona inbetween. In spite of the distinctive differences in appearance, body language, and even way of talking, all of them were equally as much Fang as the others – quick-wit, determination and all. Even Resonance, tough as nails and rough as guts, was still an aspect of Fang that grew from her true self. Maybe it was because of Fang's genderfluidity that compartmentalisation of her Vigilante self came so easily to her.

Shockwave knew plenty of others like this. Vigilantes who, while not necessarily having as distinct a personality split from their day selves, managed to differentiate their two selves just enough so that they could separate them and carry on with their regular lives during the day, untroubled by the problems their night expeditions might have brought them.

Shockwave was no such Vigilante.

Compartmentalisation, unlike with Fang, did not come so easily for him. If there were an obstacle or a difficult task, he would become fixated on it until the problem was solved, even if it meant other priorities temporarily fell by the wayside. His Vigilante self and his true self were virtually the same – or perhaps, his true self had become too much like his Vigilante self in time. It was hard to know anymore. He would find himself ready to leap into action at any moment and constantly on high alert for danger. He didn't restrict his duties to the night like most Vigilantes were ought, instead opting to keep his scarf on him at all times, to slip on when he felt the need arise.

Rather than impeding his capabilities as a Vigilante, however, it made him all the more effective. His drive gave him more opportunities to flex his skills, and so more experience to lend to his duties. If nothing else, for all the potential issues he might come up against, Shockwave's dedication made him even more deadly.

And so when the situation arose, Shockwave, absolutely determined to seek out the people who had murdered his friends, spent every moment that he could spare, regardless of whether he was in class or at work or otherwise, planning and thinking and searching for something, anything, that might give him a lead on his mission. Day after day his investigations would turn out fruitless, his lack of progress leaving him with feelings of frustration and restlessness, constantly itching to go run or fight – whatever might release the pent up anger and energy he'd accumulate over the day. Sometimes he would run and sometimes he would find a fight. Sometimes he would wind up doing both. His long-held aspirations to be *good* grew into a strong urge to become *great* – as great a Vigilante as he could be, so that he could avenge his friends, and so he would never find himself in a position of weakness or vulnerability ever again.

When Shockwave arrived back at the Base that night, air was cold but he felt warm. He could feel the heat of his breath against his face beneath his scarf, the blood in his cheeks flushed red from adrenaline, and he could feel the sting of the grit in the grazes on his knuckles. His jacket, shirt and trousers felt constricting on him compared to the t-shirt and sweatpants he usually wore for his Vigilante activities, and his bag felt heavy on his shoulder. He fished out his keys, unlocked the front door, and stepped inside the house.

As he shut the door behind him the light clicked on in the hallway and he looked up to see Fang standing at the kitchen doorway, in slouchy cargos and a loose grey t-shirt, one hand over the light switch to her side. Upon seeing Shockwave she regarded him with a strangely blank expression of almost-surprise, which he answered with a raised brow as he loosened the collar of his shirt; Fang's surprise then gave way to a groan of frustration and she raised a hand and put it to her face.

"Half an hour," she muttered. "If you'd been here half an hour ago..."

"What happened half an hour ago?" Shockwave pushed his hood back off his head and slid his bag onto the floor, kicking off his thick-soled skate shoes and nudging them to the edge of the hallway with his foot.

"I got involved in your mess is what." Fang sighed and waved her teammate towards the kitchen. Shockwave followed, all but throwing himself into a chair, and Fang pulled open the fridge and tossed him a clear plastic bottle.

"Thanks."

"Sure."

Fang leaned back against the fridge, her arms crossed, studying Shockwave as he gulped down mouthfuls of icy water, taking in his appearance from his tousled, almost dishevelled hair to his freckled, dirt-smudged face and grazed knuckles. She glanced over his attire –blue-black anorak, grey button-down shirt and belted tan chinos – and knew they were the same clothes he had set out to class in that morning.

"So what happened while I was out?" Shockwave asked, but Fang shook her head.

"You first," she replied. "Where have you been? I thought you were coming straight back after class."

"Changed my mind."

"And?"

"Nothing."

"Your clothes and your knuckles aren't saying 'nothing'."

"Nothing important I mean." Shockwave's bitterness was evident in the furrows between his brows. "Some guys raising Cain on Eastside. Big deal. Doesn't help me any on this mission." His grip tightened on his bottle of water and he put it down onto the tabletop with more force than was necessary. Fang watched him silently fuming then uttered a sigh, unfolding her arms and standing before him at the table.

"Those kids were here again," she said. "From the other night."

"I saw them on my way back." Shockwave picked up the bottle again and raised it to his lips. "What did they want this time?" For a moment, but only for a moment, Fang hesitated on her decision to tell her teammate what it was that she'd been told. A small and anxious voice in her head warned her to consider the consequences of giving Shockwave exactly what it was that he wanted – if he was already throwing himself so hard into the investigation alone, what might happen if he finally had a target to set his sights on?

That troublesome anxiety again; always getting in the way when she least wanted it to. She ignored the voice, pushing past her worries and recommitting herself to her decision.

"They found out who the Vigilante killers are."

The sudden look that Shockwave gave her was hard and steely. He put the bottle down again and leaned into the table.

"Tell me," he said, and it was not a voice to be argued with.

"A musician's manager and his crew," Fang replied. "Leader's name is Shaan Mehra. Works for Cavall Robinson, some electronica guy playing at The Niterie at the moment. No apparent Ability but seems proficient in the use of knives. His team are Robinson's technician and security detail. You've met the technician – rope dart, has some kind of electricity Ability."

"Yeah, I know the one. Name?"

"Faye. Don't know her surname."

Shockwave grunted. "And security?"

"Not sure on name, but he's a big Russian guy who looks like he can pack a punch, apparently. Managed to keep up with Fisticuffs in a fight the other day, or so it seems."

"So a strength Ability."

"Maybe. Probably not to be underestimated at any rate."

"Is that all they said?"

"Yeah."

Shockwave leaned back in his seat and ran his hands through his hair, forehead creasing into a frown. Fang knew those gestures well; it was the same motions every time, the unmistakeable tells that meant that he was considering new facts and weighing up his options. The signs that he was coming up with a course of action, and the tokens of the acumen that made him such a good Vigilante.

After a moment of silence he emerged from his meditative state and glanced up at Fang.

"I need a favour," he said.

"I'm not joining your cause," Fang warned, but Shockwave shook his head.

"No, I know," he said. "I meant something else."

"Then fire away."

"I want you to take me to see Gravitas."

Fang raised an eyebrow.

"Are you sure? If I won't help…"

"You say that, but from what I've heard he's a lot more benevolent than you."

"Cute. Why can't you go yourself?"

"I'm shy around strangers."

Shockwave's deadpan response was met with a laugh from Fang, which he answered with an easy smile.

"No, you just know him better than me is all," he said. "I don't know how to approach him."

"Fine," Fang replied, shaking her head. "I'll take you. Nine o'clock tomorrow, from here. Don't be late. Okay?"

"Wouldn't miss it for the world."

For better or worse, Clare wasn't one to agonise over things she couldn't change.

It had always been that way for her, whether the issue was big or small. If it seemed fit to go with the flow, then she would roll with all the punches and let them glance off her shoulder. Her cat had gone missing once when she was still in primary school – from the time she disappeared until the time she came back, Clare was nonplussed. She knew cats had their own mysterious agenda, and if she wanted to come back then she would come back. Sometimes, when you weren't in control of events, you just had to patiently wait and see the outcome.

But Mallory, now missing for two nights, was not a cat. Clare knew Mallory inside out, and if there was one thing that Clare had learned from ten years of friendship it was that Mallory was any-thing but secretive and mysterious. Mallory was straightforward and to-the-point, a person who couldn't see a purpose to beating around the bush and who was very clear about her intentions in just about anything she did. She was the cautious one of the group, the one who made sure that they all had a plan for whatever they were doing and knew where they were going and when they were coming back.

So up and disappearing out of the blue, without any notice whatsoever, was not something that Mallory would do if she could help it. Her vanishing was unusual at best and distressing at worst. For the first time in a long while, Clare felt anxious and genuinely restless.

Well, restlessness was nothing out of the ordinary – or at least for a Vigilante. Since she'd acquired her Ability (almost seven months ago now), Clare was always feeling restless. She'd had trouble getting to sleep any night for all the energy coursing through her veins. That was par for the course in her situation.

But no. The restlessness that Clare was experiencing was quite a different sort as of late. Rather than being plain adrenaline, the cause of her wakefulness was due to unease, the uncomfortable feeling that somewhere along the line, things had started to go very wrong and there was nothing she could do to stop it. Mallory's conspicuous absence was gnawing away at her and Linus both, and repeated attempts to call or message her were to no avail – in the beginning all their calls just rang out, but after a while they just went straight to voicemail. Neither of them were sure if that meant Mallory's phone had just died or if she was intentionally ignoring them for some reason.

Still, Clare tried her best to stay on course and to keep on going with her daily life. She tried to make herself believe that Mallory would come back soon, that everything would be okay, and that their lives would soon go back to how they were before – not as far back as before their change, but after that. Uni during the day and patrols and occasional butt-kicking at night. The good life with good friends.

So Clare woke up as usual, took her longboard to classes as usual, did her best to sit through her lectures as usual, and half-heartedly took down notes on things she was, in truth, struggling to pay attention to. Five o'clock couldn't have come sooner – her lecturer had barely dismissed the class before Clare had shoved her notebooks back into her bag, grabbed her board, then made her way out of campus and back into the thrum of the CBD, full of faces all eager to get home, just as she was. She jumped on her board, launched herself onto the road, then kicked her way off down High Street. Wind in her face, deep in her thoughts, she sped past the crowded footpaths when she thought she saw, just for a second, a familiar face walking amidst the throngs of people.

Mallory.

Clare broke from her trance and looked up with a start, abruptly slamming a foot into the tarmac and jerking to a short stop. A car honked angrily at her from behind; Clare hastily scooped up her board from the road and ducked onto the sidewalk as it shot past. She craned her neck to try see over the dozens of heads in her path and – there. She would recognise that ponytail anywhere.

Clare called out but her voice was lost amidst the buzzing of the swarm and the tumult of heavy traffic – cursing, she began to beat her way upstream, weaving in and out between pedestrians as she tried to catch up to Mallory, lost in the masses.

There was a sudden jerk as she accidentally caught someone with the tail of her board; an indignant *"Watch it!"* prompted Clare to turn her head and blurt out an automatic "Sorry!" and although the exchange took less than a second it cost her. When Clare whipped her head back around she could no longer see that familiar brown ponytail in the crowds ahead anymore.

An exclamation of exasperation slipped from her mouth before she knew it. Digging her phone from her pocket, she brought up Mallory's number and hit the call button, but once again her attempt went straight to voicemail, the sound of her friend's answer message muffled and faint, drowned in the blaring sirens of a police patrol car as it squeezed its way through the rush hour traffic to her side.

Four blocks away, towards the other end of the CBD, a young man in a grey and green hoodie and khakis ducked into a narrow alleyway and stowed himself out of sight. He eyed his surroundings, then jumped up and grabbed onto a nearby fire escape and began to climb.

Since Fang had told him what she had been informed of the previous night regarding the Vigilante killers' true identities, Shockwave had not been able to think of anything else. All night his mind had been fixated on his next course of action – where next he would go, what he would do, planning out every single detail of how exactly he would exact his vengeance for his felled comrades. Not that it ever did, but sleep did not come easily for him that night – he knew that he wanted to get the jump on his newfound targets as soon as possible. But still, as fired up as he was to make progress on his mission, he couldn't go much further until Fang took him to see Gravitas, in whom he could hopefully find a willing ally.

Shockwave didn't know a lot about Gravitas, nor how it was that Fang knew him, but one thing that he did know about him was that he was a force unto his own. He was one of the oldest Vigilantes that Shockwave knew of, one of the earliest generations to have undergone the Change. His Ability wasn't very well-known (in fact, he was known to keep it on the down low) but rumour was that he had been just as (if not even more) powerful and infamous as Fisticuffs in his heyday. He had been a much more active Vigilante in the beginning, but over the years he'd become much more peaceable – or perhaps more jaded. Eventually he'd opened up a small café/bar in town to which he now devoted most of his time to managing, putting his life as a Vigilante on the backburner and refraining from getting involved in Vigilante matters if he could. Even so, he was known to be a generous man, and wouldn't turn down a person in need if he was asked. Shockwave hoped that generosity extended to active Vigilantes as well; perhaps Fang being an old friend would give them – him – some kind of leverage in the matter.

In the meanwhile, eager as he was to meet him, Shockwave knew he ought to make an effort to retain some semblance of his normal life, even if for no other reason than to keep up appearances. So he got up in the morning as usual, walked to classes as usual, did his darndest to sit through his lectures as usual, and impatiently scribbled down vague notes on things he was, in truth, only half paying attention to. Five o'clock couldn't have come sooner – his lecturer had barely dismissed the class before he had shoved his notebooks back into his bag, pushed his way out the doors, then made his way out of campus and back into the thrum of the CBD, tuning out the noise of the crowds as he set off downtown with one very clear objective in mind.

There were few places left in the City that Shockwave hadn't explored. Be it in his night patrols or in his parkour training, he had gradually become familiar with its buildings and its streets and backalleys and the lines that they drew across the city. As a result of this, he could see exactly in his mind's eye the best route to take to the nightlife district in order to remain unseen. Barely making a sound, he clambered quickly up the fire escape of an apartment block, scaling six storeys until he reached the top of the metal staircase. Swinging himself over the side of the railing to perch over the alley below, he glanced over to the building opposite, calmly judged his distances, then suddenly launched himself out into the air – stretching out his arms and legs, he landed perfectly and noiselessly at the lip of the building, gripping tightly with his fingers at the edge of the brickwork before propelling himself upwards with his legs, pulling himself over the parapet and onto the rooftop.

Straightening up and brushing the brick dust from his hands, he strode over towards the opposite end of the building and glanced out over the cityscape. All the tall office blocks and skyscrapers of the City were behind him in the CBD, and a more or less clear line of sight towards the nightlife district lay stretched out before him. Adjusting the straps of his backpack, he began his run – light-footed steps over the bridges between rooftops, smooth traverses along the cables between buildings. A stride here, a precise jump there; slick lines across the breadth of the City stretching out from the centre of town towards its waking edges.

The only time Shockwave really visited the nightlife district was in his night patrols, and even then he felt his presence was superfluous at best. At night, when the district was thrumming with life, it was well-lit and well-looked after by bouncers and security guards. Trouble was usually stopped before it started and swiftly dealt to if it did occur – and besides which, Shockwave didn't like to draw attention to himself if he could help it. Civilians, authorities, whoever – during its waking hours, this district was much too lively for him.

Still, while it wasn't his usual choice of haunt, he wouldn't come here if he didn't have reason to. After half an hour of traversing over the tops of clubs and bars, he finally reached the end of his journey – crouching down beside the ventilation shaft on the rooftop of a bar, he gazed out across the street at the tall, dark blue façade of the Niterie.

Shockwave had done his research. He knew that the Niterie, as well as being a nightclub, also reserved at least one of its five levels above the main floor of its soundproofed building to accommodate the talent that it hosted – and that currently, Cavall Robinson was one such act staying in their rooms. Problem was, he didn't know which floor or which room.

He slid his backpack off his shoulders and let it drop by his heels behind the ventilation shaft, scanning the vast windows across from him for any sign of the musician. From the pictures he had seen online, Robinson couldn't have been that much older than Shockwave himself – there was something about his gaze that made him seem keener and wiser than his young face would suggest, however.

He wasn't here for Robinson though – he was much more interested in his crew. He was already familiar with Faye, the chaindart wielder, having fought her, but he was still out on the other two, the brawler and the knife-wielder. His plan was to get eyes on them and observe them, to tail them for a while. He still had plenty of time before he had to meet Fang.

As Shockwave sat and watched and waited, a stream of people crossed back and forth along each of the upper floors of the Niterie, irregular in their rhythm, slipping in and then out of his field of vision. Staff and technicians no doubt, and other miscellaneous folk – none of them raised any red flags to him, a cursory glance clearing most of any suspicion right off, a further few seconds of scrutiny absolving the rest. After nearly three hours with no sign of his target, Shockwave was beginning to feel impatient. He had already shifted his position several times to circumvent the buzz that signalled an oncoming wave of pins and needles. It was already well past eight o'clock – the surrounding area was well filled with people, streetlamps and building lights alike had already flickered into life, and the sun had long since disappeared behind the shadow of the cityscape. He sighed, shifting his weight, and began to look away when a dark-haired figure appeared in a window on the fourth floor.

Shockwave glanced over then did a sharp double take, a spark of adrenaline jolting him to his senses. Standing at the window and looking down at the street below, broad-shouldered, tall even with a slight slouch, was Cavall Robinson. He was wearing a slouchy hooded sweat-shirt and he had an easy, relaxed way of holding himself, almost as if one unaware of or indifferent to his own fame. It was because of this insouciance that Shockwave had almost glanced right over him, looking back only when he recognised his face from his concert posters.

And if Robinson was here, then that meant...

The musician turned away from the window suddenly, as if called. Someone else approached him from behind and placed a hand on his shoulder – someone taller, darker-skinned, lean in build, with the striking good looks of an Indian prince. He was smartly dressed in a crisp blue shirt and black sweatervest, a jacket over his arm and a phone held up to his ear. Shockwave sat up a little straighter – the chances of this being Shaan Mehra, Robinson's manger and the knife-wielding figure in black, seemed pretty good.

Shaan lowered the phone to share a few words with his employer and Shockwave took the opportunity to give him a once-over. In stark contrast to Robinson's relaxed demeanour, there was a certain dignity to way Shaan stood. For the supposed mastermind behind the rash of mostly-violent Vigilante deaths, he didn't seem like the type of guy who would get his hands dirty. Then again, Shockwave had learned a long time ago that you couldn't judge a person just by their appearance... especially not when they led a secret double-life.

Robinson brushed past his manager and out of view, leaving the latter at the window alone. He raised his phone to his ear again, returning to his conversation. Shockwave checked his watch to find that time had crept up on him and it was already past nine o'clock. He cursed and stood up quickly, snatching up his backpack in the same motion. He'd been so distracted by his task that he'd lost track of time – Fang had no patience for tardiness, but if he returned now she might still be at the Base. After all, as she had stated many times, it was his mission, not hers – the likelihood of her having left without him was low, especially considering the request he had made of her.

He'd better return now in any case. Slinging his bag onto his shoulder, he glanced back one more time at the windows of the Niterie, then began to run once more over the rooftops, back the way he came.

In the cool quiet of the apartment kitchen, Fang, already in her Vigilante gear, sat and waited for Shockwave. Behind her the refrigerator uttered its low and steady hum, and from the direction of the living room the television could be heard giving off distant chatter. Although she had turned it on, Fang wasn't paying it any real attention– it was only on as background noise, a buffer to prevent any silence-induced anxiety from creeping into her periphery and disrupting her preparations.

Fang was much too impatient to feel the affects of any anxiety though. The kitchen clock indicated it was already past nine o'clock and Shockwave still wasn't back yet. Not that he was always a shining paragon of perfect timeliness, but when it came to things that were important to him he was nearly always ready and where he was needed long before he was due. Tonight, apparently, seemed to be the exception to the rule.

She uttered an irritated sigh. No messages nor calls ahead to indicate a late arrival. Either he was so preoccupied with something that he'd forgotten or lost track of time or he'd gotten himself tied up in some kind of trouble. Either way, her partner's tendency for secrecy as of late was making coordination of shared duties incredibly difficult. She would have to have a word to him about his fixation on his mission and apparent communication issues when she next saw him. Maybe give him some kind of warning.

That would have to come later though. Even though she wasn't on board with his mission, Fang understood its importance to Shockwave – so if it was an audience with Gravitas that Shockwave wanted, then it was an audience with him that he would get. Gravitas' time was precious and Fang didn't want to waste it. Though she didn't like it, it looked as if she might just have to go and speak to him herself in her partner's stead.

She couldn't afford to wait any longer. Fang rose from the table, entered the living room and switched off the television. Silence enveloped the house, but Fang didn't linger to hear it. She moved swiftly, slipping on her shoes and slinging the blue and brown triangle-patterned strap of her drawstring bag over her shoulder.

Resonance opened the door, took a deep breath, and stepped out into the night.

"You saw her *where*?" Linus' eyes were bright and the knuckles of his clenched fists had gone white. Clare was pacing the floor of the garage, wringing her hands and frowning.

"High Street. But I lost her."

"But how could—"

"I tried, okay? I tried calling out to her but she didn't hear me or ignored me or something. I tried her cell too but it was off."

"Doesn't sound like Mallory to ignore anyone."

"Doesn't sound like Mallory to run off and disappear to begin with." Clare gave a sigh and stopped her pacing. "I don't know, Linus. Maybe this is just way bigger than we ever thought. Ever since we learned that there were other Vigilantes nothing's been going right. Going out on patrols doesn't feel the same anymore when you know you're just as much prey as the bad guys we go out trying to catch."

Linus was a little taken aback. It wasn't often that Clare sounded so concerned; usually she was the pillar of optimism that kept their little team trucking. He paused for a second, uncertain as to what to say.

"I kinda felt like, when we got these Abilities of ours," Clare went on. "That we were sort of invincible, you know? I mean, how many other people can say that they can disappear into fog, or use transparent reflective surfaces as portals. It just made me feel like I could handle anything, you know?"

A tense silence fell. Clare buried her brow in her hands. Linus stared at the floor, teeth worrying at his lip, his fingernails curled into his knees and digging into his skin. He suddenly stood up from the couch with such abruptness that it startled Clare. His jaw was set and he looked determined.

"Let's go," he said, the conviction in his voice taking Clare aback for a second. She made a frustrated sound, flinging her arms out in exasperation.

"Go? Go where? We don't even know where to begin."

"So? When has that ever stopped you?" Linus glanced around the garage before spying Clare's softball bat and seizing it from its resting place against the wall. He held it out towards her handle-first.

"I know you freak out sometimes when things start looking tricky," he said softly. "Especially when you realise you've bitten off more than you can chew. And yeah, things seem to have gotten more dangerous over the last week or so. I'm not going to deny that. But I guess it was always complicated and secretive and a little bit dangerous and we just didn't realise it. Maybe this kind of thing was inevitable. But let's just try keep it together for now, okay? Just until we know Mallory is safe. We'll get out there and go look for her. And after this mess is sorted out and we're all together again, we'll probably be able to get back to night patrols like we used to."

Clare looked at the softball bat being offered to her then up at

Linus. Her friend offered her a resolute nod, his attempt at confidence belying the worry that he felt inside.

"What happened to wanting to lay low?" she asked.

Linus shrugged a shoulder.

"Mallory is more important," he replied. "Come on. Things are going to be fine. You'll see."

After a moment of hesitation she uttered a faint laugh and took the bat from him, resting it across her shoulder.

"Yeah," she said. "You're right. Thanks."

"Sure." Linus smiled. "Now let's go, yeah?"

Shockwave returned to the Base at half past nine to find the lights off and the flat deserted. He cursed and threw his bag down onto the hallway floor – of all the ways tonight could have gone, this was going in the wrongest way possible. Making quick strides back to his room, he fumbled with his cellphone with one hand while clumsily stripping off his hoodie with the other. Throwing the garment onto the floor, he pulled clothes from his dresser with unnecessary roughness while pulling up his teammate's number on his phone – the dial tone sounded and it rang and rang but Fang wasn't picking up. Swearing under his breath, Shockwave tossed the phone onto his bed and hastily finished changing out of his shirt and khakis, snatching the device up again as he left the room. As he yanked open the front door he glanced down at his bag on the floor – he stopped himself short, bent and half ripped it open, and pulled his green scarf out from inside.

Slamming the front door shut behind him, Shockwave set off down the street at a run, trying to call Fang's number again. Once again it rang and rang but to no avail. He hung up to try again when suddenly someone leapt out into the dimly lit path before him. Someone tall, broad-shouldered, and all in black with a dark hood.

There was a hard, dull collision and two bodies were sent tumbling over the concrete. The phone slipped out of Shockwave's hand and fell skittering over the pavement. He looked up from the ground to see the hooded figure he had collided with getting up again – blind anger and adrenaline taking sudden hold of him, he scrambled to his feet, and before he knew what he was doing, launched himself at them with a raised fist and an enraged roar.

The hooded stranger blocked his punch with crossed arms but Shockwave was undeterred and he punched again. Fast, almost faster than he could have registered, his opponent deflected his punch away with a sweep of a forearm and grabbed hold of his wrist with one hand – before he knew it, his legs had been kicked out from beneath him and he was crashing onto his back, the breath being driven from his lungs with a pained and surprised cry.

The stranger let go of Shockwave's arm and placed one heavy combat boot on his chest.

"Got that out of your system now?" they said, in a voice quite unlike what he had been expecting.

Shockwave, confused, looked up at the person standing above him. The stranger swept their hood back to reveal the last person that he could have ever anticipated.

CHAPTER SIX

URBAN LEGENDS

Urban legends were the stuff of gossip for Vigilantes. Okay, sure – urban legends were the stuff of gossip for anyone, but they were a particular favourite thread of conversation for the night folk of the world. When you were a Vigilante with a secret double life and tended to have limited contact with many Vigilantes outside your immediate team, it was a good, fun topic to talk about.

Being a Vigilante meant secrecy and discretion. There was no secret society where they all got together and created a nation-wide network through which to communicate – not all Vigilantes would use their Abilities in the same way, and the probability of somebody exploiting such a network for nefarious purposes was just enough that nobody had ever tried. Knowing who-in-where-is-capable-of-what could be a sensational thing, for sure, but it would also be too easy to let slip that so-and-so with such-and-such an Ability lived in the next town over, and that could carry terrible consequences for everyone involved, especially when Vigilantes were wont to making up their own codes and ideas like revenge weren't totally off the table.

But urban legends... now those were exciting. Urban legends rarely came directly from Vigilantes themselves, but were instead borne by the people who had supposedly seen them in action. Not knowing all the details meant that the privacy of the Vigilante in question (whether or not they really existed) remained intact, and regardless of whether or not the stories were true, Vigilantes in cities all over the world were able to secure a sense of solidarity, and maybe even inspiration, just from hearing these tales. Somewhere out there, there was somebody else just like them, a Vigilante using their Ability to own the night – and even if for a moment, it meant that they felt a little bit less alone.

Fisticuffs didn't care much about feeling less alone, but she *was* interested in urban legends.

Working alone was just something that Fisticuffs preferred to do. Most Vigilantes liked to work in little teams, but that was never something that appealed to her. It wasn't that she'd never been offered the chance (because she had, several times); she just found she worked better in solitude. Other Vigilantes were welcome to go about things as they saw fit and she would go about things the way she saw fit.

But now something had changed to threaten the way that both Fisticuffs and other Vigilantes worked. Vigilantes everywhere were getting slowly picked off, one by one, and now the threat was here in the City, *her* city, and so far it had been going unchallenged. For the first time, Fisticuffs found herself considering the possibility of collaborating with or contacting other Vigilantes (for this, it seemed, was a formidable opponent) and she didn't like that at all. No – collaborating could be much too risky on a mission like this, especially when the task required the gathering of so much intelligence. Finding another Vigilante whose methods or Ability complimented your own was not always an easy thing, and how could she be sure that the culprits weren't already amongst the Vigilantes living in the City?

So it was on this night that Fisticuffs thought about an urban legend that she had once heard in the earliest nights of her Vigilante career, just four years ago. Supposedly, in a town not too far from the City, there was a Vigilante by the name of Kinetic. No-one was quite sure what his Ability was, but one thing was for certain – he was a pretty incredible scout, and a genius at collecting intelligence. That is, when he wanted to – word also was that he only did things if they aligned with his own wants, so it couldn't be assumed that he fought the good fight. He wasn't completely without moral compass (neither was he opposed to working with other Vigilantes, in contrast to Fisticuffs), and he had taken down a few bad people in his time, but if a mission didn't interest him then he wouldn't lift a finger.

Well, Fisticuffs supposed, even Vigilantes could have preferences sometimes. Fisticuffs would have liked to be able to contact this Kinetic to propose an alliance, or even to possess his capabilities for herself, as being able to gather intel on a mission like this would have been extremely helpful. But she hadn't heard any further news about Kinetic in years, and she wondered if he was still even around.

No matter, she figured; after all, you couldn't always rely on others. Besides, even if she didn't have the sleuthing prowess of this fabled Vigilante, she was perfectly capable of being able to investigate matters on her own – or at least, in her own ways.

Only two nights ago Fisticuffs had exchanged blows with a Vigilante who possessed, it seemed, more or less the same Ability that she had. It was a battle that ended without a clear winner, as her opponent had taken off abruptly in the middle of proceedings. But it had been long enough – during the skirmish she had seen his face, strong-jawed, sharp-featured, bleach-blond spikes and green eyes; and this information was a major turning point in her ongoing investigations.

These investigations, however, led to some intriguing revelations, one of which made her realise she needed to make contact with certain other Vigilantes around the City after all. And in this case it was a certain Vigilante whom Fisticuffs had seen protecting two youths from a chain-wielding hooded figure and a massive black dog just the other night.

It was just past half past nine when Fisticuffs spied a young man running along a dimly lit suburban street. She attempted to call out to him, but he didn't seem to hear her shouts. So she ran to catch up and stepped out before him on the footpath, only for him to crash straight into her then get up and start throwing punches at her.

So Fisticuffs did as she only could do and blocked his punches, kicking out his legs from beneath him for good measure and pinning him to the ground.

"Got that out of your system now?" she asked, mildly annoyed. She drew back the hood from her head and watched the expression on his face segue from confusion to one of astonished recognition. She took the opportunity to study him herself.

He was only a fraction shorter than she was, with a thick shock of wavy brown hair and sober brown eyes. He was wearing black sweats and a grey t-shirt, dressed, as she was, in appropriately practical gear for his Vigilante duties. There was a graze on his freckled face just under his line of his cheekbone and a long, black smudge of dirt on the outside of his forearm.

"Shockwave, I presume," Fisticuffs greeted him, when he seemed to have calmed down. "I'm…"

"Fisticuffs. You're Fisticuffs." The Vigilante looked as if he'd been thrown for a loop.

Fisticuffs nodded shortly. She'd expected as much. Although she did her best to keep a low profile, same as any other Vigilante, she knew that she herself was something of an urban legend amongst other Vigilantes, though the concept bemused her some-what. She removed her boot from his chest and extended a hand to help him to his feet.

"Sorry about the punches," he said, more equable now. "I thought you were… well. Somebody else."

Fisticuffs shrugged a shoulder and picked his cellphone up from the pavement, handing it to him.

"Occupational hazard. I'm used to it."
Shockwave dusted himself off and held out his hand to shake hers.

"Shockwave," he introduced himself. "But you already seem to know that."

"I do. I've been hoping to make your acquaintance for a while now."

"Given your reputation, it's an honour. How can I help?"

Fisticuffs could appreciate a Vigilante who could jump straight to business.

"I came because I saw your fight the other night, with the black dog," she began. "You probably already know about the Vigilante deaths, am I right?"

"That's right," Shockwave replied carefully. "I've been looking into it a little bit myself."

Fisticuffs briefly looked back over her shoulder to survey the empty street then took a step closer towards him.

"I found something out," she said in a low voice. "About the guys behind the incidents. Information I don't think anybody else knows yet. I'm not sure how much you already know, but I think it's something worth sharing."

Shockwave considered her words. He glanced down towards the end of the street, seeming to inwardly debate with himself, before giving a faint sigh and turning back the direction he'd been running from, gesturing at Fisticuffs to follow.

"Come on," he said. "Let's talk somewhere private."

After Gravitas had more or less retired from his Vigilante duties, he had pursued a long-sought after dream of running his own food establishment and gotten a lease for a small building only a few streets away from the town square. He transformed the ground floor into a modest café called The Estaminet and kept the two floors above as living space for himself. He would run the café during the day, and after closing up he would diligently conduct his nightly managerial business upstairs in his living quarters before going for a breath of fresh air. Though he was now more a café owner than a Vigilante, Resonance knew first-hand that his Vigilante capabilities were nothing to shake a stick at. She understood why Shockwave would be as keen as he was to meet him.

When Resonance arrived at The Estaminet, however, there were no lights on in the café below or either of the top two floors above.

She *hmm*'d to herself.

"Odd," she murmured. "I know he's been open all day…"

She trailed off midsentence then traipsed up the concrete steps to the flat above the café. Resonance paused to listen for a moment, then reached out a hand and knocked on the door. There was a soft creak and the door opened slightly under her touch. The Vigilante frowned deeply. She pushed open the door slightly and peered into the dark.

"Grav?" she called into the flat. "Are you home? It's Resonance."

No response. Resonance could feel the cords in her neck tense. She pushed open the door a little more and stepped inside. It'd been a while since she was here last, but her friend's apartment was exactly the same. Immaculately tidy and spotless; no chair at the table nor book on the bookshelf was out of place, and the coffee table was a meticulously arranged array of remote control rows and magazine stacks. Though the Base was far from being untidy, this house put their quarters to shame.

Resonance looked to a little dish on the table next to the front door to see a set of keys and a wallet sitting within. A pair of shoes were at the entryway and a stack of books were on the dining table. He should have been at home, however…

She crossed the living area to a small staircase and took the steps, two at a time, to the upper levels.

"How much do you already know about the culprits?" Fisticuffs asked.

Shockwave sat down at the basement table.

"Well," he began. "We figured out their true names. Two of them anyway."

"Nice work."

"Can't take credit for that one, I'm afraid. Neither can my partner, and she was the one who told me. Those kids you saw me fighting for the other night, they found out and told her."

"Those kids were Vigilantes?" Fisticuffs echoed. She seemed sceptical. Shockwave shrugged a shoulder.

"They've been in the business a couple months, half a year. Still have a lot to learn, but they've got the determination, in any case."

"Right." Fisticuffs seemed unconvinced. "Anyway, what did they tell you?"

"The leader of the crew is a guy named Shaan," Shockwave said. "He's the manager for some musician in town at the moment. The theory is that he's using the tour as a way to get from city to city easily. His associates are a technician and one of the security personnel. The girl's name is Faye. Don't know security's name though."

"His name is Anton," Fisticuffs said smoothly. "He's head of security for Cavall Robinson's tour group. Faye is Robinson's chief technician. The two of them have been working with him for about two years, Shaan for almost three. Shaan goes by the Alias of Artifice. Faye goes by the name Faraday and Anton calls himself Meteor Hammer."

"They have Aliases? If they have Aliases then it means..."

"They've been Vigilantes for a while? Not sure. If they have, I haven't been able to figure out where they came from. Do you know much about the dog?"

"Can't say so."

"Pity. Neither me. I'm going with the assumption that it's just a pet, but none the less dangerous. They call it Cave Canem, supposedly. Good stuff though, your information matches up with mine."

"That's good to hear."

"In regards to Abilities," Fisticuffs continued. "How much have you learned there?"

"Less concrete, but a bit," Shockwave responded. "Shaan, or Artifice... he hasn't displayed any sort of Ability to any of us in our encounters with him, besides a proficiency with knives. We're not sure if he even has one. The girl Faraday seems to be able to manipulate electrical currents to some extent. Handy for a technician. Seems like she uses her weapon to her advantage on that one as well. We're guessing the big one, Meteor Hammer, has something to do with strength, since the kids said he was able to keep up with you."

"More or less," Fisticuffs nodded curtly. "Meteor Hammer is much the same as I am. Faraday's Ability, to be specific, is the absorbing and transferring of electrical energy. She can drink it in from whatever source is nearby and store it, then transfer it later."

"Sounds a bit like Resonance's Ability," Shockwave murmured quietly. "Alright. Thank you for informing me."

"I'm not finished just yet," Fisticuffs cut in. Shockwave was taken aback.

"What do you mean?"

Fisticuffs sighed deeply.

"This is something I've only just discovered," she said. "I haven't told anyone else about this yet."

Shockwave raised his brows at her and made a gesture urging for Fisticuffs to continue. She paused before she spoke again, in a heavy voice.

"Artifice," she began. "He has an Ability as well. It's not like any Ability I've ever heard of before and I doubt I'll ever hear of such a thing again."

Something about the weight of those words was making Shockwave begin to feel unsettled. Fisticuffs noticed the expression on his face and shook her head.

"Believe me, I've done my research and it's the only thing that makes sense. I'd never think it true myself otherwise."

"Well, what is it?"

Another hesitant pause. Fisticuffs seemed disquieted herself.

"Through touch," she said. "Artifice has the Ability to absorb the energy present in all Ability-wielding Vigilantes. The energy that allows us to have Abilities. Via skin-to-skin contact, he can choose to drain this energy to increase that of his own, or even to transfer it to others."

Shockwave felt the blood drain from his face.

"You mean..." he began. Fisticuffs nodded solemnly.

"He can take away the Abilities of others."

There was a silence as Shockwave registered this information. Then suddenly his eyes grew wide. He stood up from the table abruptly.

"Fang," he said.

Resonance arrived at the upper floor of Gravitas' apartment to find it as dark as the floor downstairs. It was quiet – there was not the sound of breathing, nor of footsteps, nor anything. The presence of the keys and wallet and books downstairs were a clear indicator that he *must* be at home, but there was no sign of him at all.

The bedroom was dark, the bed neatly made. Resonance checked the closet – the clothes that she remembered to be part of Gravitas' Vigilante getup were all still here, so he couldn't have gone out on patrol.

She went to the window and looked out over the street. Beneath, she could see the awning of the café that Gravitas was so proud of. It was impossible that he would have up and left it without good reason. She heaved a sigh.

There was a sudden rhythmic buzzing at her side. Resonance dug her hand into the pocket of her sweatpants and pulled out her phone. It was Shockwave calling. She frowned at the screen.

"Are you going to answer that?"

Resonance started and whirled around.

Next thing she knew she was hurtling through the window and out onto the street below.

Though Linus had done his best to encourage Clare into action, in truth he was just as unsure as she was in terms of where to start searching. They returned to some of the places they liked to hang out in during night patrols, but the chances of Mallory actually being there were slim at best. If Clare really did see her before, then it seemed that she was at least safe – but if she was able to wander around the city freely, then why didn't she just come back home? It didn't make sense.

Then again, there were a lot of things happening nowadays that just didn't make sense. Having Abilities, for example – that barely made sense. That having an Ability was apparently some kind of widespread phenomenon, that also didn't make sense. And the thing that made the least sense of all was the fact that people – other Ability-wielding individuals, even – were willing to kill other human beings over the possession of one. It didn't inspire a lot of confidence in him, that was for sure.

Linus wasn't one to pretend that he knew all the answers, nor was he sure that going out and searching for Mallory would be the sure-fire way to find her; but there was one thing he did know, and that was the way that the night had a calming effect on Clare's mind.

So he talked his friend into going outdoors for a walk. During their conversation at home she had been noticeably agitated, but as they continued walking in companionable silence through town, aimless in their navigation, he could tell she was starting to relax.

"You know," Linus said, breaking up the quiet. "If – I mean, when."

"Yeah?"

"When Shaan and Faye and such have been put away or whatever and this is all over... I think we should ask Shockwave and Resonance for some advice on how to be good Vigilantes, you know?"

A smile spread across Clare's face.

"Do you think they'd actually give us any apart from 'go home and stay out of trouble'?"

Linus laughed.

"Okay, point. But Resonance might be more forthcoming than Shockwave, you know? Either way, they have a lot of experience. Could make for some interesting stories."

"Sure. I guess. Maybe." Clare shrugged. "I dunno. I guess I just like the idea of being able to learn for ourselves, the way they probably did. But yeah, it'd probably be cool to learn from their experiences too. Know what to do and what not to do and all that. Avoid any big mistakes they might've done."

"Right." Linus gave a nod. "You don't have to be hit by a car to know it hurts."

It was at that moment the sound of shattering glass pierced the night.

Everything hurt.

She could taste blood on her lips and smell the tar of the rough asphalt underneath her. Everything was blurring in and out of focus and something was screaming shrilly in her ear and everything hurt.

Just metres away from her there came the vibrations of rhythmic buzzing. She glanced up, dazed, and out of the periphery of her vision she could see her phone ringing with an incoming call. Shockwave again.

She tried to reach out a hand towards it but there was glass in her arms and in her back and her phone was just out of reach.

At the sound of breaking glass, Clare and Linus had stopped dead in their tracks to look at each other, wide-eyed and startled.

"...That sounded like it was just around the corner," Clare said in hushed tones.

There was a moment of hesitation then the two of them broke suddenly into a run and rounded the corner onto the next street. What they saw ahead made Clare utter a horrified gasp and Linus clasp a hand over his mouth.

Sprawled out on her side in the middle of the street, surrounded by shards of glass in all directions, was Resonance. For a moment Linus was afraid that she was unconscious, but then slowly she began to move – little by little, pain obvious from the expression on her face, she began to push herself up onto her hands. Pieces of glass were embedded in her; with shaking hands, she reached for a shard back near her shoulder blade and yanked it out with a strangled cry of pain.

"Come on!" Clare grabbed at Linus' arm and ran forward towards her.

"Resonance!"

The Vigilante looked up from the ground and when she saw them her eyes widened. As they drew close she gestured violently at them and tried to push them away.

"Go!" she demanded. "Get out of here!"

"What happened to you?!"

"It doesn't matter, just go!!"

Clare and Linus were bewildered.

"But what—"

"You should do as she says," a voice said, and they all looked up.

A cluster of silhouettes emerged from the upper level of the building before them to descend the concrete steps. As they stepped into the light their faces became clear – in the forefront, Shaan Mehra, shortly followed by Faye, a massive man with bleach-blond spikes, and a huge black dog with glowing amber eyes.

Shaan smiled pleasantly at them. Faye's gaze fell on Clare and her eyes narrowed. Clare's grip on her bat tightened involuntarily.

"Nice to see you again," Shaan greeted them warmly. "Better go while you still can."

For a moment time seemed to freeze.

Resonance was first the break the silence.

"*Go!!*" she yelled again, and this time Clare and Linus obeyed, leaping into action and turning back the way they'd come. The black dog tore after them with a vicious snarl; Linus gave a shout as it almost snapped its teeth on his ankle and he fell against Clare; the dog lunged at them but missed and shot over their heads as the two of them tumbled hard down over the street, Clare's softball bat falling from her grasp and clanging away.

Clare pushed herself to her knees and hauled Linus to his feet, throwing him forwards. As she was about to get up a foot caught her in the side and threw to the left, and she looked up as someone stood above her – Faye, with her long ponytail and dangly silver earrings, her chain dart in a coil in her left hand. There was something gentle and pretty about her face but a kind of intensity was apparent in her eyes as well – an intensity that, at that moment, was directed at Clare.

"That was some pretty dirty fighting the other night," she said. Her voice was soft. Charming. Dangerous. "Fights should be fair and even-handed. Not dishonourable and below the belt. Don't you think?"

She reached for the end of her chain with her right hand.

Linus stumbled towards the footpath and tripped on the curb. He tried to get up but the black dog was suddenly there and it hunched over him, hackles raised, growling and ferocious.

Shaan stepped into view and stood over him, smiling.

Resonance pulled out another shard of glass and reached once again for her phone when the man with the bleach-blond hair seized her and threw her into the front wall of The Estaminet. At the last second she absorbed the impact, the force giving her enough energy to get back up onto her feet after she fell. She tore the last piece of glass from her arm as she stood and faced her opponent with a fierce glower.

"Come on then," she growled. "Show me what you got."

A mid-to-long range weapon. That's what Resonance had said

about the rope dart. Clare tried to keep this in mind as she frantically dodged Faye's lances but could barely find a way to get close. Was getting close even advisable? Would it help her at all?

A few metres away, behind Faye, Clare could see her softball bat lying on the pavement. There were the barest traces of fog on this street – it wasn't much but it was better than nothing. Clare concentrated hard, narrowly escaping another strike from the chain dart, and tumbled into the fog. She reappeared again on her knees beside her bat and she snatched it up – Faye whirled around to face her and Clare tried her best to look confident, preparing to attack or dodge or disappear, when suddenly she noticed the lights coming fast down the street towards them.

Pinned down and clearly in danger, Linus couldn't help but feel something flutter in his chest as Shaan smiled that charming smile down at him. Perhaps, he thought, this was true fear. The kind of fear that an injured bird might feel when confronted by a hungry cat. Or when you had a fierce predator above you and another to your side.

There was a stiletto in Shaan's right hand; he tossed it easily to his left and Linus felt his stomach go cold. Shaan knelt down by Linus' side.

"It's a shame," he said. "I would have liked to hear your tunes someday. But now you know who we are, you definitely can't be allowed to live."

He took hold of Linus' wrist in his right hand, and Linus felt a sensation like a static shock run through him. Instantly, he knew something had changed. A physical tiredness weighed him down and he suddenly felt heavy.

"What did you–" Shaan winked at him. He raised the knife.

There was the sound of an approaching engine and he looked up to his left.

Resonance dodged another punch and threw herself at the blond-haired man with as much energy as she could muster. She might as well not have done anything at all – the man batted her aside with a mere sweep of his hand and she was sent toppling to the ground again, absorbing the energy from the impact as she fell. She looked up to see her phone on the ground before her and quickly snatched it up, twisting herself onto her back and kicking at her opponent's knee as he approached.

The man stumbled back and Resonance used the opportunity to get back up onto her feet again. This much she was sure of – she was not at all prepared for this fight.

She thought about Gravitas and realised he was probably already dead. As soon as she had realised something was wrong she should have left immediately and come back during the daytime. But instead they were getting thrashed –

There was the screeching of car tyres and she turned to look behind her. An ancient-looking blue car came screaming down the street towards them, skidding sideways down the middle of the road. Clare vanished into the fog and it passed through where she had just been; the car clipped Faye and sent her crashing to the ground. Resonance jumped away just in time as it came towards her – the man with the bleach-blond spikes was not so fast and the side of the car slammed into him and threw him backwards into a power pole.

The driver's seat window of the car was rolled down – Resonance looked towards it and the familiar face of a girl with a long brown ponytail stuck her head out and shouted at her.

"Get Clare and Linus!" Mallory yelled.

Resonance nodded, dazed, and turned back to look for the others. She shouted Clare's name – Clare locked eyes with her and took her cue, almost immediately vanishing into the fog, reappearing by the car and throwing herself inside through the open backseat window.

Resonance ran towards Shaan, who had a knife raised in his left hand – with an almighty roar of *"Get away from him!"* she tackled him and the both of them went skittering across the ground, Resonance overshooting and skidding further away. Shaan threw the knife towards her and she barely dodged, the blade glancing off her shoulder.

In the confusion the black dog had taken his attention away from Linus and Linus took the opportunity to shove it off him with an almighty heave that made him realise just how much his body ached; the dog was thrown backwards with a yelp and Linus pushed himself up to his elbows.

Then for a second – just a second – the dog's form changed. Instead of a great black beast, another figure crouched on the ground before Linus. A figure with a handsome face, dark hair and startling blue eyes. A figure that only three nights ago Linus had watched on the stage at The Niterie.

Cavall Robinson glowered back at him.

Resonance avoided a slash from another knife and threw a punch at Shaan's face – Shaan dodged almost effortlessly, twisting around, and Resonance stumbled past him – she used the momentum to fall into a roll and came back up, almost turning back to face him again, but then instead choosing to run.

She ran towards Linus, who half-lay on the ground, petrified in the gaze of the huge black dog, who growled at him with livid eyes and bared teeth.

"*Linus!*"

Linus looked up at her at the sound of his name and the black dog lunged at him; Linus was knocked back onto the ground, his head striking the concrete and rendering him unconscious. The dog turned its attention to Resonance and leapt – Resonance dodged and it missed her, careering into Shaan who was only a few metres behind her.

Further down the road Mallory had revved up her engine again and was speeding back towards them, the backseat door flung wide open. Resonance seized Linus and pulled him up with all her might; as the car approached Resonance used a burst of strength to throw him into the backseat and began to run after the vehicle. Shaan and the black dog leapt out of the way as the car shot towards them; Clare hauled Linus' unconscious body into the backseat and yelled "*Come on!*" back at Resonance, who used her last ounce of energy to leap and grab Clare's hand, every muscle in her body screaming –

The car door slammed shut. Resonance lay on her back on the seat, breathing hard and fast, blood trickling from the cuts in her arms, her formerly grey sweatpants now stained with patches of red. Clare sat looking stricken beside her and Linus lay in a senseless heap at their feet. Clare gulped down breaths of air and found it in her to say a single name.

"Mallory."

The girl in the front seat turned to smile shakily at them.

"Looks like I made it just in time," Mallory said.

CHAPTER SEVEN

NO SECRETS

When they were certain that they hadn't been followed from The Estaminet, Mallory pulled the car into a sidestreet and switched off the lights.

"I don't understand," Clare stammered. "Mallory, where have you been? We haven't seen you in days!"

Mallory killed the engine and turned around in the front seat. Clare was taken aback at how worn out she looked; there were shadows under her eyes and she looked drawn and grey. Her hair was a mess and she was still in the same clothes that Clare had seen her in last.

"I'm sorry," Mallory said, an apologetic smile on her face. "I meant to come back. I really did. My hands were tied though."

"What even happened?"

"Not now. I'll tell you later. How's Linus doing?"

Clare pulled Linus up onto the seat beside her and brushed the hair away from his face. There was blood at the side of his head and he was still out cold.

"I don't know," she answered, worried. "I can't tell, but…"

"He'll be okay," Resonance said. She hadn't said a word during the car ride up until now, instead wordlessly applying pressure to one of the wounds on her arm with her scarf. "The dog got the jump on him and he hit his head. He's lucky it wasn't the back of his skull."

"So he'll wake up soon?"

"I'm not sure. He could be out for a bit while his body takes time to recover. But he's a Vigilante. He'll survive. The energy that gives us Abilities helps us to heal as well."

"Cave Canem," Mallory said. Resonance and Clare looked up at her.

"What was that?"

"The dog. His name is Cave Canem."

"How...?"

"They all have Aliases."

"All of them?"

Mallory nodded.

"Yeah. The leader, the one with the knives, he's called Artifice. The girl is Faraday. The big guy is Meteor Hammer. Meteor Hammer's Ability is super strength and Faraday can absorb and transfer electrical currents."

"Hang on, how do you know all this?" Resonance looked at her in bewilderment. "And how did you even know where to find us?"

"Turns out a lot can happen in a couple of nights," Mallory replied, uncharacteristically cryptic. She flashed a quick smile at the Vigilante. "Enough about that though. Are you two alright?"

Clare cautiously felt her side below her ribs, where Faye had kicked her.

"Just bruised, I think," she said. "Nothing broken."

"Resonance? You look like you've been through the wars."

Resonance smiled grimly.

"Wars, third-floor window, same difference. Nothing I can't handle." She took her scarf away from her arm and inspected the bloodstains. She made a face. "My scarf is going to need some serious care though."

Mallory sighed.

"Sorry I couldn't be there sooner," she said. "I wasn't even sure if I'd make it in time."

"Hey, you turning up was nothing short of a miracle." Clare pushed herself up so she was sitting a little straighter. Her muscles ached and her knees felt bruised. "You're a lifesaver, Mal. Thanks."

"Yeah." Resonance placed her scarf back over her arm. "Thanks, Mallory. I owe you one this time."

"Just call it even and it'll be enough. I haven't forgotten about the fire just yet." She turned back in the driver's seat. "Here, buckle in and I'll take us all home."

"Thanks," Resonance replied. "But I can get home myself. It'll be fine."

Clare looked at Resonance in surprise and Mallory turned back around to stare at her with a similar expression.

"Resonance, are you sure?" Clare asked, concerned. "You got thrown out a window, for crying out loud."

"Yeah, and it's a pain in the neck but it's nothing I haven't handled before. I'm a professional, remember? Besides," she pointed out the windshield down the street ahead. "Look. I'm only a couple of blocks away. Seriously, I'll be fine."

"I don't know about this," Mallory muttered. "For all we know they're still out there. Looking for us."

"You clipped one of them with your car and slammed another one headfirst into a power pole," Resonance reminded her. "Even if we are targets, I don't think they'd come hunt us down right away. They'll be back, for sure, but they'll need time to recover. And so do we, for that matter."

Resonance tied her scarf around her arm and opened the car door. Carefully, gingerly, she stepped outside onto the street. Clare leaned over to look out at her.

"Just be safe then, okay?" she called. "We'll come see you after Linus has woken up again. So you better be there."

Resonance winked at her.

"You got it," she replied. She looked to Mallory, who had rolled down the window. "Thanks again, Mallory. You'll have to tell me how you found out all this information at some point. Could always do with a tale about danger and espionage."

A smile flittered across Mallory's lips.

"It's nothing as grand as all that," she replied. "But alright. I'll see you soon."

Resonance waved and departed, going off slowly across the street to disappear into the shadow of the buildings ahead. Mallory watched after her as she left; Clare moved across the backseat and laid Linus down across the upholstery.

"Are you ready?" Mallory glanced at Clare in the rear-view mirror. Clare nodded and Mallory started up the engine again. They went the rest of the way home in silence.

In the wake of the chaos, Artifice slowly sat up, dusted himself off, and turned to regard the black dog lying by his side. The dog lay still, eyes closed, its back rising and falling with its breathing.

"Cavall?"

The dog didn't respond. Artifice reached a hand towards it when the dog's eyes flew open and it snapped at his fingers with a vicious bark, spittle spraying from its jaws; Artifice jerked his hand back and shot to his feet, moving back a few steps. The dog glared at him then closed its amber eyes and put its head down again, growling under its breath.

Concern on his face, Artifice reluctantly turned away and approached Faraday, picking herself up off the ground on unsteady feet. She accepted the hand that Artifice offered her, giving a sharp hiss of pain as she straightened.

"How's Cavall?" she asked through gritted teeth.

Artifice paused then shook his head gently. He glanced over his comrade.

"Does it hurt anywhere?" he asked.

Faraday shook her head and waved a hand at him.

"Nothing I can't handle," she muttered. "Go help Anton."

"I'm fine," a rumbling voice said. Gingerly, Meteor Hammer pushed himself up, using the power pole to support himself as he stood. As he stretched, a few sharp cracks could be heard as he stretched his back and worked out the kinks in his arms and legs. He looked back to Artifice.

"Go help Cavall," he said.

Artifice looked back behind him to see that the black dog wasn't a dog anymore. He let go of Faraday and walked towards the person now sitting in its place, head down, legs drawn up and elbows resting on their knees.

"Cavall?"

Cavall Robinson looked up at Artifice through tousled hair and red-rimmed eyes.

"It's getting worse," he said.

Artifice heaved a sigh then sat down beside him.

"I know," he replied. Cavall looked back down at his shoes again.

"That kid saw," he said. Artifice frowned.

"I know," he replied.

Wordlessly, Cavall held out a hand and Artifice took it. A faint white glow appeared in the space between their palms, intensified, then was gone.

"Better?" Artifice asked. Cavall nodded and rose to his feet.

"For now."

Upon returning home, Clare and Mallory both changed into some fresh clothes and Clare tended to her injuries. They laid Linus down on his bed and Mallory did her best to clean the blood from his hair and the wound on his head. Clare peered out through a gap in the curtains to look out at the street below. It was still, but it was a deceptive sort of stillness; it was quiet, but somehow now that quiet had become ominous. A dark and foreboding silence.

Clare gave a sigh. Mallory turned to acknowledge her with a questioning look on her face. Clare hesitated for a moment, wondering how to phrase her thoughts.

"Just before we went out and got into that fight," she said. "Linus was saying how everything was going to be alright soon. We're out of the house for ten minutes and then Resonance gets thrown out a third-storey window." She gave a chuff of mirthless laughter. "I think we're in a lot deeper than we realised."

"…Yeah." Mallory nodded solemnly. "You're not wrong."

It was Clare's turn to look at her friend with a questioning gaze. Mallory leaned forward, resting her elbows on her knees. She studied Clare carefully for a little while.

"Do you want to know a really awful secret?" she asked. It was a second before Clare nodded, tentatively, in response. It was another second before Mallory spoke again.

"I don't know when exactly," she said. "And I don't know how. But somehow, after the night with that fire… I lost my Ability."

Clare frowned.

"What do you mean, 'lost'?"

"I mean as in I wasn't able to use it anymore. I was exactly the way I used to be before we got them."

"But… how is that even possible? Was it because of the fire, or…?"

"Like I said, I don't know. It's as much a mystery to me as it is to you. I was worried about telling you and Linus because I wasn't even sure what had happened and I was afraid of what it might mean for us as a team. I was working on something to emulate it. I was going to show you after you came back from patrol, but…"

"…But we didn't come back for ages." Clare finished. She looked away, out the window, feeling guiltier now more than ever. How could she not have noticed something was different about Mallory? Surely there must have been signs that she didn't pick up on.

"I was going to come out and look for you," Mallory continued. "But on the way I... met someone."

Clare glanced back at her in alarm.

"Not–?"

"No, no," Mallory shook her head, guessing Clare's thoughts. "Not them. Someone else. A Vigilante. I said that I was one as well but it didn't take long for it to come out that I didn't actually have an Ability. Not anymore at least. I got recruited to help research Artifice and co, though."

"But... why?" Clare was confused. "If you didn't have an Ability..."

"Yeah, that's what I thought as well. But apparently having had one and knowing what it was like to be a Vigilante was a plus. I was literally picked up off the street, so I get the feeling I wasn't the number one candidate for the job, but 'desperate times call for desperate measures', or so I was told. I wish I could have contacted you guys or something but I wasn't allowed to. Not while we were in the middle of investigating, anyway."

"This Vigilante..." Clare began. The unfinished question died on her lips.

"You'll probably meet soon," Mallory replied. She rose from the bed. "Sorry. I really hate to desert you two all over again but I have to go back and report what just happened."

"We'll see you again soon, right?" Clare asked, concerned. Mallory nodded.

"Yeah. Do you know where Resonance lives?"

"You mean the Base? Sure, but how do you–"

"Tomorrow night," Mallory said. "If – and I mean when – Linus is peachy keen again. Come by and see us. That's where we'll be. There's a lot of things to talk about and Shockwave wants to see this whole business done and dusted as soon as possible."

"You've met Shockwave?" Clare asked numbly. Tonight was bringing no end of surprises. Mallory smiled.

"Who do you think told me where you guys were going to be?"

She crossed the room and drew Clare into a tight hug. Clare returned it gladly.

"Thanks again for coming to get us," she mumbled.

"Like I would leave you guys unsupervised for too long," Mallory replied casually. "Look what happened. I disappear for two days and you're already off getting into fights. I even broke speed limits for you."

Clare made a sound that was half laughter and half dry sob. Mallory patted her on the back comfortingly.

"I'll see you guys soon, alright?"

"Yeah. See you soon."

The lights in the Base were still on when Resonance returned to the flat. She thought she could see a shadow moving along the floor through the window. Shockwave, no doubt, she thought. Pacing in that way he did when he was thinking long and hard about something. Soon he would throw himself down in a chair or a beanbag or the crash mat in the corner of the room to brood some more, until he came up with a satisfactory solution or gave up due to the headache he'd gotten from frowning so deeply.

Any other time she might have gone down to join him and offer him a penny for his thoughts. Things were always easier solved if they worked together. They weren't a team for nothing.

Not tonight though. Tonight Resonance made her way slowly up the steps to the front door and turned the handle, reaching inside to unhook the chain and stepping inside. On the nights when either of them were out, they always left the front door unlocked. Taking keys with you on patrol wasn't always practical, especially when you had no idea what exactly you would come up against when you left the house. When nobody was going to be at home, they locked up from the inside and left through the storm-cellar doors of the Base, the key of which was taped underneath the flowerpot with the geraniums.

Resonance stepped inside and closed the door quietly behind her, replacing the chain and turning the lock. Slipping off her shoes, she placed them aside and made her way to the bathroom with silent footsteps, clicking on the light and untying the scarf from around her arm, dropping it onto the floor. She leaned over the sink, grasped the edge with both hands, and threw up into the basin.

Red liquid spattered onto the porcelain and trickled into the drain. Resonance drew the back of her hand across her mouth and spat a wad of blood into the sink. She breathed out a long, rattling sigh and shakily lowered herself to the floor to lean against the side of the bathtub.

She tilted her head back against the edge and closed her eyes, breathing slowly, in through the nose, out through the mouth. She relaxed her shoulders and allowed the feeling to spread through her body, and as it flowed through her she allowed herself to return, slowly but surely, to being Fang again.

Pain shot through her and she winced. She hadn't had any time to react before Meteor Hammer had thrown her through the window and so had taken the full force of hitting the glass, and almost as much so when she had slammed into the ground. Mercifully nothing was broken and the energy she had acquired from some of the hits she'd taken in the short brawl afterwards had given her enough strength to be able to walk back home, but it wasn't enough to last and she was starting to feel it now.

She stayed like that for a while, trying her best not to move. Her wounds from the glass shards were mostly superficial and would heal, but there were a few that would need a bit more care. Bruises mostly, she hoped. Maybe some internal ones, but they would all heal in time.

"Looks like you've been through hell."

Fang opened her eyes. Shockwave stood in the doorway, resting a hand on its frame. She gave a faint and bitter laugh.

"So you're back, I see," she replied coolly.

A flash of something, maybe hurt, maybe guilt, passed over Shockwave's face.

"Sorry," he said, and he was gruff but genuine. "I meant to be back, but..."

"But you were in the middle of something."
"Yeah."

Fang shook her head.

"When I say nine o'clock, I mean nine o'clock. What happened? I thought this was important to you."

Shockwave frowned.

"It is important. You know that."

"Then how is it I ended up leaving here alone?"

"I never asked you to do that."

"No, you just asked me to take you to see Gravitas. No big deal."

"Fang."

In spite of her pain and exhaustion, or maybe because of it, Fang could feel a slow wave of anger starting to well up within her.

"Alright, fine. I get it. You were in the middle of something so you couldn't make it back in time. Great, happens to us all. So tell me, were you actually doing anything worthwhile or were you just off getting into more pointless scraps again?"

Shockwave's frown deepened into an annoyed scowl. He made an exasperated sound and dropped his hands to his sides.

"What else do you want me to say, Fang? I'm sorry. I honestly meant to be back in time. If my being absent was really so frustrating to you—"

"Goddamnnit, Shock, this isn't *just* about you not being here!" Fang barked, and it was in quite a different voice that she spoke. "This isn't *just* about you keeping your promises! This is about you being so involved in your goddamn mission that you can't separate yourself from it for even for a second. The moment you're finished with class or work you're straight back into it again and getting into fights for no good reason other than being angry at a lack of progress. You're so stuck in it that you don't give a damn about your own safety!"

Shockwave was momentarily taken aback, but recovered quickly.

"What do you know about what I've been doing?" he replied, angry, his voice rising despite himself. "From the very beginning you've refused to have any part in this thing. You keep telling me that it's *my* mission, *my* business, so don't you criticise me on my methods when you've clearly stated that you don't want to be involved!"

Fang uttered an ugly laugh.

"Hell's teeth, Shock, have you ever thought about why that is? I could have told you from the start that this was bigger than either of us could handle. You could have just as easily reached the same conclusion, but you're so obsessed with going a hundred miles an hour that you never even stop to step back and think about what you're doing! Do you even give any thought as to what stakes are at hand when you take on a mission or are you too preoccupied with throwing yourself headfirst into danger the first chance you get?"

"Fang, if you have something to say then just say it, but I am *not* packing it in now—"

"*This is not just about this mission!!*" Fang roared, and suddenly she was on her feet and Shockwave was looking at Resonance. "I am *not* just talking about this one time! This about you being so unable to compartmentalise that you can't even separate your Alias from your true self anymore! You're so *possessed* now by this toxic compulsion to be the absolute best Vigilante there is that every minute of every day that you're awake and breathing you're thinking about the next big thing to jump into! You don't have to tell me *jack* for me to be involved in your business – every single time that I see or interact with you I'm involved whether you or I want it or not, so don't you *dare* accuse me of being ignorant! You want to work on your own?

Fine. You want to work as a team? Fine. But learn some goddamn communication skills and sort yourself out for crying out loud! My time is precious too, Shock. If you're so insistent on chasing after your solo investigations and throwing yourself into danger at every possible chance, then be my guest! Don't stop on my account. But at least do it on your own time and *not* when you've asked me for mine!"

Silence fell over the room. Fang's words hung thick and heavy in the air, the echoes of them reverberating off the tiling on the walls and floor. Her hands were balled into tight fists, the knuckles white, and her mouth was drawn into a tight and angry line. Then, as if all of her strength and fury had dissipated with her outburst, exhaustion overtook her, and she lowered herself slowly back down onto the bathroom floor with a long and shaky exhalation of breath. She leaned her head back against the bathtub again and closed her eyes.

Shockwave's anger had left him too. There was a strange expression on his face, a mix of stony and uncompromising stubbornness and bitter guilt and self-consciousness. He crossed to the medicine cabinet and reached to open it, noticing the blood splatters in the sink below. He faltered, glancing over at Resonance, and a flicker of concern crossed his features. Opening the cabinet, he took out the first aid kit, and held it out towards her. Fang opened her eyes and looked up at him soberly.

"I don't want to be the best there is," Shockwave said quietly. "I just want to be good enough."

Fang sighed. It was a tired sound.

"Yeah," she replied. "I know you do."

She took the kit and opened it. There was a lull as she pulled out cotton pads and rolls of tape.

"…I'm sorry I have to say this," she said, after a pause. "But Gravitas is dead."

She took a bottle of disinfectant from the kit. Shockwave's mouth tightened and he swore coldly under his breath.

"I'm sorry," he said stiffly.

"Yeah." Fang's face was drawn. "Me too."

There was silence again while Fang began cleaning the blood off her wounds. Shockwave leaned back against the sink and crossed his arms tight against his chest. He picked up Fang's bloodstained scarf off the floor and twisted it tightly around his fingers.

"Fisticuffs was here," he said. Fang looked up at him.

"Actually?"

"Yeah. She gave us some valuable information." He dropped the scarf to his side. "I'll tell you about it later."

Fang pressed a cotton pad to the biggest of the cuts on her arms and fumbled with the tape, tearing off a length with her teeth.

"Guess this thing really is a lot bigger than I thought," Shockwave muttered.

"Yeah," Fang replied. "I guess it is."

She tore off another piece of tape.

"Doesn't look like it can end well."

"No. You're probably right."

Another piece of tape. Shockwave watched her from the corner of his eye.

"Think you might change sides?" Shockwave spoke casually but

Fang knew he was only half joking. She put the tape back into the kit.

"I've thought about it." Her tone was similarly offhand, but he knew she was speaking frankly. He nodded curtly.

Fang took a box of bandages from the first aid kit.

"I'll stick around for now though," she said. "I think I've passed the point of no return. Besides, can't have you going into this one alone. I know how scared you get of the dark."

Shockwave was stunned into speechlessness. He looked at Fang with a disbelieving expression, uncertain of how first to react. Then his disbelief lifted with an astonished and relieved chuff of laughter.

"Dark? It's not the dark I'm afraid of."

Fang smiled wryly.

"Sure, chicken-wuss."

"It's *you* I have a problem with."

"Now that I can believe."

Shockwave looked at the scarf still in his hand and held it up.

"I'll sort this out for you."

"Thanks."

He moved to the door, as if making to leave, but then paused.

"Fang."

She looked up. Shockwave exhaled through his nose.

"If you do ever think about going back," he said. "To the way things used to be."

The rest of his sentence hung in the air. Fang understood. She shook her head.

"Thanks," she said. "But that's not happening anytime soon." She closed the lid of the first aid kit. "Being who I was. Doing what

I did. It was challenging and it was good, but it wasn't what was right for me anymore."

"What changed?"

"I don't know. My environment, I guess. New city, new team, new way of working things. New attitude."

"I have noticed less of a propensity for violence."

"Yeah, but that's none of your doing. Don't forget, you're still number one at ticking me off."

"Funny. I could say the exact same thing."

He made to leave.

"Hey, Shock."

Shockwave turned back around.

"What?"

Fang pushed herself up to sit on the edge of the bath.

"We're going to win this one," she said, firmly. "Aren't we?"

It was only half a question. One thing was for sure, she sounded more certain than he felt. Shockwave raised a shoulder in a shrug, then let it drop.

"Gotta commit to succeed," he responded. "Right?"

Fang chuckled and reached over to turn on the faucet.

"Right."

The first thing Linus noticed when he woke up was that it was dark. The second thing that struck him was how much his head hurt. He winced and uttered a groan, rolling over onto his side. Then he pushed himself up onto his hands.

He was back home in the flat, he realised. He was lying on his own bed in his own room at home and he was safe. But what was he safe from? Linus tried to think, but found he couldn't recall what had happened. Strange, he thought. He was certain something dangerous had happened, and that he had been in danger somehow. But he couldn't quite remember the details.

The door creaked open. Clare poked her head into the room and started as she saw him.

"Linus!" She ran towards him, looking as if she were going for a hug, but caught herself at the last minute, instead sitting down on the bed beside him.

"How are you feeling?"

"Like I got hit by a train." Linus shifted gingerly into a sitting position. "What happened?"

"You don't remember?"

"Well…" he tried to think. He recalled going with Clare on a walk to go find Mallory – no, not exactly to find Mallory. To help clear Clare's head. That was right. And then somewhere, something had gone horribly wrong.

"Resonance," he said, remembering suddenly. "Is she alright?"

"She's fine," Clare replied. "Or at least, she said she was fine." The look on her face spoke multitudes about how she thought about the statement. "What else do you remember?"

"I think… I got thrown into a building? And Shaan was there… I can't remember what happened after that though."

"You hit your head."

"Did I?" Linus felt the bump on the side of his head. That sure would make sense.

"Yeah." Clare reached over and turned on the bedside lamp. "You've been out for a whole day."

"A whole day, huh." Linus looked down at his feet. He felt put out for some reason. Even more so when he couldn't remember what had actually happened to him.

"We were just about done for," Clare continued. "But then Mallory showed up and saved us."

Linus looked up very quickly and immediately regretted it.

"Ow. Mallory? Mallory's okay?"

"More than okay, it sounds like. She said that night we didn't come back for ages, she went out looking for us and ended up getting recruited by some Vigilante to help investigate the Vigilante killers. That's why she disappeared all of a sudden."

"Is she still here?"

"No," Clare looked as disappointed as Linus felt. "She had to go somewhere."

There was silence for a moment.

"She lost her Ability," Clare said quietly. Linus looked at her with the same expression of horror and confusion that Clare had given Mallory. "She didn't tell us because she didn't know how it was going to change things. She doesn't know how or why. It just happened somehow."

"Sounds like I missed out on a lot while I was out," Linus murmured. Clare tried to smile.

"Damn straight," she replied. "Sleeping on the job. Pretty sloppy work, Linus."

"Sorry, leader. I'll remember to bring my helmet to battles next time."

Clare laughed lightly and rose from the bed.

"I'll get you some water," she said. "Mallory said to come see her after you woke up but we'll wait a little while. Be right back."

She disappeared out into the corridor. Linus could hear her footsteps pad down the hallway and down the stairs and he lay back down on the bed. Outside the window he could see the faint glow of the streetlamps up the road, the gentle swirl of the light night fog, and the soft silvery light from the moon. That's right, he thought. He closed his eyes. He was safe here. Here in his room in the flat he shared with his friends, there was nobody trying to throw him anywhere or threaten him with pointy knives.

That's right... he remembered. A slow frown creased his forehead. Somebody *had* threatened him with a pointy knife. That guy from The Niterie, the one who was secretly a Vigilante. Shaan. But what had happened after that? He had grabbed his wrist...

Linus immediately recalled the static shock-like feeling that had run through him when Shaan had grabbed him. Something about that simple movement had changed him somehow, he knew it. But what? Moreover, he couldn't shake the feeling that something else important had happened, but what? He tried to concentrate on the memory. They had tripped over each other, Clare had pushed him away, then someone had thrown him across the street... Shaan was there and he had a knife and the black dog was on top of him.

The black dog...

His eyes snapped open. Suddenly he remembered. Resonance had said before that whatever energy it was that gave them their Abilities didn't affect animals, but they'd never once considered transformation might be somebody's Ability. Shaan had never been the leader of the Vigilante killing operation, it had been Cavall Robinson all along.

Linus rolled out of bed and onto his feet. He had to tell Clare. His bedroom door opened again and he looked up, expecting to see his friend, but instead froze as Shaan Mehra stepped into the room.

Linus opened his mouth to shout, call for Clare, anything, but Shaan raised a finger to his lips and instead Linus found himself falling silent, a lump rising in his throat. He took a step further back into the room, keeping his distance. Shaan seemed cool, relaxed. Underneath his hooded black coat he was wearing the same clothes that Linus had first seen him in; a red shirt, perfectly ironed without crease or wrinkle, a well-fitted dark waistcoat and black jeans. His eyes were as bright as ever.

"Nice to see you again, Linus," Shaan said in a pleasant, soft voice.

"What are you doing here?" Linus demanded. Mentally he cursed himself for sounding less brave than he'd have liked. "How did you get in?"

"There are plenty of ways to get in a house," Shaan replied. "You just have to be creative. And as for why..." A flick of his wrist, and suddenly a stiletto knife was in his hand. Linus took another step backwards. "Sometimes we just have to tie up loose ends. Apparently you figured out a certain someone's true identity, and that's been our best-kept secret so far. I can't let that go in good conscience."

"You mean Cavall?" Linus asked, trying to stay calm. He kept his eye on the knife. Watched Shaan twirl it between his fingers easily. "Cavall Robinson. He's the black dog, isn't he?"

"If you like." Shaan stepped forwards. "I say Cavall is Cavall. But the dog... that's Cave Canem."

"Cave Canem?"

"Well. Every Vigilante worth their salt has an Alias, right?" He flashed a smile at Linus. Linus tried to ignore him and pulled his gaze away, chancing a quick look towards the window. That's right, the window. If he could just –

"I wouldn't risk it, if I were you," Shaan cut in, watching Linus closely. Linus scowled at him.

"Why not? Afraid I can leave faster than you can throw?"

"Oh, any other day I wouldn't doubt it. That Ability of yours is quite something." He tossed the knife to his other hand. Showed his teeth. "*Was... something.*"

Then Linus suddenly understood what had happened when Shaan had grabbed him the previous night. Why he felt like something about him had changed so drastically. The colour drained from his face.

"Come on then," Shaan said, rolling his shoulders. "I'm feeling tired today. So let's just make this easy for the both of us, yeah?"

He tossed the knife back to his right hand and raised it into the air.

"Linus?"

Shaan turned. Clare stood in the doorway, stunned, a glass of water in her hand and a look of horror on her face. Linus swiped his arm frantically at her, trying to gesture at her to run.

Shaan smiled at Clare.

"Hello again," he said.

Clare looked to the glass in her hand, glanced back up, then pitched it hard at Shaan. Shaan threw up an arm and the glass shattered; in the same instant, Clare yelled "*Run!*" and Linus bolted past Shaan and out of the room.

Clare grabbed Linus by the wrist and they ran for it, half-sprinting half-falling down the stairs and bursting through the front door out into the night – as they ran out onto the street a silver blur suddenly cut through the space between them with a shrill whistle and a knife embedded itself in the concrete before them. Clare gasped and the two of them came to a sharp and stumbling stop and spun around to find that Shaan was no longer in the house but instead standing in the street behind them.

Linus grabbed Clare by her sleeve and tried to say something but his words came hushed and faint. Clare glanced at him.

"What?"

"Don't let him touch you," Linus hissed. "*He can take away Abilities.*"

Clare stared at Linus for a second, mouth agape, then whirled back to face Shaan, advancing towards them.

"Don't you take one step closer!" she shouted, her voice shaking.

Shaan seemed to consider her words for a moment. He tossed a knife to his left hand, then back to his right. Twirled it between his fingers. Shrugged. Then he raised the blade and threw the knife.

There was not enough time for Clare to grab Linus and disappear into the fog. Shaan, or Artifice, had been counting on that much. There wasn't enough time for Clare to do much of anything, but there *was* sufficient time for Clare to raise her arm, on instinct, as if she could block or deflect the knife, and incredibly... that was enough.

Clare's eyes were screwed shut and she waited for the pain, but instead all there came was a dull *thud* and then silence. She opened her eyes, slowly at first, expecting to see a lot of blood, but instead found something else quite different. Something amazing.

Artifice's stiletto knife sat suspended in midair not even a foot away from her face, buried deep in the middle of a solid shield seemingly made of thick white fog.

Metres ahead of her, Artifice stared, wide-eyed, his up-until-now composed demeanour upset by surprise. Beside her, Linus stared in a similar fashion. Clare lowered her arm and the shield and knife moved with it; she unclenched her fist and the shield vanished and dissipated back into the fog, the knife clattering to the ground. For a moment, nobody spoke.

Artifice took a step back and Clare raised her hand again, re-gaining her composure, her expression one of fervid intensity.

"I said, don't you move!" she yelled. Braver now somehow. Artifice raised his hands in an expression of surrender.

"Relax," he replied easily. "You got a one-up on me this time. Truth is, after last night I wasn't expecting much of a real fight from you guys but it seems you proved me wrong. I'm not in much of a mood for a scene tonight and I was told to avoid one if possible, so I'm going to let you off this time. Seems like it's your lucky day today. But you and I..." he looked to Linus. "...We'll see each other again. I don't doubt it. Then we'll see."

He winked at Linus then turned and ran, rounding the corner into the next street. A moment of astonishment took Clare aback for a second, but then shaking herself to her senses, she dashed after him, turning the corner only to find that Shaan had vanished.

She stared down the empty street, dismayed, and Linus came after her, seizing her by the shoulder and grabbing her attention.

"Clare." His voice was hushed but agitated. "Clare, come on. We have to see Resonance and Shockwave *now*."

Clare frowned.

"Why, what's wrong?"

"*We* were wrong, Clare. We were so wrong. Shaan isn't the leader of the group, it's Cavall Robinson. *Cavall* is the mastermind behind the Vigilante killings. It's his Ability. *He* is *the black dog*."

CHAPTER EIGHT

INTELLIGENT CONVERSATION

There would never be as many people in the Base at one time as there would be on this night. Shockwave and Fang didn't know it just yet, but their usually quiet headquarters were about to become a lot busier. As for whether or not it would surpass yet-unbeaten noise and chaos levels thus far was yet to be seen – the Base had seen its fair share of team domestics in the nearly-three years since Fang had moved to the City, and there had been one or two impressive exchanges in the past, so it would take some amount of tension for there to be an argument of equivocal volume.

No arguments had happened just yet, but tension was already in abundance; from the moment Shockwave and Fang welcomed Fisticuffs into the Base and sat down at the table, they all already knew that they were potentially in for a long and arduous night.

"How many are we expecting?" Fisticuffs asked, as she settled into her chair.

"I'm not sure," Shockwave replied. "A few more, maybe. At least two or three. Does that bother you?"

Fisticuffs shrugged.

"If it can't be helped, it can't be helped," she said. "I find the fewer people involved then the less you have to worry about.

Nevertheless…"

"Seems like it's kind of inevitable though." Fang shifted in her chair and winced from a nudged bruise. "You warn who you can or who you know about big threats and they'll either want to join you or they won't want a bar of it."

Shockwave threw a glance and a half-raised eyebrow her way.

"You've just highlighted the exact reason why I prefer to stay away from other Vigilantes," Fisticuffs replied.

"Seeing as we're sitting here talking, something must have changed your mind," Shockwave commented. "I don't mean to be presumptuous…"

"I'm here because there is a danger here in the City that presents a very real threat to me as a Vigilante," Fisticuffs said firmly. "Others, evidently, have failed to stop them so far, and so now that means the ones responsible are all the more powerful for it, and I am a potential target because of that failure. It's affected the way that I like to work because now they are just strong enough that I know full well I will not be able to take them down on my own.

"I'm here because I saw you fighting a common enemy that I realised I needed more information on and you proved yourself as being a capable Vigilante with both the aptitude for quick thinking and strategy, and the drive to take the ones responsible down. Right now I'm willing to cooperate as well as I can for as long as necessary, and I am grateful if you are willing to do as much the same. Don't judge my motivations as being entirely selfish, Shockwave, but don't be quick to count this partnership as a sign of amity just yet, either."

"Of course. I wouldn't be so bold to assume."

"Capable and strategic," Fang echoed, amused. "Hey, Shock, I think that's the nicest thing anyone's ever said about you."

"Yeah, and it's a crying shame."

"It's good to see you managed to return in one piece, by the way, Resonance." Fisticuffs looked to the black-haired Vigilante. "Shockwave seemed concerned after I told him the news about Artifice."

"About his Ability. Right." Fang nodded. "Thank you for having told us what you know. I did actually end up meeting Artifice last night. I'd gone out with the intention on contacting another Vigilante for assistance on this mission, however..."

"Declined?"

"Dead, actually. Artifice and his crew got there before us." Fang's expression hardened and Shockwave looked down at the table.

"I'm sorry to hear that," Fisticuffs replied. There were sincerity in her words. "Did you get away safely?"

"Got thrown out a window. Bit of a scuffle. Otherwise fine. I'm a little concerned about those kids though," Fang glanced at Shockwave beside her. "Linus especially. He was more or less alone with Artifice at one point."

"I guess we'll find out," Shockwave muttered. "Either way, we have to treat these guys as the biggest threat we've ever encountered so far."

"Believe me, they will be," Fisticuffs said in a low voice. "I've never heard of any other Vigilante having an Ability like this before. If he has the capacity for infinite energy then he could very easily expand to beyond just the draining and transference of it."

"Because the more energy a Vigilante possesses the more Abilities or sub-Abilities they can develop. Right."

"Can I ask," Fang broke in. "How did you find all this out anyway? Their Aliases, their Abilities..."

"I didn't do it alone," Fisticuffs replied. Shockwave and Fang looked at her in surprise. It was unprecedented enough that Fisticuffs was here at the Base at this very moment at all, but to hear that she had collaborated with another person for an intelligence mission...

Fisticuffs responded to their surprised silence with a curt nod.

"I had a few suspicions," she said. "About Artifice's motivations. The acquiring of power was my main one, but a lot of less-experienced Vigilantes were getting killed off as well, and it just seemed... well. If you wanted to ascend the ranks and become the most powerful Vigilante then bumping off the competition would be a logical move, but why waste time on small fry? So I started wondering if it was something else. If someone had the Ability to neutralise the Abilities of others, or to somehow take them for themselves..."

"Then it wouldn't matter who they picked because energy and Ability don't reflect on the experience of the Vigilante." Shockwave was frowning now.

"Right." Fisticuffs clasped her hands on the table in front of her. "I needed to find a way to confirm my suspicions, but I didn't want to lose my own Ability in the process. But then I managed to find someone that was both a Vigilante, yet without Ability. That's already uncommon enough, but the key difference here was that she *used* to have an Ability. Something happened recently to change that. And that was very interesting to me."

"This Vigilante," Fang began. "Who—"

There came a knock on the storm-cellar doors and they all looked up simultaneously.

"Anyone home?" A muffled voice called from above. "It's Mallory."

"Mallory." Fisticuffs and Fang spoke in unison. They looked at each other in surprise.

"You know Mallory?" Fang asked first.

"Of course," Fisticuffs replied. Shockwave got up to open the storm-cellar doors and Mallory, hair tied back as usual, wearing a cardigan and loose beige cargos, came down the concrete steps and into the light of the basement.

"She's the one who's been helping me investigate."

"Mallory." Shockwave held out a hand. "Good to put a face to the voice. Thank you for bringing my teammate back in one piece."

"Shockwave." Mallory took his outstretched hand and shook it. "Same goes for you. Unfortunately I can't take credit for having personally brought her back, since she was insistent on walking back by herself. But I'm glad if I could help."

"Was she now?" Shockwave threw a less-than-pleased glance at Fang, who pretended to ignore him. "That does sound like something she would do."

"Mallory," Fisticuffs greeted. "Good to see you've arrived." Mallory approached the table with a smile.

"Hello, Fisticuffs," she responded. "And hello again, Resonance. How are you?"

"Just dandy," Fang replied. "And please, call me Fang. Just while we're in the Base."

"Alright then. Fang. It's nice to see you again."

"Likewise. The invitation goes to you as well, Fisticuffs."

"Thanks, but if it's all the same to you, I'd prefer to stick to formalities for now."

"Absolutely."

"I didn't realise Mallory was also the one who'd been helping you with your investigations," Shockwave said, returning to the table. "Though seeing as you had her on call last night... it makes sense in hindsight."

"Yeah." Fisticuffs pulled something out of the waistbag at her back and placed it on the table. "Disposable cell," she said. "Makes it easier to issue instructions without having to meet up constantly."

"Tell me about it," Mallory chipped in good-humouredly. "You've been running me all over town with that thing."

"Mallory's provided invaluable assistance in my investigations," Fisticuffs said. "Since she had both Vigilante experience and, at one time, an Ability, I was able to send her to gather intelligence where I couldn't."

"And where was that?"

"The Niterie," Mallory replied.

"I happened to see Meteor Hammer's face in the middle of our fight," Fisticuffs went on. "And then I recognised him later, standing guard outside The Niterie. He would have recognised me as well so I sent Mallory in my stead."

"Since Clare and Linus and I hadn't even met any other Vigilantes until a week ago, and I'd never been to The Niterie before, I wouldn't have been recognised. So it was safe."

"Safe, indeed," Shockwave muttered. "What if she'd been caught?"

"I don't actually consider myself a Vigilante as much as I am a mechanic," Mallory answered. She pulled her phone from her pocket; a few quick swipes of the screen and she turned the phone to face Shockwave and Fang. "Why risk getting caught when you can send a machine instead?"

"That's impressive." Fang regarded the app with admiration. "You coded it yourself?"

"Yeah. Didn't take very long. Modified some cheap tech and set it up. It wasn't like they laid out all their plans for me or anything, but it at least let me monitor their activity and keep tabs on where they were going."

"Beats a stakeout," Shockwave muttered. He nodded at Mallory. "Good work. You'll make a great Vigilante yet."

"Thank you. I appreciate that."

"So this is how you were able to find out about Artifice's Ability?" Fang asked.

"Not quite," Fisticuffs replied. "There was no 'one way' we found out. My suspicions weren't even confirmed until just before I came to see you. Mallory didn't even know until I told her after she came back last night."

"I think that's how I lost my Ability," Mallory said quietly. "That night of the fire, after the explosion… there was someone who helped me get up. I heard Clare and Linus calling my name and I thought that was what had woken me up, but there was a feeling like a static shock... I think that may have been Artifice."

"You lost your..." Fang put a hand to her mouth. "Wait, if Artifice was there, then that means..." she looked to Shockwave and he replied with a nod, a troubled expression on his face.

"It must be," he replied in a hollow voice. "I think we were very lucky that night."

There came another knock on the storm-cellar doors. Frantic.

"I'll get it." Fang rose from the table and went to the steps.

"The next question is what Artifice hopes to achieve by doing all this," Fisticuffs continued. "And how he managed to rope Faraday and Meteor Hammer into being accomplices. It'd be so easy for him to run this one alone, and much less conspicuous. So why..."

"It's because it's not Artifice." Shockwave looked up and Fisticuffs and Mallory turned in their chairs. Clare, Linus and Fang came down the stairs from the storm-cellar doors, looking shaken.

"Clare! Linus!" Mallory stood quickly. "What happened to you? Are you alright?"

"Artifice came to pay us a visit," Clare said grimly.

Everything seemed to stop for a moment. Shockwave rose abruptly from his chair.

"Did he touch you at all?" Fisticuffs demanded. Clare shook her head.

"No. Well... I didn't let him near me at all. But Linus..."

"He grabbed me last night, when we were fighting," Linus broke in. "Took away my Ability."

Shockwave sat back down again and put a hand to his brow.

Despondent.

"He came back to finish the job," Clare continued. "Got into the house somehow. *This* guy says he was literally about to throw himself out the window to get away."

"Oh, Linus," Fang said. "When Meteor Hammer threw me out the window last night, I wasn't trying to set a precedent. Are you alright?"

"Believe me, if Clare hadn't come up then I'd probably have done it." Linus lowered himself into a chair. "He was going to kill me because I saw something I shouldn't have."

"And what was that?"

"The black dog," Linus said. "It's not a dog at all. It's Cavall Robinson. *He's* the leader behind the Vigilante killings. Being able to turn into a dog... that's his Ability. Artifice was never number one, Cavall was heading this thing the whole time."

A stunned silence fell while everyone processed the news.

"*Cave Canem*," Fisticuffs muttered. "So that's how..."

"An employer in more than one way." Shockwave sighed, frustrated. "No one could have suspected because animals can't possess Abilities and there's no definitive list on what kind of Abilities people can possess."

"Artifice said it was their best kept secret so far," Linus went on. "And that he was going to come back and we'd see him again soon."

"Scumbag," Mallory cursed. "First me and now you. I'm sorry, Linus."

"Hey, it's not your fault. I'm just glad to see you again."

"So Cavall, or Cave Canem, is leading a group of Vigilantes to kill other Vigilantes so that he can take away their Abilities and, presumably, use that energy for himself. This just keeps getting better and better." Fang sat back in her chair and crossed her arms. "Just peachy."

"How does he do it?" Clare asked. "Artifice, I mean. How does he take away Abilities?"

"Do you know what Abilities are?" Fisticuffs fixed her gaze on Clare. "How they work?"

"Fang said it was like... some kind of extra energy, right?"

"Almost. Not quite." Shockwave folded his arms on the table. "Think of the thing that allows us to have Abilities as a kind of omnipresent 'dust', so to speak. It's more of a recent phenomenon, the last five, six years or so, and it tends to affect teenagers and young adults more than most. The effects this 'dust' has on us varies from person to person, maybe even from area to area, but it's generally agreed the influence it has on us is felt strongest at night. Some people are more sensitive to it than others, and the ones who are take in this 'dust', this energy, and it develops into the Abilities that we have."

"The more energy a person has," Fisticuffs added. "The more potential they have to develop sub-Abilities from their main Ability. For instance, if Faraday can both absorb and transfer electrical currents then that means she possesses more energy than Meteor Hammer, who has extraordinary strength. It doesn't dictate how strong these Abilities will be or how experienced the Vigilante is, but it gives an indication of the potential they have."

"Didn't you say that the energy we have from our Abilities helps us to heal as well?" Clare looked to Fang. She nodded.

"That's right. And that's how Vigilantes possessing accelerated healing Abilities work as well. They manage to possess an incredible amount of energy that allows them to heal much faster than most other Vigilantes, and in some cases they can transfer that energy to others and help them to heal, too. If they could develop other, different Abilities from the energy they have, then I'm pretty sure healers could easily take over the world."

"And this is where Artifice's Ability comes in." Fisticuffs placed her hands flat on the table. "You're not far off the mark. Artifice is, for all intents and purposes, a Vigilante with a powerful healing Ability. Think of the way he can neutralise the Abilities of others as a bastardised offshoot of the Ability to regenerate. Instead of just being able to give the energy that he has to others, he can take it away if he so chooses instead. Suddenly you're just the way you used to be all over again only more dead, and you got four killers away laughing to their next destination, ready to do it all over again."

"But if he can take away Abilities..." Mallory began. "That's the part that I don't understand. Neutralising another Vigilante's Ability means that he gains the energy that they had to fuel his own, sure. And he shares that energy with his teammates, fine. I get that part. But the moment he takes away a person's Ability, they're basically defenceless. They no longer present a threat to him and they probably couldn't beat him even if they tried. So why kill them? What's the point?"

"It's to eliminate the chances of their Ability ever returning to them."

Everyone turned. A light clicked on in the stairwell from the living area and somebody came down the wooden steps and into the Base. He was dressed in shades of charcoals and burgundies and a red bandanna was tied around his arm. A young man, tall, broad-shouldered, with a strong build; Māori, with short dark hair, dark eyes, and a kind smile.

There were a pair of glasses with thick black frames on his face this time, but otherwise Mallory recognised him instantly. Clare and Linus looked to each other in surprise. Shockwave rose from his seat and greeted the newcomer with a hand outstretched; the latter took his hand and drew him into a one-armed hug, which Shockwave returned.

"Joshua. Welcome back."

"*Kia ora*. It's good to be home."

Fang glanced at the stunned expressions around the table and smiled.

"Clare, Linus, Mallory," she said. "I believe you've met before. Fisticuffs, this will be your first time. This is Rehua. He's the third member of our team."

"Please, call me Joshua if you like." He approached the table and regarded Fisticuffs. "The legendary Fisticuffs." He held out a hand. "It's a pleasure to meet you."

"The pleasure's all mine," Fisticuffs replied, shaking his hand.

The young man looked to Clare, Linus and Mallory and gave them a bright, sunny smile.

"Clare, Linus and Mallory," he said. "It's good to finally meet you. I owe you all a debt – you three helped saved my life."

CHAPTER NINE

CARDS ON THE TABLE

Joshua had never been a very adventurous teenager.

Adventures, he rationalised, were for people who had the bravery to believe that everything that they did would come out right in the end, even if they had no reason to think so. And 'brave' was the last thing that Joshua would consider himself. That's not to say that he lacked self-confidence; he was perfectly confident in his self and his abilities. You couldn't practice activities like kickboxing or parkour without self-confidence, after all. But he also preferred quiet nights in to big nights out, and he'd pick loyally following over leading any day of the week.

His best friend, however, was something of the opposite.

For as long as Joshua had known him, Louis had always been someone who had no problem venturing out of his comfort zone – not out of recklessness, but rather because of his unshakeable sense of faith in himself. Whether it was trying new tricking skills or furthering the strengths he already had in parkour, he was a person who would ultimately choose fight over flight. Though he often came off as being more of the solitary sort, there was no doubt in the fact that he had all the qualities of a natural-born leader. 'Brave' was definitely a word Joshua would use to describe him.

And adventures were exactly the kind of thing he went in for.

So the week after Louis' seventeenth birthday, when he found he had come into so much energy that he couldn't sleep, there was no doubt in Joshua's mind that his friend would choose any other option than to take to the night and use that energy to train to his heart's content. And it was during this time that he discovered his Ability; the power to change his body's density at will, to be able to even crack the earth with a single punch.

A month later, following his eighteenth birthday, after undergoing his own change (and experiencing the restless nights that subsequently followed), Joshua partnered up with Louis. He soon found out his own Ability; the power to heal at an accelerated rate, and to even help make well others if he wanted. The two of them became a fearless night-time freerunning duo, exercising both their physical prowess and the limits of their newly acquired Abilities under the starlit sky of the small town they'd lived in all their lives.

Crime fighting didn't enter the picture until a few months later, when the two of them happened to meet a skilled Vigilante by the alias of Siren. After that, inspired by the things Siren had said to them, Louis made the decision to become a Vigilante, and Joshua made his own decision to follow suit.

The alias Louis chose was Shockwave.

The one that Joshua chose was Rehua.

One who could split concrete if he so chose and one who could heal others with a single touch.

It didn't take long for them to grow into their new responsibilities and get used to their identities as Shockwave and Rehua. Sometimes there were moments in which Joshua would think that, perhaps, his friend was a little too used to wearing his Alias. About a year later the two of them moved out of their hometown and into the sprawling concrete jungle of the City where they made their base. Less than a year after that, through a series of singular circumstances, they gained the addition of a new and decidedly more experienced member to their team – Resonance.

Resonance, or Fang as they came to know her, opted to keep the methods she was used to from her time as a solo Vigilante while Louis and Joshua continued to work as they always had on their joint nightly patrols. Nights where they all worked together were infrequent but not uncommon, and nights where all three of them went on individual patrol were even more rare, but not totally unheard of.

It was on one of these rare nights, a week after hearing that Equilibrium and Shooting Star had been killed, that Joshua encountered two strangers who cornered him in the dilapidated structure of a long-since disused warehouse, beat him unconscious, then set the building alight and left him there to die. It wasn't long after he regained consciousness (due to part of the ceiling collapsing onto his legs) that he realised something was very wrong. His Ability allowed him to recover from just about any injury in a few moments, but when he awoke there was nothing but pain and it didn't go away.

The loss of his Ability made Joshua feel useless, especially when they had only just recently decided to investigate the long-festering rumour of the Vigilante killers. Up until a week ago Louis hadn't wanted anything to do with it, but now – as he saw it – they had a personal reason to get involved, and they were going to do their best to see this problem done with. But what could he do without his Ability? He was no longer as much help on the battlefield, that was for sure, and without the extra energy he would be hard pressed to keep up with his team in a fight.

So he decided to make himself useful in other ways. Two days and one night after the fire that had nearly killed him, he set off on his own to investigate how he might have lost his Ability and whether he was the only Vigilante this had happened to. The loss of his Ability meant that he didn't have the energy that he used to during the night, but he did his best to soldier on where he could. His investigations took him to a few of the cities where the Vigilante killers had purportedly already been, in an attempt to seek out some of the more older and more experienced Vigilantes for advice; that is, if they weren't already dead. It wasn't easy – most of what he had to go on were a bunch of urban legends he had collected over time, and while his compilation was extensive it was hardly solid fact.

Through some bizarre circumstances, however, while in the Easternmost City, he managed to come across the very same Vigilante that he and Louis had met as teenagers, who had inspired them when they were just two kids fooling around back in their hometown – Siren. Siren, who had been laying low, was able to shed some light on the situation by suggesting a motive – power – and a theory that the killing of Vigilantes was at once both arbitrary and done in order to cover up something even bigger. Something that everyone was missing.

It was at this point that Joshua began to consider the idea that his losing his Ability was not the random accident that he had initially thought it to be. It was on his way home that he realised that he did not feel as affected by his injuries and his long day and near-sleepless night as he had five days ago.

"So what you're saying..." Fang began.

"*Āe.*" Joshua nodded. "I think there's a possibility of a person's Ability coming back to them after having been stolen. I can't say how long it'd take or if it would return in the same way at all, even. That might be up to the Vigilante and their Ability and how much energy they possessed in the first place. But there's a chance."

Mallory and Linus looked at each other. Both of them had the same look of hope in their eyes.

"You do realise," Fisticuffs said slowly. "What you're saying – there's no way to prove that any of it is true, strictly speaking."

"No, I understand." Joshua dipped his head. "But I think with everything that we've seen so far, it makes sense. If there is that chance that a person's Ability can return to them, and that it can come back to the same level, or maybe even come back stronger... then that gives a perfect explanation as to why so many Vigilantes are being killed."

"If they left them alive and their Abilities were to return," Shockwave murmured. "Then Vigilantes all over the show might band together to get their revenge."

"Right. And who'd want to risk that?"

Clare raised a hand and Fang acknowledged her with a nod.

"Sorry," Clare said, lowering her hand. "This is probably going to be a stupid question. I know there's no Vigilante 'secret society' or whatever, and you all try really hard not to contact one another if you don't have to. But seeing as this is like a 'common enemy'..."

Shockwave shook his head.

"I'm afraid not," he replied. "I think we already told you before, but the Vigilantes we have tried to contact don't want a bar of it. If you knew there was an enemy out there who killed Vigilantes for their Abilities, would you want to go in needlessly?"

Clare sighed and slid down in her chair.

"I guess not," she mumbled. "This kind of stinks."

"Tell me about it." Fang clapped Clare on the shoulder.

"While you were in the Easternmost City," Shockwave said to Joshua. "Did Siren…?"

It was Joshua's turn to shake his head.

"Sorry," he responded. "Tried, but no dice. Too risky even for a Vigilante of Siren's calibre, apparently."

"While we're on the subject of recruiting," Fisticuffs broke in. "Joshua. You said that you managed to track down some of the more 'renowned' Vigilantes, so to speak, with some of the older Vigilante urban legends, is that correct?"

"That's right. A few of them, anyway. I narrowed it down to the ones that were at least three years old. I didn't find all of them, but that's to be expected." Joshua smiled. "I count having found even one of them to be a miracle, to be honest."

Fisticuffs hmm'd for a moment.

"During your expedition," she said. "Did you ever track down a Vigilante named Kinetic?"

Much to Fisticuffs' irritation, Shockwave gave a sudden loud bark of laughter. Fang and Joshua looked similarly amused.

"That guy?" Shockwave scoffed. "Waste of time. Not if there's nothing in it for him."

"Supposedly his knack for stealth is nothing to be disregarded." A slight scowl crossed Fisticuffs' features at having been rebuffed in such a way. "If we knew where he was based…"

"The City Over," Joshua replied, still smiling. "It was the City Over. But no, Shock is right. Kinetic's no good."

"Is that so?" Fisticuffs tone was frosty and she turned her scowl onto Joshua. "That's a fine way to regard another Vigilante before you've even tried contacting them, even with their reputation."

"Oh, no, he'll help," Fang said lightly. "They're right, he is no good. But he'll help."

"Oh really?" Fisticuffs regarded Fang coolly. "And how do you know?"

"Well. I said 'he'll help'." Fang smiled. Pointed to herself. "I guess I should say 'he's already helping'."

Fisticuffs fell into stunned silence, then sat back in her chair.

"So it's you," she uttered under her breath. "You're the fabled Kinetic. Who'd have thought."

Fang winked at her.

"I'm sorry," Linus cut in. "I'm lost. What's going on here?"

Fisticuffs turned to look at him.

"There was a Vigilante I'd heard of," she said. "Back in the early days. Went by the alias of Kinetic. Incredible at stealth and gathering intel, skilled fighter, but supposedly only did things if he had something to gain from it."

"It's one of the oldest Vigilante urban legends," Joshua added. "About five years old maybe. The mysterious Kinetic. His Ability was anyone's guess."

"From the lack of further news I'd assumed he'd either disappeared or dropped off the radar somehow."

"Truth is, we met Kinetic on a mission a few years back," Shockwave said. "Our investigation led us to the City Over and we ended up working with him to finish it. It was a pain in the ass for everybody involved."

"Yeah, and that's precisely the reason why you invited him to join us in the City." Joshua nudged Shockwave with his elbow. The latter rolled his eyes.

"Seemed like a good idea at the time. I don't think I'll ever be more wrong in my life."

Joshua laughed.

"So then this 'Kinetic'." Mallory looked to Fang. "That's you?"

Fang nodded.

"Kinetic was the first name I chose for myself when I became a Vigilante," she explained. "He was every single good and bad decision I made as an amateur and every single hitch that I came across on my way up. He wasn't always a nice person but he was pretty good at what he did, if I might say so, and he got the job done as he saw fit.

"Resonance was the name I changed to when I moved to the City. New place, new team, new attitude. New name. Resonance is everything that Kinetic learned on the way up and is the person he was starting to grow into towards the end. She benefits from his knowledge and experience without any of the bad attitude problems he had."

Shockwave snorted in derision. Resonance swatted at his arm with the back of her hand.

"So…" Clare hesitated. "Which one is Fang?"

Fang smiled.

"Fang is Fang. No more, no less." She winked.

"So now I know we actually have the infamous Kinetic on our side. Couldn't have imagined this happening four years ago." Fisticuffs seemed to allow herself a smile.

"Don't hold your breath," Shockwave said in a low voice. Fisticuffs frowned at him.

"I'm honoured if you had a high opinion of me," Fang replied. "But my teammate has a point. It wasn't until last night that I decided to join the fray, so I can't take any praise in good conscience. Nevertheless, I hope I don't disappoint."

"Better not," Shockwave muttered. "We can't afford it this time."

"Yeah, and that's where the bad news comes in."

All eyes turned back to Joshua. He looked grim.

"Louis – Shock – has been keeping me updated," he said. "He called me about Cavall Robinson, who to look out for. Cave Canem and Artifice and the rest, right?"

"Right."

"After I got the message I decided to come back right away. But I saw something on my way home."

Joshua pulled a folded square of paper out of the pocket of his hoodie and opened it out on the table. He smoothed out the creases then turned it around so everyone could see.

It was a poster advertising the tour dates for Cavall Robinson's shows. Clare and Linus could see the date for the show that they had seen at The Niterie four nights ago, and the one they had heard faintly in the distance two nights after that.

Joshua pointed at the next and final dates on the poster. The next two shows were in the City After and the first was set for two nights from now.

Mallory frowned.

"But then that means we've basically run out of time," she said. "Assuming they leave tomorrow and continue what they've been doing like we thought..."

"They might have already left for all we know," Fang broke in. She seemed agitated. "We might have missed our chance."

Fisticuffs uttered an oath under her breath. Linus bit his lip, anxious, wondering whether if he should speak or keep his mouth shut. Lest he make things worse.

"I don't think so," he finally said. Joshua cocked his head.

"*He aha ai*? What do you mean?"

Linus fell silent and glanced at Clare. She seemed anxious herself, but gave him an encouraging nod. Linus tried to speak, failed, then cleared his throat and tried again.

"Shaan – Artifice, I mean. He was definitely intending on shutting me up for good tonight. He didn't get to, but he said we'd see him again. I don't know much about him, but I'm willing to bet that he's a man of his word. On top of that, we..." he gestured at Fang and Clare. "We've actually *seen* them. We know their faces. And every single person at this table knows who they are and what they're capable of. I don't think they're about to let us off the hook with that kind of knowledge if they can help it."

"So what are you saying?" Fisticuffs raised an eyebrow. "They'd rather come back for a final showdown than make an easy exit while they can? Listen, I actually fought Meteor Hammer, all right? He seemed perfectly content to run off in the middle of a scrap without any regrets about it."

"Yeah, but the three of them also do exactly what Cavall – Cave Canem – tells them to do," Clare chimed in. "Artifice would have fought us tonight, no qualms about it. But he was told to avoid a scene if possible, so he backed off. I mean, look at them! They *know* they can beat us if they want to, and they almost did. We would have been killed the other night if Mallory hadn't shown up when she had."

"She's right." Fang leaned back in her chair, her arms crossed, frowning into space. "The four of them are insanely powerful when they're together and they know it. How else would they have made it this far otherwise? They may well come back to finish us all off before they leave. It might actually be that *we're* the ones who should be running."

"I'll be damned before I run away from a fight," Fisticuffs retorted. "These guys are raising Cain and I'm sure as hell not backing out when my life as a Vigilante is at stake."

"If we had more support, maybe we'd be able to get in a few punches, but as we are..."

Shockwave, who had been silent until now, sat back in his chair and ran his hands through his hair with a frustrated exclamation.

"We're not ready," he growled. He slammed his hand down on the table, making Clare and Linus jump.

"We're not ready!" he repeated, and he sounded angry. He stood up abruptly. Joshua looked up at him, concerned. Shockwave walked away from the table, an expression of vexation on his features, running his hands through his hair again.

There was a silence, fraught with tension. Fisticuffs had her elbows to the table and her hands at her temples, almost scowling in her concentration. Linus had a faint look of guilt on his face and Clare looked similarly nervous; Mallory placed her hands on top of her friends' and gave them a comforting squeeze. Joshua studied Shockwave carefully as he paced the basement floor in agitation.

With a sudden roar of outrage, Shockwave raised a fist and slammed it into the wall. The sharp *crack* made everybody start; the concrete under the Vigilante's fist gave in and a crater appeared from beneath his knuckles, the web-like fractures splintering and spidering outwards.

"Damnnit!" Shockwave barked. "How did we even get into this mess?!"

Joshua took off his glasses and placed them upside-down on the table. He looked up, gazing coolly at Shockwave. Completely composed.

"You know exactly how we got involved, Louis," he said calmly. Firmly. "We made our decision when Equilibrium and Shooting Star died. That we were going to see to it that the ones responsible would regret it. You made your decision then. And you can make a decision again now."

A pause. Shockwave breathed out slowly through his nose and turned back around. He lowered his fist to his side, blood freckling his knuckles. He looked at Joshua and Joshua nodded. Shockwave closed his eyes, breathed a slow and heavy sigh, then opened his eyes again. He returned to the table and sat down in his chair. He beckoned to his teammates and the two of them leaned in to listen.

"Alright," Shockwave said, and he seemed himself again. "Team discussion. We've established that Cave Canem and his group are powerful. More powerful that even we might be able to handle. We all know that. So we can choose to back out of this one and not fight. We lay low and wait until they're out of the City. Or we can stand our ground and take up arms. There is no guarantee we will come out of it the same, or even come out of it at all, but we can damn well try. So which one will it be?"

Joshua nodded solemnly.

"*Kakari*. With you to the end, leader."

"Yeah." Fang smiled. "Let's give these jerkwads what they're owed."

A flicker of a smile passed over Shockwave's face then was gone again.

"Right."

He turned to look at Fisticuffs.

"I assume you've made your decision as well?"

Fisticuffs nodded.

"Damn straight, I have."

"Good. Thank you."

"Thanks to you as well."

Fisticuffs pushed her chair back and rose from the table.

"Seeing as we have the fight to end all fights coming for us tomorrow, I think I'll take my leave now. I'll return here in the evening, if that's acceptable to you."

"Absolutely." Fang raised her hand in a salute. "I look forward to working alongside you, Fisticuffs."

"And you, Resonance. Or should I say, 'Kinetic'."

Fisticuffs turned to look at Mallory.

"I'll thank you here now as well, Mallory," she said. "In case I don't get to later. You were of great assistance during my investigations. Thank you."

"I'm glad if I could be of service." Mallory extended a hand and Fisticuffs shook it. She then regarded Clare and Linus.

"Clare, Linus," she said. "Our introduction was rather abrupt in nature, but it was good to meet you as well. Your contributions to this mission are also appreciated."

"Thank you," Clare replied, a little flustered. "It was good to meet you too."

"Maybe I will see you again some time. Until then."

Shockwave got up to open the storm-cellar doors for Fisticuffs and she ascended the concrete steps and disappeared out into the night.

"Right," Shockwave said, after Fisticuffs had gone. "Now that that's been decided, Clare, Linus, Mallory. You three should head home too. Lie low 'til the storm blows over."

Clare, Linus and Mallory glanced at each other. They were all thinking the same thing. Shockwave saw the looks on their faces. His eyes widened, and then narrowed into a scowl.

"No," he said. "Absolutely not."

"But why not?" Clare challenged him, matching his frown. "If you need support then all you have to do is ask! You said so yourself, these guys are dangerous and they need to be stopped. We might not have been Vigilantes long but right now we're the only ones you know of willing to help. I found out a new thing with my Ability, too–"

"This isn't just about being *willing* to help, Clare, it's about being able to. Look at you three. You've only been in the game for half a year at most. Two of you haven't even got Abilities anymore. How do you expect to be able to keep up?"

"Shock–" Fang began, stepping forward. Shockwave held up a hand and turned to look at her and Joshua. He pointed a finger to the stairs leading up into the flat.

"Go upstairs," he commanded. It wasn't a question. Fang glowered darkly at him and made to give a sharp reply but Joshua nudged her and nodded his head towards the stairs. Nettled, Fang threw her hands up and turned heel, tramping up the wooden steps to the living area, Joshua following close behind. The light clicked off in the stairwell and it was quiet.

Shockwave closed the storm-cellar doors and came back down into the Base, standing to face Clare, Linus and Mallory.

"Let me ask you a question," he said, and his voice was quiet. "I don't expect you to give me an answer right away. But just listen. Why are you so eager to take down Cave Canem?"

"Because he's clearly dangerous." Mallory seemed almost indignant at the question. "He needs to be stopped–"

"No," Shockwave interrupted, and he was firm. "That's not what I'm asking. I know why he needs to be stopped, but why do *you* want to fight him?"

"I don't understand," Linus said. There was an edge of suspicion in his voice. "What are you implying?"

Shockwave sighed and pinched the bridge of his nose. He folded his arms.

"I am asking, what, specifically, are *your* motivations? You are three inexperienced and largely powerless Vigilantes. What reason do *you* have for wanting to take down Cave Canem? Why is it that you're so insistent on fighting when two of you don't even have Abilities anymore? Is it stupidity?"

"No!" Clare shot back, offended.

"Alright then, so it's not stupidity. So what is it? Are you in it out of the goodness of your hearts? For ideals like 'justice'? To set right a wrong? Or are you in it for more selfish reasons? Revenge maybe, or recognition as a big hero?"

Clare opened her mouth to object but Shockwave held up his hand.

"Stop," he said, an edge of anger creeping into his words. "Look, I don't want any knee-jerk responses. You figure out which one it is and come to term with it yourselves. You want to know my motivations for going through with this? Vengeance. That's all. Nothing more, nothing less. I want to get back at the garbage who thought they could throw my friend off a building and I want to make them pay for what they did with their lives. If you thought being a Vigilante was about doing the right thing then I'm sorry to disappoint, but you're wrong. We make up our own rules. We do what we want to because we have the power to and so we can get a decent night's sleep every once in a while.

"We knew about the Vigilante killings long before they came anywhere near here but I had no intention of playing any part in it until somebody that I knew died. If I fight for good it's because it aligns with my interests. If Joshua fights for good it's because he follows my lead wherever I go. And if Fang fights for good then it's only because she has something to gain from it and bad doesn't interest her enough. She might put on a good show of being calm, but I know for a fact she's never more alive than when she's in full flow, and back when we first met her she would have done anything to keep moving, no matter what it was.

"So as you can see, our motivations are far from being selfless or just. We're not heroes. There is no justice, and there are no more heroes. Not in this world. Just Vigilante idiots and fools rushing in."

Clare, Linus and Mallory fell silent. They looked at each other, and somehow they felt confused and guilty all at once. Shockwave regarded them soberly.

"I can't say who you thought we might have been," he said quietly. "But we're not good people. Good people don't leave killers to go unchecked for the sake of their own safety then dive right in when they feel like it. So go somewhere safe. Rest up. Keep a low profile until these guys are gone, whether they're dead or somewhere else; either way. Be better people than we are. Do what you like – just stay out of this war."

After Clare, Linus and Mallory had left, Shockwave went upstairs and sat down in the dark of the living room, his head in his hands. He closed his eyes and breathed very slowly.

"Are you sure you should have sent them away?"

He looked up. Joshua stood in the doorway, silhouetted by the light from the hallway. Shockwave lowered his hands and stared at his bloodied knuckles, noticing them for the first time.

"They would have hindered more than helped." He nursed his hand. "They don't have the experience, they lack sufficient fighting skills... Two of them don't even have their Abilities anymore. What would you have done?"

Joshua pushed himself off the doorframe and came into the living room, sitting down on the sofa next to his friend.

"I don't know if you've forgotten," Joshua said gently. "But I've also lost my Ability. I'd be about as useful as a mouse up against a lion. Fang's obviously been through the wringer lately, and there's somebody's blood still in the sink. Is anyone going to tell me whose?"

"Fang's fine," Shockwave muttered. "Her Ability has always been the strongest of all of us. She'll recover. As for you, you have fight skills you can use without an Ability, which you seem to believe you're getting back anyway. And we have Fisticuffs."

Joshua uttered a laugh.

"*Kātahi rā*, Louis, my Ability isn't going to come back overnight and I'm not even sure if it'll come back the same way. What if I can't keep up? What if something goes horribly wrong with Fisticuffs? What if Fang decides she'd rather switch teams?"

"She won't," Shockwave replied, almost as much to himself as to Joshua. "She said she'd stay."

"Alright, so she promised. Probably made some glib comment about holding our hands or something, am I right?"

"Yeah. Pretty much."

"Knew it. Look..." Joshua sighed. "All I'm saying is that the backup might not have hurt. They might be inexperienced but they're obviously pretty damn eager, whatever their reasons might be. You're the strategist. You could have come up with a plan. They might not have needed to fight at all."

Shockwave shook his head.

"No," he said. "It'd have been too dangerous. It's already too dangerous and I can't risk any decision that might make things worse than they already are. Maybe if we'd had more time, I could have come up with something. Maybe I'd have let the kids help. But we *don't* have time. We barely have time to process the information we learned tonight. So unless something miraculous happens soon, then I'm standing firm by my decision."

Joshua paused, then nodded.

"Alright," he said. "Well, I know how you stick by your decisions. And I'll stand by you because *e aua hoki*, God knows, I've done it all my life." He rose from the sofa and dropped a handful of bandages into his friend's lap. "I just hope you're right."

Joshua clapped Shockwave on the shoulder and walked out of the living room. Shockwave leaned back on the sofa, closed his eyes, and uttered a deep, heavy sigh.

"I hope so too."

Out in the hallway, Fang stood at her door and watched Joshua disappear back to his room. She glanced towards the living room, breathed out her own sigh, then slipped back into her bedroom and quietly shut the door.

CHAPTER TEN

COMBAT READY

When Fang had been a teenager she'd had issues with anxiety.

It had been a debilitating condition, and more often than not exhausting and physically incapacitating. Some days she found herself in a perpetual state of agitation for no reason whatsoever, the adrenaline wracking her veins and fraying her nerves leaving her unable to sleep. Other days the things that might only make others feel ill at ease sent her into a full-blown panic attack.

It was a hard affliction to describe to anyone who didn't have it, and it was almost impossible to understand for anyone who hadn't had experience with it. Fang didn't even try to explain – being unable to successfully communicate how she felt was almost as draining as going through her day to day. To be able to calm herself down in the moments preceding a spell, she found ways to control her racing heart and queasy stomach through grounding and controlled breathing. When there was so much adrenaline coursing through her that she found herself unable to keep still, she went out and ran; in this, her discovery of parkour came as a blessing, and due to her persistent restlessness she was able to train often and improve very quickly, learning how to both strengthen her mind as well as her body.

Though for most others the acquiring of Ability was seen as a gift, for Fang it was nothing short of hell. While others were ecstatic at their new fortunes, Fang felt nothing but dread. Her anxiety left edgy on the best of days and insomniac on the worst; receiving an Ability meant receiving the immense energy that enabled it, and suddenly breathing exercises and hour-long runs didn't cut it anymore. Her agitation soon turned to anger and frustration and her anxiety became a fuse for explosive fits of uncontrollable rage, as much directed at herself as the world around her.

So seeing no other alternative, Fang became a Vigilante and took to the night to ease her mind and stop her fidgeting hands. She took up an Alias and assigned to it the persona that would allow her to express herself unrestrainedly without caring about being brusque or brutal – in this case, the boyish Kinetic. Kinetic allowed Fang a channel through which she could turn her adrenaline into motion and her rage into the almost self-destructive pursuit of action. Any challenge, any mission would do, so long as it might use up the mass of her overflowing adrenaline.

In the process, she came up with new ways to try abate her anxiety. When she knew she had a big fight coming she would sit quietly in the dark of her room and strap her hands, winding and unwinding the tape tightly around her wrists, her palms, between her fingers; doing and undoing the bandages over and over again until it was perfect. Even when she didn't have a mission she would indulge in this process, and she continued to practice it in the years following. As the years went on and her anxiety got better she kept this habit still, and even after she had moved to the City and changed her Vigilante name she continued to practice it from time to time. Shockwave and Joshua came to learn about her patterns and she, in turn, came to learn about theirs.

They all had their rituals. And tonight was a night for rituals.

In her room, Fang sat on her bed, her curtains drawn, shifting herself bit by bit into her identity as Resonance, strapping and unstrapping her hands over and over until the bandages were perfect. She was already dressed in the black singlet and grey marle sweatpants that made up her usual Vigilante gear, having painstakingly cleaned and repaired the latter after her ordeal at The Estaminet the other night.

Downstairs in the Base, Shockwave paced restlessly back and forth, back and forth, his hands clasped fast behind his back. His eyes were red-rimmed and cast to the floor, his brow furrowed; his steps were measured and rhythmic but hushed. He had on his grey and blue hoodie, navy sweatpants and canvas sneakers; his scarf, green, matching the colour of his t-shirt, was tied neatly around his arm, the tear that had been in it now repaired with clumsy but careful needlework.

In the kitchen, Joshua sat straight-backed in a chair at the table, dressed like his teammates in a simple t-shirt and loose sweatpants, red on black, his scarf tied around his arm and his glasses perched atop his head. His hands were placed flat on the table before him and his eyes were closed. He breathed slowly, in and out, inhaling and exhaling. Meditating.

These were the rituals that they were engaged in when Fisticuffs finally knocked on the storm-cellar doors of the Base at precisely half past eight, just after the sun had started to set. Shockwave broke from his reverie to let her in and upstairs Resonance left Fang's room, hands immaculately strapped, wristbands on and bag slung on her back. She passed by the kitchen and stuck her head in. Joshua still sat meditating at the table.

"Hey," she called. Joshua opened his eyes, saw her and offered her a smile.

"Hey." He pulled his glasses down from atop his head to sit them on his nose. "Are we going?"

"Soon. Fisticuffs just arrived, it sounds like."

"Alright." Joshua pushed his chair back, rose and stretched his arms. Resonance studied him for a moment and he caught her gaze.

"Something the matter?" He raised his brows at her and lowered his arms. She looked at him in a troubled manner.

"Are you going to be alright out there tonight?" she asked after a pause. "I know you said you might be getting your Ability back, but it's still a far stretch from actually having it. Cave Canem and Artifice and the lot… they're going to be a tough opponent to beat."

The smile slipped from Joshua's face and became an expression of concern.

"I think I should be the one asking you that question," he said, sombre. "Louis told me what happened the other night. You got thrown out a window?"

Resonance shrugged.

"Minor injuries. There was a confrontation, I had it covered."

"Did you? Because I'm pretty sure I heard someone say last night that if it hadn't been for Mallory then you'd have all been killed. Fang, I know you're fast, but if you were so taken by surprise that you couldn't avoid getting grabbed, did you even have time to absorb the impact?"

"Excuse me, but do you see any bandages on me?"

"I did yesterday. In fact, I did this morning as well."

"And now they're all gone and there's no damage left. All fixed, no need to worry. Everyone's happy."

"*Aeha*! Damn you, I'm not happy and I *will* worry. What if things had gone worse for you out there?"

"Hey, I came home in one piece, didn't I?"

"How am I supposed to know? I wasn't there. You might not have broken anything, and thank God for that, but I saw your scarf and I'm pretty sure that was your blood I saw in the sink when I got back home. I've had just about a week to recover but you've only barely had a day. I can fight without my Ability, but can you?"

Resonance gave a laugh.

"I'm pretty sure the last time I checked, I had more Vigilante experience than you and Shock did."

"Yeah and I'm pretty sure the last time we checked you were also pretty cavalier about getting into dangerous situations, 'Kinetic'. I can't stop and heal you in the middle of a fight this time around."

"And I couldn't stop and heal myself in the middle of a fight for the three years I was a solo act as well. Funny that, isn't it? Look," Resonance held up her hands. "You're fine, and I'm fine. Similarly, you're *not* fine, and I'm not fine. Neither of us is ready. Shock is downstairs pacing holes into his shoes because he's also not ready. We can't switch out our hands this late in the game, so we might as well make the most of what we've got. Okay?"

"Cute." Joshua pushed his chair back in and removed his glasses. "Does that actually work for you?"

"Sure it does. Come on, we're probably leaving soon."

Joshua placed his glasses on the table and it was Rehua who followed Resonance out of the kitchen towards the wooden steps to the basement. Shockwave and Fisticuffs looked up at them as they descended and the latter gave them a stoic nod. She was wearing her usual Vigilante gear and her long brown hair was drawn back into a loose braid, as always. The leather gloves adorning her hands were not the fingerless ones she always wore, however; these ones covered her whole hand and had silver studs on the knuckles. Likewise, her boots were not the same as before, and appeared to have a steel plate fixed on each foot, about an inch wide, starting at the front around the toes and curving down the outside of the foot to stop just at the arch.

"Evening, Fisticuffs," Rehua greeted. "Ready to go?"

"We'd better be," Fisticuffs replied. "We can't afford to slip up tonight. Not when it might be our last chance."

Shockwave picked up something off the table and handed it to Resonance.

"Here," he said. "Scrubbed up best I could."

It was her scarf. Resonance held it up and shook it out – it was clean now and free of the heavy bloodstains that had spotted it the night before last.

"Wow, good job. Thanks." Resonance folded the scarf neatly and tied it around her arm.

"Alright." Fisticuffs folded her arms. "So here's how it's going to go. Our number one priority tonight is to track down Cave Canem and co. and get the jump on them, preferably before they get the jump on us. Assuming that they're all extremely proficient at fighting as a unit, our best bet might be to tackle them one by one. However, under no circumstances must we let Cave Canem escape." Fisticuffs gazed sternly at the three Vigilantes before her. "If we let him go, it's game over."

Shockwave made a doubtful face.

"Shouldn't Artifice be the priority above Cave Canem? He's the one who can take away Abilities after all. Without him they won't be able to accomplish their objective anymore."

"Yes, but he does the things he does at Cave Canem's bidding, whether voluntarily or otherwise. Take down the leader and they won't have a directive anymore. Whatever his true motivations are, even if Artifice is out of the picture, if Cave Canem is hellbent enough on getting what he wants then he may find another way to achieve his goals."

"Hm. I'm not entirely sure I agree."

"We can work from the outside in," Resonance cut in. She put a hand on Shockwave's shoulder. "Lackeys first, get them out of the way. Then Cave Canem. We can still knock Artifice out of the running first, we just can't let Cave out of our sight in the process."

"Right." Fisticuffs nodded. "We keep him in check at all times if possible. We can't really do much in the way of planning on this one, since we still don't even really know what they've got up their sleeves. But we can do that much at least."

Shockwave processed this information then gave a stout nod.

"Fine. We better make tracks then. I don't want to get out there and find them already on our doorstep."

Some blocks away from the town square there was a long-neglected shopping street, a wide, half-lit pedestrian zone lined on each side by wooden benches and closed-down shops with graffitied roll-down doors. Old streetlamps dotted the edges of the stretch of cobblestones, only a few of which were working properly; of the remaining, one was dead and another flickered on and off at irregular intervals, an audiovisual Morse code puncturing the stillness with throws of light and abrupt, high-frequency buzzing sounds.

By the time the four of them arrived on this street, it had been almost an hour since they'd left the Base and so far they hadn't come across any sign of their enemy. It was difficult to know whether this was a good or a bad sign, but it was clear that nobody was taking it well. The atmosphere was growing more and more tense and the four of them communicated less and less as time went on, with Fisticuffs falling into an edgy silence as they continued on their way.

"You don't suppose they already left or went after the kids first or anything, do you?" Resonance asked quietly. Rehua grimaced.

"Maybe we should have checked in with them before we left," he said. "Should we go back that way?"

"No," Shockwave replied firmly. "We'll continue towards the highway out of town for now. If we keep going this way we're bound to intersect them at some point, whether they decide to go after the kids or end up trying to skip town."

"Skip town?" A deep, gravelly baritone rolled out of the darkness ahead and made them all instantly alert. Towards the end of the street, a massive silhouette stepped out of the shadows and into the glow of the streetlamps; imposing, intimidating, with broad shoulders and huge arms. They wore dark clothes, a hooded leather jacket and heavy jeans, with heavy boots on their feet and leather gloves on their hands.

The new arrival pulled the hood back off their head to reveal a face that both Fisticuffs and Resonance had seen before – strong-jawed, sharp-featured, with bleach-blond spikes and piercing green eyes. There were small silver rings in his ears this time, and a weighty-looking chain dangling from the loops of his jeans.

Meteor Hammer bared his teeth in a grin.

"You didn't think we'd leave without saying goodbye, did you?" he asked, his accent thick and pronounced. "How insulting."

"Insulting?" Fisticuffs shot back, her tone curt. "What's insulting is running off in the middle of a fight without so much as an 'I surrender'. That's just common courtesy."

Meteor Hammer threw back his head and laughed, a loud, rich sound that bounced off the buildings surrounding them and trailed away into faint echoes.

"I'm sorry," he chuckled. "Surrender? That's optimistic. If my retreating slighted you then I apologise, but I can assure you it was no surrender."

"Where's your employer?" Resonance called. "Is he hiding somewhere, or did he sent you out here all on your own tonight?"

"Cave Canem? He'll be around. He's a busy guy, after all. I've just been sent to tie up loose ends before we leave."

"A diversion," Shockwave muttered. "He's here to delay us."

He made to move, his muscles tensing, but Fisticuffs held out an arm before him.

"No," she said in a low voice. "You three go on ahead. Track down Cave Canem and don't lose him." Her lip curled back into a bellicose grin. "This one's *mine*."

Shockwave paused, then nodded. "Alright then. Good luck."

"Godspeed."

Shockwave gestured to Resonance and Rehua.

"Ready?"

Rehua smiled.

"Ready as we'll ever be."

Without another word, the three of them ran forwards towards Meteor Hammer, Shockwave leading his team into the fray. Meteor Hammer grounded himself, holding his arms out wide as if to invite them to do their worst; Shockwave ran straight at him and Meteor Hammer swung a fist forward but Resonance put herself in the way, her body hunched and arms raised in a cross-arm block, absorbing the energy of the blow. She quickly twisted her arms and trapped Meteor Hammer's forearm in a vicelike grip and Shockwave leapt up over her and launched himself off Meteor Hammer's arm, flying over his head and landing in a roll behind him. Rehua drew close to their right and Meteor Hammer pivoted into the beginning of a roundhouse but Resonance threw down his forearm and hurled herself towards his outstretched leg with both arms raised, stopping the kick and absorbing the impact of the blow once more; Rehua continued past, following Shockwave out and away from the street.

Resonance shoved Meteor Hammer's leg up and ducked underneath, following the trail of her two team mates; Meteor Hammer went with the momentum of the throw into a roll and came back up, moving to run after her, but suddenly Fisticuffs was there and she threw a punch at him with a roar; he twisted backwards, narrowly missing her fist, and spun backwards into a ready stance, set to face her.

Fisticuffs pulled her studded gloves down tight and flexed her fingers, taking a few steps backwards and rolling her shoulders. Meteor Hammer cracked his neck from side to side and curled and uncurled his massive fists.

"You better watch yourself," Fisticuffs growled. "I'm not about to let you get away a second time."

"And I'm not about to give you the satisfaction of having that *choice*." Meteor Hammer lunged forwards, his fist drawn back, and threw himself at Fisticuffs. Fisticuffs ran forwards and met him halfway with her own battlecry, blocking his fist with a forearm and deflecting his fist to the side, causing him to shoot past. She grabbed Meteor Hammer by the shoulders and drove her knee into his back, forcing him down onto his knees on the cobblestones.

Meteor Hammer reached back and grabbed Fisticuffs by the scruff of her collar, yanking forward and throwing her down hard while simultaneously pushing himself back and up into a standing position again; Fisticuffs landed heavily on her back with an *oomph* and twisted out of the way in time to miss a stomp from a boot and pushed herself back up onto her feet again. She ran forwards and drew her fist back and he moved to block but it was a feint; instead she sprang up and twisted into a spinning backwards roundhouse that caught him on the side of his head and knocked him on an angle into the ground.

Meteor Hammer rolled over the stones onto his back, drew back his knees, and kipped himself up back onto his feet. He wiped the blood away from his left ear and laughed again.

"Oh, this is good," he said, amused. "This is very good." He drew the chains from his belt loops and wrapped them around his knuckles. "I'm glad I'm allowed to beat you this time, because I have no intention of holding back."

"I wouldn't have it any other way." Fisticuffs grinned. *"Bring it on."*

Shockwave, Resonance and Rehua continued to make haste from the abandoned shopping street and entered the night-dead business district, leaving Fisticuffs to fight with Meteor Hammer on her own.

"Do you think she'll be alright by herself?" Rehua asked as they ran. "I know she's legendary and all..."

"We've got to trust that she can handle it on her own," Shockwave muttered. "We can't afford to hang back. If Meteor Hammer was sent as a distraction then we have to make sure to avoid that distraction, or there may be hell to pay later on."

"I should have stayed," Resonance said under her breath. "Strength for strength, Fisticuffs might match him, but with my Ability..."

"No," Shockwave interrupted her. "Let Fisticuffs handle it. You may be right, but we need to stay as a unit as much as we can. Coordination is going to be key in this one."

"Look who's finally talking about coordination—"

A flash of silver suddenly lurched out of the darkness to their right and caught Resonance at the corner of her eye.

"Watch out!"

With a great burst of strength Resonance shoved Rehua forwards and twisted back; a length of chain, buzzing and crackling with blue electricity, shot towards them, intersecting the street and cutting through the space between Resonance and Rehua, barely missing Shockwave as he too jumped back.

The metal chain whipped backwards in the direction from which it came and Resonance, Shockwave and Rehua whirled around to face the right, looking for its source. To their right was the mouth of an alleyway, its length of which was shrouded in shadow.

"We know you're here," Resonance shouted. "Show yourself!"

With her long black ponytail and dangly silver earrings, someone stepped out of the alleyway with the soft tinkling sound of jingling chains. She wore a long hooded cardigan over a dark tunic and black leggings. Black, soft-soled martial arts shoes adorned her feet and there was a thin belt slung around her hips.

Faraday smiled charmingly at them, her weapon coiled in her left hand and the dart end hanging loosely from her right.

"It's nice to see you again," she said.

Shockwave glanced around surreptitiously but could see no other enemy; Faraday caught his gaze and shook her head.

"If you're looking for Cave, he's not here." Her smile widened. "He's not one to fight unless he feels like it."

"He's perfectly welcome to it," Resonance replied. "But why don't you call him out here and he can not-fight while we knock his lights out?"

Faraday laughed; a sweet, pretty sound that seemed to light up her eyes.

"You're very funny," she responded. Her chain dart jingled in her right hand. "I like you."

Faraday suddenly swung the dart forward and launched it towards Resonance and Rehua; the two dove out of the way and Shockwave kicked up a leg and brought it down hard onto the chain, pinning it to the concrete. Faraday gave a sly smile and a jolt of electricity shot down the length of the chain; Shockwave removed his foot just in time and Faraday yanked the chain back, twining it around her leg, kicking forward and shooting it towards Rehua.

Rehua flung himself sideways to avoid the dart as it flew towards him; whirling forwards, Faraday gripped the chain tight and twisted sideways, whipping the chain to the side. Shockwave was forced to throw himself back over the chain and landed in the beginnings of a backwards roll, changing tack halfway and kipping himself back up onto his feet; Resonance dove over the silver links and rolled, landing forward on her hands and knees.

Shockwave glanced at his teammates and swore under his breath. He made a fast decision; a decision he didn't like.

Inwardly cursing at himself and his circumstances, Shockwave ran towards Faraday, who had already recalled her weapon, wrapping it around her forearm and preparing to swing it forward again. He dropped to his knees as he drew close and skidded forwards, throwing his torso back to avoid being sliced by the chain dart; as soon as it had passed over his head he threw his upper body forward again, curling his hand into a tight fist and throwing a punch at Faraday. He caught her in the solar plexus and she stumbled backwards with a cry, her weapon slipping from her hands and skittering over away the road.

Shockwave pushed himself up off his knees and turned his head to look at Resonance and Rehua.

"*Go!*" he shouted at them. Resonance gave him a stunned look but then recovered quickly and nodded, scrambling to her feet; up ahead, Rehua offered him a salute before turning and running with Resonance down the street, away from Shockwave and Faraday.

Faraday got to her feet, holding her stomach with one hand, and laughed that sweet, tinkling laugh again. It was a sound of genuine amusement.

"I haven't had such a good fight in a long time," she said. "I think I'm going to really enjoy this."

Shockwave narrowed his eyes and gave a tight-lipped smile.

"Yeah," he said, almost to himself. "I think I'm going to as well."

Given that Artifice had already paid them a personal visit, it was agreed that the flat was no longer a safe place while Cave Canem and co. were still in town. So in the interest of remaining alive for one more night, Clare, Linus and Mallory decided to hole themselves up in Mallory's car, which they parked in a darkened backstreet around the corner from the flat. As a safety precaution they had taken their Vigilante weapons with them; Mallory had her crowbar stashed in the foot of the passenger seat and Clare, riding shotgun, had her softball bat in her lap. In the back, Linus had Mallory's tyre iron sitting on the seat beside him.

"Are you guys still thinking about what Shockwave said?" Linus asked.

"...Yeah," Clare replied quietly. "And I still don't like it."

"Which part?" Mallory turned to look at Clare. "The part where he forbade us from fighting, or the part where he said that they weren't good people?"

"I dunno. Both, I guess." Clare sighed and leaned her head back on the headrest. "I just kinda thought... having an Ability and being a Vigilante. I guess I thought there was something exciting and kind of noble about it. But maybe we really are all just in it for our own selfish reasons, whether it's to get our kicks or be able to go to sleep every other night."

"Do you remember how we got started?" Mallory asked. It was a rhetorical question; of course they all remembered. Almost seven months ago, within only a matter of weeks from each other, the three of them had found that they had acquired strange powers. Mallory, tinkering at her workbench late one night, had reached a hand out for her wrench and almost instantly found it in her grasp. Linus, who had gone to look out his bedroom window one evening, had cupped his hands against the glass to get a better look outside, and fallen through his own reflection to come tumbling out the window of the downstairs living room and onto the street below. And Clare, during a late night walk with Linus and Mallory, had turned around to talk to her friends when she suddenly vanished into the fog without any warning whatsoever, ending up only metres away from the convenience store they had set out to visit.

Two months later, after tiring of energy-fuelled all-night gaming sessions, they decided that there was probably something to be better done with their newfound powers and restless nighttimes, and settled on going out to fight petty crime and beat up bad guys. Well – it was mostly Clare's idea. Linus agreed almost immediately, saying they could be like the comic book superheroes they had grown up on. Mallory, erring on the side of caution as always, was unconvinced as to the validity of the idea, but chose to join her friends rather than leave them to run amok on their own.

"We literally decided to go out and fight crime to be like superheroes. I dunno, Mal." Clare shrugged glumly. "The more I think about it, the more it seems like we just wanted to do something other than play games all night."

"Does that have to be a bad thing though?" Clare and Linus looked at Mallory.

"What do you mean?"

Mallory raised a shoulder then let it drop.

"So we got in over our heads a little bit. Maybe there are no more heroes like Shockwave said and maybe we are in it for selfish reasons. Does that invalidate the consequences of our actions though? We still stopped a couple of thieves in our time. Maybe it made us feel big and important and that's the kind of thing we were looking for, but it's still something that we did. That goes for the rest of them, too. Shockwave might just be in it for revenge and Resonance might just be in it for kicks, but they're still putting themselves out there tonight to try take down a dangerous enemy."

"Are you saying we should go back out and help them?"

Mallory laughed in uncertainty.

"I don't know," she replied. "Noble and grandiose ideas are more your fashion."

"Shockwave would get mad," Linus said dubiously. "And what

could we do without our Abilities?"

"Why does it have to be about Abilities? We might not have them anymore, but we still have our brains, and we've still got *some* energy in us. Every little might help in this fight. Look," Mallory reached over and opened the glovebox, pulling something that looked like a modernised medieval gauntlet out of the compartment. She slid it onto her right hand and held it up.

"I started working on this almost right after I realised I lost my Ability," she said. "It does pretty much everything my Ability used to do. It's a bit clunky, but it's just as good. I might not have my Ability anymore, but if anything else, doesn't that give us a one-up on Artifice? He doesn't have anything to take from us anymore."

There was silence for a moment while Clare and Linus processed this thought.

"Well," Clare said, a smile creeping onto her lips. "I would like to see how much I can do with my new Ability."

"I'm not getting left behind if you guys are going," Linus interjected.

Mallory held up her hands.

"Hey, I didn't say anything about going. Plans are for the leader to give, right? So how about it, leader? What's it going to be?"

Clare looked down at her softball bat, scuffed up from years of use both on and off the pitch. She ran her hands over the aluminium then gripped the handle tightly in both hands. She looked up at Mallory and Linus, eyes gleaming.

"Alright, gang," she said, twisting towards them, and a new resoluteness was in her voice. "New plan. We're going to go out there and we're going to help Shockwave and Resonance and the rest of them give Cave Canem and Artifice and their lot the ol' one-two. We've been warned; we know it's dangerous, and it might not go well. Maybe Shockwave is right and there are no such things as heroes anymore. But I'll be damned before we let them fight the others alone, even if they are more experienced than we are. So who's with me?"

Mallory winked at Clare.

"We're with you, leader," she said. Linus picked up the tyre iron beside him and grinned.

"Count me in."

Clare laughed and reached towards the car door handle.

"Alright then!" she said. "Let's go beat up some bad guys. On the count of three. One... Two..."

They opened their doors and stepped out of the car.

CHAPTER ELEVEN

ALL OR NOTHING

Shockwave had made many mistakes in his lifetime.

He did his best to avoid them, but usually he didn't mind them much. Mistakes usually meant that he still had things left to learn, and he was always willing to learn. Whether it was making a move before he was ready or choosing the wrong course of action at a crossroads, he would quietly reflect back on what it was he had done, acknowledge that he could do things better next time, then pick himself back up and try again. Learning from his mistakes was how he had improved both as a Vigilante and as a freerunner in the time that he had been involved in either venture.

Mistakes were how you learned to become a better person, provided that whatever that mistake was didn't kill you first. And right now, Shockwave was in very real danger of being killed.

The first thing that he had done wrong was underestimate exactly how strong an opponent Faraday would be. In his previous encounter with her less than a week ago, he had been able to push both her and Cave Canem into a retreat – but a lot could happen in four nights, it seemed, and in that time no less than two more Vigilantes had had their Abilities taken away by Artifice, the energy from which had apparently been shared amongst Cave Canem and co. to fuel their own strength.

The second thing that he had done wrong was think that Faraday would be easier to defeat without her weapon in her hands.

Shockwave was paying dearly for those errors now. As soon as Resonance and Rehua had left he rushed at Faraday, drawing in close, and thought to himself that without her chain dart he might be able to get in a few punches. Faraday had moved to lunge for her weapon in the same second but abandoned her attempt as Shockwave threw a punch at her. He tensed his muscles, changing the density of his arm, and drove his fist towards her, but Faraday swivelled out of the way; whirling back around, she raised both hands and swept them at the outside of Shockwave's extended arm. It wasn't even a very hard push, but it was enough that Shockwave was caught off guard; taken off balance, he stumbled and fell, tucking into a hasty roll and coming back up on his knees.

He turned his head to look at Faraday behind him, surprised, and she narrowed her eyes at him and smiled. She turned and went for her chain dart again and Shockwave twisted around and threw his fist into the ground; the concrete beneath their feet suddenly cracked and split into pieces, sinking into a massive crater with Shockwave at its epicentre, the edges of the cavity going as far as where Faraday's weapon lay on the road. Faraday stumbled with the force of the quake and Shockwave took the chance to get back up and launch himself at her again, both arms outstretched as if to tackle her.

Faraday turned and met him halfway, grabbing his hands and interlocking her fingers with his, her hands crackling with electrical energy; she buckled her knees and went down into a backwards roll, bringing up a foot to slam into Shockwave's stomach and launching him back over her head with the momentum of her turn. As the electricity ran from Faraday's hands to Shockwave's and through his body he let out a strangled yell; thrown through the air, he landed in a clumsy tumble across the road, the shock causing his body to spasm. Fighting the feeling, he pushed himself back up on his feet, his legs almost giving way.

Faraday rolled over and snatched up her chain dart from the ground, holding the coil in her left hand and the end with the dart in her right. She began to swing the chain in a circle, letting out more of its length as she swung, the radius of the circle increasing as she went. Shockwave tried to shake his head clear and regain his composure, pulling into a ready stance with his hands raised in loose fists before him.

"Just give up already!" Faraday called. "You've lost this one." The chain made a faint, jingling *whp whp whp* sound as she swung it in the air. Shockwave shook out his limbs.

"Not hardly likely," he muttered. Faraday launched the chain forward. Shockwave ducked back as the dart shot past his head and he grabbed the chain; he grounded himself with his Ability and *pulled*, yanking the chain hard towards him, attempting to catch Faraday off guard and disarm her as he had once before, but she was ready for the trick – instead of trying to hold her ground she let herself move with the pull and suddenly Shockwave was nose to nose with her and he found that he was the one who had been taken off guard.

Faraday bared her teeth in a sharp-toothed grin and wordlessly slammed the heel of her palm into his diaphragm. Shockwave doubled over with a gargled cry, instantly winded, and Faraday grabbed him by his the back of his hair and pulled down sharply, driving her knee upwards to slam into his face; Shockwave was thrown backwards in a bloody-nosed arc and he landed hard on his back, the remaining air in his lungs forcefully knocked out by the impact. He drew in a deep, rattling wheeze for breath, his hands shaking, blood on his lips, and tried to push himself up on his elbows, but Faraday placed a foot on his chest and forced him back down.

The air around Faraday's shoe crackled with thin blue lightning and a surge of electricity shot through Shockwave and he thought his heart would stop; his back arched as every single muscle in his body tensed and he roared with agony, feeling as if every part of him was on fire, and then Faraday let him go and the horrible sensation was gone as suddenly as it had begun. Faraday lashed her foot out at him in a kick but Shockwave grabbed her by the ankle with one shaking hand, gripping as tight as he could manage; he pulled with as much strength as he could muster and Faraday's other leg gave out and she toppled onto her back with a cry.

Shockwave rolled out of reach and pushed himself back to his feet, whirling back three steps and turning around to face his opponent in one fluid, if shaky, movement, the night fog creeping in swirling around him as he moved. He tried to draw himself upright but couldn't quite manage it; his chest and shoulders rose and fell as he fought to regain his breath, his tousled hair fell into his eyes and the front of his t-shirt was singed. Try as he might, he couldn't stop himself from trembling, and his vision was swimming in and out of focus. He raised a hand to his burned chest; the adrenaline rushing through his veins from the electric shock was causing his heart to race out of control and he thought his knees might buckle beneath him at any moment.

Faraday picked herself back up, looked at Shockwave and laughed.

"Aren't you a sight?" she said in a teasing voice. "Maybe I should put you out of your misery."

She brought up the chain and whirled it around it a circle; bringing up her leg, she swung the chain underneath, catching the dart on the backswing with her left foot. Shockwave could see the attack coming and tried to move but only stumbled backwards; Faraday sent a bolt of electricity snaking down the length of the chain and kicked the dart towards him –

– But Shockwave wasn't there.

The dart pierced the empty space where he had been only a split second ago, the thickening fog swirling rapidly in his place. The chain and dart fell to the ground with a metallic tinkling and Faraday, surprised, looked around for her vanished target.

"Hey, Faraday!" someone shouted. Faraday turned towards the sound.

Two figures, silhouetted by the night fog, walked up the road towards her. It took Faraday a moment to recognise their faces, but when she did, her eyes narrowed into a glare.

"Well look who it is," she murmured. Despite herself, she found herself smiling.

Linus and Mallory walked out of the fog and stopped in the middle of the street. Mallory gazed intensely at Faraday, her gauntlet on her hand and her crowbar resting on her shoulder. Linus held the tyre iron at his side, doing his best to look confident.

"I thought I told you to stay out of this!"

Faraday turned back around again at the sound of Shockwave's voice and she finally spotted him – some ways up the road, Shockwave lay awkwardly back on his elbows near the sidewalk, Clare crouched at his side. Shockwave looked furious, glaring at Clare with an intensity that would have made her cringe any other day. But right now she didn't care.

"I don't mean to sound rude, Shockwave," Clare said. "But save the lecture for later. We've made our decision and we'd like to help."

Shockwave laughed in disbelief.

"Help? It's barely been fifteen minutes and I've been knocked down three times. What makes you think you can do better when you've only been a Vigilante for the fraction of the time that I have?"

"Well, we don't." Clare grinned sheepishly. "We don't expect to be able to win. Not at all. At least, not by ourselves. But if we can damn well try help you guys get the upper hand."

"Sorry to burst your bubble, but 'try' isn't going to cut it."

"Well, that's the best we've got, so we're going to run with it. Where are the others?"

Shockwave scowled at Clare but she didn't flinch.

"...up ahead," he finally muttered. "The plan was to intercept them before they left town. Fisticuffs is back with Meteor Hammer."

"Then go."

Shockwave was incredulous.

"*What?*"

Clare nodded fervently.

"Cave Canem and Artifice are the priority, aren't they? Go join your team. We'll handle Faraday."

"You're not planning to run off with my fun, are you?" Faraday called, reeling her chain back in. Clare looked over and grinned.

"Not on your life," she replied. "The real fun starts now!"

"Where do you get off being so confident?" Shockwave growled. "You'll get slaughtered!" Clare glanced back at him and shrugged lightly.

"Well, you know what they say. Fake it 'til you make it, right?"

She grabbed Shockwave under the arm and began to haul him upright and all of a sudden he felt a light-headedness, an all-around feeling that he was as weightless and insubstantial as a cloud. Everything around him turned white for a second, and suddenly Shockwave was on his feet and he found that he was far away at the end of the street, fog swirling around him; Faraday was now a long way behind, and he stood facing the direction that Resonance and Rehua had run off in before.

Clare took her hand away from his arm and Shockwave turned to face her, both confused and angry. Clare stepped back a few paces, pushing up the sleeves of her anorak, and offered him a reassuring smile.

"Just go!" she urged. "Leave Faraday to us. We'll catch up with you later." A pause. "...Hopefully."

Before Shockwave could react, Clare had turned and whirled back into the mist, vanishing into the whiteness. He cursed under his breath and looked back towards the direction his teammates had gone. He didn't feel good about leaving the kids to Faraday; not at all. He hadn't been much use against her alone, so what hope would they have? But he also wanted to rejoin his teammates and to be there himself when Cave Canem and Artifice were taken down.

Shockwave let out a snarl of frustration. He didn't like this – he didn't like this at all. But he would have to trust Clare, Linus and Mallory to at least stay alive and keep Faraday distracted. He drew the palm of his hand across his mouth and wiped the blood from his nose, streaking the red along his fingers, and turned to spit a mouthful of blood and saliva into the gutter. Pulling himself together and trying to ignore the pain Faraday had dealt him, he shook his head at himself and began to run off down the street.

He hoped he wouldn't regret this; or that if he did, he would at least live to do so.

Out of all the members of their little team, Rehua was the one who exercised the most amount of caution in the face of potential danger.

Even with Resonance's time as a solo Vigilante, she had the greatest tendency to barge right into a situation, damn the consequences, because she trusted her quick reflexes and adaptability to get her out of trouble. The nature of her Ability meant that she could tank almost anything without getting hurt, and her light-footedness and physical prowess at parkour meant that even if she did need to bail, she could do so quickly and quietly. Shockwave was also a fast and adaptable thinker, which served his capability as a strategist in good stead, and he tended to be more careful, but occasionally let his emotions cloud his judgment. Nine times out of ten he would be calm and level-headed and avoid going into situations unprepared, but the remaining one part meant that he was sometimes overly aggressive and tactless in his manner.

The Abilities of his teammates were hugely adaptable. They could be used both defensively and for attacks. They benefited Shockwave and Resonance well, but at the same time they allowed them to be careless. But Rehua – Rehua was only a healer. Or rather, he had been. Being a healer didn't mean that he was impervious to injuries, just that he healed from them faster than most. His Ability was useful, no doubt, but it wouldn't help him win a fight; Rehua had to go into those on his own merits. So as it was, when the three of them were faced with a potential trap, he would always be the one to want to back away from it first.

And Artifice, sitting alone on a bench outside the Epic Theatre, was most definitely a trap.

The Epic Theatre was an old, run-down cinema complex at the end of the old theatre square, situated near the edge of town. The place had been a thriving hub of activity once, but that had been before the establishment of the new entertainment district years back. Recent damage done to the theatre by a gang of arsonists (whom Shockwave and Rehua had later apprehended) meant that it was now far from the grand structure it had been, and a sign posted on its massive double-doors, chained shut, indicated that it was facing eventual demolition in three weeks time.

His back facing towards them, Artifice sat in front of the Epic, one ankle crossed over his knee, his arms spread wide along the back of the bench. His head was tilted up at the dilapidated building, as if imagining what it might have been like in its prime.

Resonance stopped at the edge of the square and looked as if she were about to shout some manner of insulting greeting in Artifice's general direction, but Rehua put a hand to her shoulder and stopped her. She looked back at him and he raised a finger to his lips.

"Wait," he said in a hushed voice.

Some distance away, at the opposite end of the square, Artifice moved his head, as if he had heard them. He shifted in his seat, swivelling around so that he was looking straight at them, and gave them a dazzling smile.

"Would you look at that," he called out to them. His voice bounced off the walls of the closed-down buildings surrounding them. "So you made it this far after all."

Resonance shrugged off Rehua's hand and began to walk forward.

"Don't sound too excited," she retorted. "You'll make me cry. Or were you expecting somebody else?"

"As a matter of fact, I was." Artifice rose from his bench and turned around to face them, sliding his hands into the pockets of his black winter coat. "I was waiting for my friends, you see. You haven't seen them, have you? Although..." he grinned. "You appear to be missing some of your company as well."

Resonance scowled, stopping in her tracks, but it was Rehua who stepped forward to answer.

"Our friends are fine," he called back. "They can take care of themselves. But how about yours?"

Artifice laughed lightly.

"Oh, they're capable," he replied. "They're very capable. I'd trust them with my life. And I'm definitely counting on seeing them again soon, after they're done with your lot."

"Wanna bet on it?" Resonance growled.

"Absolutely. We have one last show to do tomorrow night, after all. We have to make tracks; otherwise we'll be in no fit state to perform. Especially Cavall."

"Yeah, speaking of that guy." Resonance folded her arms. "Cave Canem, right? Where's he at, anyhow? Is he biding his time or is he just letting you guys do his dirty work?"

"'Dirty work'? That's adorable. If you think having to deal with you is anything else but important and necessary then you're underselling yourself and underestimating him."

"Res," Rehua called in a low voice. Resonance turned to look at him and he gave her a meaningful kind of expression. She took on a look of concern.

"Are you sure?" she asked.

Rehua smiled and held out his arms in a shrug.

"Hey, he already got me one time," he replied. "There's nothing else left to take from me."

"That's pretty morbid, dude."

"Bit rich coming from you. Just go, alright? I'll catch up with you later."

Resonance paused, then nodded.

"Alright," she said. "Good luck then."

"Likewise. See you later."

Resonance turned and began to run up the square towards an exit at the northeast side of the square, but all of a sudden there was a flash of silver from her left; a stiletto knife whistled sharply past her and embedded itself at the ground before her feet, stopping her dead in her tracks. She glanced left.

Artifice hardly seemed to have moved at all, but it was clear that he had thrown the knife. His right hand now rested at his side instead of in his coat pocket, as it had been a moment earlier. He smiled pleasantly at Resonance and began to shrug off his coat to reveal the dark red shirt and black jeans underneath. His sleeves were rolled up and folded precisely just below his elbows and she could see the henna tattoo going from the fingertips of his right hand and up his arm.

"Sorry," he said. He folded the coat and laid it neatly on the bench. "But I can't let you off that easy. Between the fact that I need what you have and you know something you shouldn't... you understand, don't you?"

He rested his hand on his hip and Resonance noticed for the first time the utility-like belt slung around him, the loops in which at least a dozen closed stiletto knives were stowed.

Artifice pulled one of the knives from his belt, flipped it open with a flick of his wrist, then vaulted over the bench and strode towards Resonance.

Resonance acted quickly, reaching down to grab the knife embedded in the ground and pulling it out of the concrete. She gripped it in her hand and ran towards Artifice, meeting him halfway as she darted across the square; she slashed wildly at him with the blade but he easily dodged, pivoting out of the way. Resonance whirled back around to face him, holding up the knife before her. Artifice looked at her stance and laughed.

"Kind of stupid to think you can use my own weapon against me, isn't it?" he asked, openly taunting her.

"I never said I was smart," Resonance growled, and lunged forward with her arm outstretched. Artifice tossed his knife into his left hand and swatted Resonance's arm out of the way with his forearm; in the same move he seized her wrist and pulled her forward, and suddenly he was behind her with his knife to her throat and his chest pressed against her back. He tightened his grip on Resonance's wrist so that she could feel the edges of the bandages she'd strapped around her hand pressing into her skin and the bloodflow from her wrist being cut off. She grunted in discomfort but didn't let go of the knife in her hand.

Artifice pressed the blade of his stiletto closer to her throat so she could feel the sharp edge almost cutting into her skin.

"*Drop the knife*," he hissed, only inches away from her ear.

"Hey!!" A bellow came out of nowhere. Artifice turned his head in time to see Rehua sprint up behind him and launch a flying kick into his back that knocked both him and Resonance forward; with a grunt Artifice loosened his grip on Resonance and she used the opportunity to reach behind her and grab him by his collar and the belt of his jeans, throwing him bodily over her head and slamming him into the ground, eliciting from him a sharp grunt of pain. Rehua grabbed Resonance's arm and pulled her back a few steps.

"Did he –?" Rehua began, his voice low and urgent. Resonance shook her head quickly and held up her arm, indicating the wraps on her wrist.

"Only touched the tape," she muttered back. "Knew I strapped my hands for a reason."

Rehua's shoulders relaxed as he gave a sigh of relief.

"*I pai ai.* Losing both our Abilities would all we need."

Still on his back, Artifice made a sound that was half spluttering cough, half winded laughter and Resonance and Rehua took a step back and became alert again. At once they remembered that they were essentially up against a Vigilante with a strong healing Ability, and that it would be twice as hard to beat him as any other opponent. Resonance fastened her grip on the knife still in her right hand and Rehua flexed his fingers, curling his hands into tight fists.

Slowly, Artifice pushed himself back up onto his feet and turned around to face them.

"Good to see you've still got some fight in you, even after I took away your Ability." He brushed off his shoulders.

"Yeah, well," Rehua shrugged, eyeing the knife still in Artifice's hand. "You know what it's like being a healer. Doesn't really help you throw your punches better."

"No, you're right. It doesn't. We have to find other ways of fighting, don't we?"

Artifice shifted back into a ready stance, holding his knife in his left hand and holding his right up and open before him.

"Well, alright," Artifice said. "Two against one, is it?"

"*Make that three.*"

Artifice, Resonance and Rehua turned at the sound of the voice to see, walking up the square towards them, Shockwave, his hair a mess and faded streaks of dried blood smeared over his mouth and chin. His hoodie was zipped up over his t-shirt now and his scarf had been wrapped around his right hand in a kind of makeshift bandage.

"Shock," Rehua breathed, surprised. Shockwave strode up to stand beside him, a scowl on his features.

"The kids showed up," he muttered under his breath. Resonance looked at him, aghast.

"They *what?*"

"Yeah. They're still with Faraday now."

"And you *let* them?!"

"Who the hell do you think I am?" Shockwave hissed back, irritably. "They bailed me out so I could meet back up with you. Didn't exactly give me a choice in the matter."

"Hell's teeth, Shock."

"When you're done whispering amongst yourselves," Artifice interrupted. "Mind telling me how you managed to escape Faraday?"

"...That's easy," Shockwave replied coolly. "I beat her."

Artifice looked Shockwave's dishevelled state up and down and gave him a mocking smile.

"Well that's a lie if I ever heard one," he replied.

"That's priceless, coming from you," Shockwave retorted. "How about you give me a few answers? Why all this? Why go to the trouble of killing other Vigilantes?"

Artifice laughed.

"So they don't come back and give me lip about taking away their Abilities, of course."

"Damn you, you know what I mean. Why do it in the first place? Why do you even need so much energy?"

"For a capable Vigilante such as yourself, you sure seem to be in the habit of asking a lot of silly questions. Why don't you take a wild guess?"

"Quit deflecting, Artifice. What's your endgame?" Resonance cut in. She was starting to get impatient. "You could use your Ability for your own gain but instead you're at someone else's beck and call. Why fuel the ambitions of someone else when you could easily be king of the world on your own?"

The smile on Artifice's face changed. Suddenly it became softer, kinder. Almost sad. He lowered his hands and stood at ease.

"Have you ever had that one person," he began. "That you want so badly to succeed at everything they do? Someone you would do anything for if it meant they could get what they want? You would give them the world if they asked. They try so damn hard and they deserve it. But then something happens. A part of them that they can't help starts to take them over, like a sickness. They can't control it. How can you then stand by and do nothing?"

Rehua shifted his stance slightly, in a reflexive and almost self-conscious kind of way. Artifice glanced at him.

"I can see you know what I mean," he said. "You're a healer. You and I are the same. It's in our nature to want to fix things. To want to set them right."

"*Was* a healer, no thanks to you," Rehua broke in, frowning. "We're nothing alike. Is this what this is about? Someone you care about is sick? So fix it already. You've got enough power."

"What if they don't want to be fixed?" Artifice asked softly.

"More answers, less vague rhetoric, Artifice. You still haven't explained how Cavall ties into all this."

Artifice laughed and it was a combination of arrogance and disbelief.

"Get a clue, *Rehua*. I think I've already made myself perfectly clear."

"Great, so you're some benevolent guardian angel now on some great and noble quest." Resonance scoffed. "Right. You'd hurt others for the sake of this one person you care about so much? Some saint you are. Where's your moral compass?"

"Look at you, sounding so high and mighty," Artifice shot back. All of a sudden he sounded irritable, his calm demeanour disturbed. "As if you don't already go out at night and beat up petty crooks for the fun of it. I may be no saint but neither are you, so I'd appreciate it if you got off your high horse and admitted you and I are just doing what we think is right."

"Sorry, but I don't think that highly of myself," Shockwave growled. "I'm here for one reason and one reason only, and that's to make you suffer the consequences for having killed our friends."

"Aren't you going to give me a chance to surrender first?"

"Please, I'd rather you put up a good fight. It'll make it that much more satisfying for me when I punch your face in."

Artifice chuckled.

"In that case, I guess I'll do it your way."

Seeming to have regained his temperament he moved back into his ready stance, one foot forward of the other, his left hand clutching his knife and his right hand up and open before him. For a split second, Resonance thought she could see his palm crackling with a faint white electricity. She mirrored his bearing, shifting her right front forward and holding up her stolen blade; beside her, Rehua raised his clenched fists to the level of his chin and Shockwave tensed his muscles, his hands curling at his sides.

"Come on then." Artifice beckoned to them with a smile.

Shockwave moved first, swinging his fist forward with a roar of rage.

Clare, Linus and Mallory didn't particularly have a plan when it came to dealing with enemies on night patrols. They tended to wing it a lot of the time. They hadn't had a great deal of experience with fighting, since they'd never really come across many targets that required anything more than strategic herding and cornering. The fact that Clare and Linus possessed Abilities that allowed them to essentially teleport meant that they could afford to just go with the flow of things and still manage okay, although that annoyed Mallory to no end. Their Abilities may have been useful but they also enabled her friends to rush into situations without thinking things all the way through, which occasionally made trouble for them when they could have avoided it completely.

In this situation, however, things were decidedly different. Thanks to Artifice, Linus and Mallory no longer had their Abilities, leaving Clare the only one who could even hope to match another Vigilante in a fight. Still, just having an Ability wouldn't be enough – not against this opponent. Faraday had just proven she could knock Shockwave down in a fight, and he was no amateur Vigilante himself. This time they couldn't afford to make mistakes or be careless; this time they had to be strong and think fast.

So when Faraday launched her chain dart towards them, there was nothing else they could do but run for it. Mallory and Linus threw themselves to the side, Clare twisting and vanishing into the mist; she reappeared behind Faraday and swung her softball bat as hard at her as she could but Faraday was faster. Bending and sweeping underneath the bat as it passed over her head, she came back up again, raising a leg and slamming her heel into Clare's stomach. Clare was knocked back with a gasp, dropping her bat, stumbling backwards and beginning to fall; Faraday brought her chain around and whipped it towards her, but as Clare fell she disappeared back into the fog again, reappearing several metres away and rolling clumsily back over her shoulder.

Pushing herself to her feet and darting forwards, Mallory launched her crowbar at Faraday with a little extra assistance from her gauntlet, the bar spinning forward at high-speed. Incredibly, Faraday used her chain dart to knock the crowbar out of midair; Mallory stretched out her arm and recalled her weapon as she drew closer, the crowbar coming back to her gauntlet hand with a *clang*. She grasped it in both hands and swung it at Faraday but Faraday only twisted out of the way, twining her chain around her arm and shooting it towards Mallory, the metal links crackling with electricity.

Mallory let herself drop, falling clumsily to the road, and kicked both her feet at Faraday's shins; her knees buckling, Faraday dropped with a shout, sprawling to the ground, and suddenly Linus was there, yelling an incoherent battlecry and swinging Mallory's tyre iron like a golf club. Faraday snapped up a hand and caught the tyre iron in mid-swing, then sent a jolt of electricity along it that made Linus yelp as it burned his hand; he let go, and Faraday gripped the tyre iron tight and swung it hard at the backs of Linus' legs, sending him toppling backwards to the concrete. She raised the iron to swing again but Mallory held out her hand and it was wrenched out of Faraday's grip and into the gauntlet.

Linus rolled out of the way and pushed himself onto his feet as Faraday reached out to grab him with an electrified hand; Mallory got up, her crowbar in one hand and tyre iron in the other, and tossed the iron back to Linus as Faraday got back to her feet again.

"Look at you lot," Faraday teased, studying them all. She began to swing her the dart of her weapon in a circle. "Aren't you an eager bunch? Especially when considering two of you don't even have your Abilities anymore. Tell me, are you brave or just stupid?"

"Well in my experience, the two are almost identical," Clare replied, before throwing herself forward. She disappeared into the fog as Faraday launched forward her chain whip again, vanishing in a swirl of mist; Mallory used the opportunity to hold out her gauntlet and the chain of Faraday's weapon shot into her hand and she held on tight. Faraday jerked her head around to look at her and suddenly Mallory felt a feeling like sharp fire shooting up her arm. With a cry, she let go of the chain, reeling backwards and tripping back over her feet, hugging her gauntlet arm close to her chest; Clare reappeared behind Faraday and threw a clumsy punch at her with a yell.

Faraday whirled around and knocked Clare's arm out of the way without missing a beat, before backhanding her hard across the face, her hands crackling with blue lightning. Clare was sent careering sideways with a cry and took a graceless tumble; Linus ran at Faraday brandishing the tyre iron but she was too quick; yanking back on the chain dart, she swung it backwards, snagged it with her foot on the backswing, then kicked it towards him. Linus twisted sideways and missed it as it shot past, but Faraday only pulled back on the chain – it jerked back, wrapping itself around Linus and binding his arms tightly to his side.

Faraday smiled and sent a shock of electricity down the length of her weapon and Linus screamed as the current ran through him, every inch of him howling in pain; then the electricity stopped and he collapsed to the ground, convulsing involuntarily and choking for breath. Faraday reached down and grabbed him by the collar, hauling him up so he was almost standing upright again, and shook the chain loose from around him. She pulled Linus close so that she was face to face with him.

"Nice try," she said sweetly. "Better luck next time."

Faraday seized the belt of Linus' jeans with her other hand, and hurled him hard towards the window of a shop nearby. Linus braced himself, screwed his eyes shut, and waited for the pain.

But the pain never came.

Or, it did, but not in the way he was expecting.

Instead of smashing through the plate glass window as he'd been anticipating, Linus felt only a sensation as if passing through a thick and heavy curtain; then all of a sudden the breath was knocked from his lungs as he slammed onto his back, and he was spilling out over the hard ground with nothing but rough asphalt beneath him.

Linus opened his eyes in shock and found that he was alone and it was quiet. He pushed himself up on his hands and looked around to find himself in the place he least expected to be – the street on which he, Clare and Mallory lived. He glanced behind him and saw he was lying just below the living room window of their flat.

Linus clambered to his feet and stumbled backwards, staring up at their home, a silent and familiar pillar of comfort in the midst of the chaotic City. All was exactly as they had left it mere hours ago.

There was no way this could be possible, Linus thought to himself, utterly speechless. It had only been two nights since Artifice took away his Ability, so how could he already have it back? Rehua said that there was a chance of a Vigilante's stolen powers to come back to them, but this was much too fast. No, there had to be a catch.

Linus walked towards the living room window of the flat. He studied his reflection – his astonishment, he noticed, was showing clearly on his face. He looked down at his hands, then reached out towards his reflection.

Whenever Linus had used his Ability before, it had been easy and effortless. Be it water or glass, passing through any transparent reflective surface felt merely as if he had passed through a flimsy veil of gauze, or walked through a light breeze. This was nothing as comfortable – as soon as Linus touched the window he could feel the resistance beneath his fingertips. He pushed at the glass and the glass pushed back – Linus pushed a little harder and his fingers sank into his reflection and he felt like he was pushing through a heavy curtain. He felt a breeze on the tips of his fingers.

Linus drew his hand back quickly. For a second he did nothing but clutch his hand to his chest in surprise. But then his surprise turned into elation, and his elation turned to determination. It wasn't as strong or as comfortable as before, but his Ability had definitely come back to him. He didn't know how and he didn't know why, but he wasn't about to argue with serendipity.

Linus took a few steps back off the sidewalk and onto the street, then began to run straight at the flat. He leapt forward into the air as he approached the living room window, his hands outstretched – his hands passed through his reflection and he disappeared into the surface of the glass with a battlecry.

Clare and Mallory, still sprawled out on the ground, had been expecting many things when Faraday had picked up Linus and thrown him bodily towards the shopfront window – but seeing their friend disappear into its surface had not been one of them. Horror and dismay turned into shock and astonishment as Linus had vanished into the glass, and they glanced at each other with surprise written all over their faces. Faraday looked similarly stunned, and for a good few seconds she did not move.

"Where did he go?" she said, stunned. She whirled around to look at Clare and Mallory.

"*Where did he go?*" she said again, this time flustered and demanding. Clare was just as flabbergasted as any of them, but she wasn't about to let this chance get away. She glanced at the ground to her side and saw her softball bat resting in the gutter. She looked to Mallory and Mallory's eyes widened in understanding.

"Looks like he got the one-up on you," Clare said. She grabbed her bat out of the gutter and threw it forwards.

Mallory reached out her gauntlet arm towards the aluminium bat; it shot towards her with incredible speed, catching Faraday behind the knees on the way and sending her crashing backwards to the ground with a screech, her grip on her chain dart loosening and the coil slipping from her hand. Mallory swatted Clare's bat aside as it came towards her and turned her gauntlet to the chain dart; it vibrated for a second and then, before Faraday could react, sped into her hand with a streak of silver. She leapt to her feet, tossed the coil into her left hand and pulled taut on the dart end, echoing the same stance she had seen Faraday taking before.

Faraday got to her feet, eyed the chain dart in Mallory's hands, and laughed.

"Really?" she said in a teasing voice. "You're going to use my own weapon against me?"

Mallory looked down at the chain. Faraday had a point; she didn't know the first thing about using a rope dart. She could understand the basic physics of the thing, but Mallory was a mechanic, not a martial artist; this was an ancient weapon that took months to learn and years to master. No, trying to use her own weapon against her would be a stupid idea. She looked back up at Faraday.

"You're right," Mallory replied. "That would be stupid. Good thing I don't have to."

At that very moment, from the same window he had disappeared into only moments ago, Linus came hurtling hands-first out of the glass with a yell and collided with Faraday where she stood, sending her crashing back to the ground again. The two of them tumbled clumsily away and ended up in a tangled heap in the middle of the road; Linus looked up, and then after a split second of realisation, frantically scrambled back up to his feet and away from Faraday.

But Faraday didn't move.

Mallory and Clare glanced at each other, and then after a moment, simultaneously began to edge closer. Linus tiptoed slowly back to Faraday's unmoving form and crouched down gingerly, reaching out a hand; he touched her on the shoulder and quickly stepped backwards as she turned and flopped onto her back, but Faraday remained still and unmoving. Her mouth was half open in a stunned kind of expression and a trickle of blood ran down her face from where her head had struck the concrete, the impact apparently knocking her out cold. Linus held a hand over her mouth and could feel the faint tickle of breath on his skin.

Drawing his hand back, Linus turned to look at Clare and Mallory, giving them both an awkward laugh.

"Well it looks like that just happened," he said shakily.

"Linus," Clare exclaimed, wrapping her arms tight around him. "Your Ability! But–?!"

"Damned if I know," Linus replied, flustered. "I'm just as clueless as you, but if it has come back..."

"Let's not look a gift horse in the mouth," Mallory broke in. She picked up her tyre iron and crowbar, slinging the latter onto the belt loop of her cargo pants, and stepped forwards to embrace Linus also, before pulling back and looking at her friends with a combination of lingering astonishment and grave severity. "And let's also agree that we were extremely lucky this time. That was a one in a million event and it'll probably never happen again."

"Oh yeah," Clare laughed in an almost hysterical way. "We were damn lucky."

Linus looked back down at Faraday's unconscious body.

"So what do we do with her?"

Mallory glanced at the chain dart still in her right hand then looked at Faraday. She bent down, grabbed her under the arms, and then gestured to Clare and Linus.

"Here, grab her feet. Help me move her over there."

Clare and Linus obeyed wordlessly, the three of them hauling Faraday over to sit against a lamppost at the side of the road. Mallory shook out the chain dart and began to wrap it firmly around Faraday's wrists, binding her tightly to the concrete pillar.

"With any luck," she muttered, straightening up again. "She won't wake up for a while. We'll come back and get her when we're done."

"We should go," Clare said anxiously. She glanced up the street to where she had dropped off Shockwave before. "I don't know, maybe they've already won, maybe not. But I want to go, just in case. Come on, you two."

Clare stooped and picked up her softball bat of the road and started walking. Mallory and Linus began to follow.

"Where did Shockwave say they were headed exactly?" Mallory asked.

"They were going to intercept Cave Canem and Artifice before they left town," Clare replied. "Resonance and Rehua were already up ahead. Fisticuffs is back fighting Meteor Hammer somewhere."

Mallory suddenly stopped in her tracks. She glanced back over her shoulder at the street behind them. Clare and Linus noticed her pause and halted as well.

"Mallory?"

Mallory looked back at her teammates and she looked thoughtful.

"I think you two should go ahead," she said. Clare and Linus looked surprised.

"What?"

"Yeah." Mallory looked a little sheepish. "Is that alright? I know she's probably okay on her own, but I'd like to go back and help Fisticuffs."

There was a brief pause while Clare and Linus processed Mallory's words, but then the startled expression on Clare's face softened into a grin.

"Alright," she said, and then: "Are you sure?"

Mallory nodded resolutely and smiled.

"Absolutely."

Clare laughed and came back to pull Mallory into a hug, which she returned.

"We'll see you later then," she said warmly. "You be safe, alright?"

"Yeah, sure thing. Same goes for you too, leader."

They broke apart and Mallory began to back down the road, waving to her friends as she went.

"You better come back in one piece," Linus called to her. "Otherwise we won't be a proper Vigilante team anymore. The family that slays together, stays together. Right?"

Mallory chuckled.

"I think you're mixing up your proverbs there again, champ."

She tossed the tyre iron to Linus and he caught it deftly.

"Here," she said. "Hold onto that for me, will you?"

"You betcha. Thanks, Mal."

Then with a wink and a salute, Mallory turned and began to run down the road, disappearing into the depths of the fog and out of sight. Clare and Linus watched her as she went.

"Alright," Clare turned to Linus. "We should get a move on. Don't want to be late."

Linus paused for a moment, then glanced to their right at the window he had been thrown into just minutes before. He looked back at Clare and gave her a grin.

"Come on," he said, and held out a hand. "I'll give you a lift."

CHAPTER TWELVE

CAVE CANEM

A year ago, if Clare had been told that she would one day possess an incredible Ability and become a Vigilante, she wouldn't have believed it. If a month ago she had been told that she would soon meet other people who had incredible powers just like her, she would have been incredulous. And if a week ago she had been told that she was soon to be in the biggest fight of her life yet... well, she wouldn't have known what to think.

But here she was, standing alongside one of her two best friends, the both of them capable (if amateur) Vigilantes, each of them possessing extraordinary powers. And here they were, perched on the balcony of the opera house Linus had transported them to, the familiar forms of four other Vigilantes scattered amongst the fog in the old square below.

They could see Resonance, slight but strong, a knife in her hand and a bloody gash on her arm; Shockwave, fluid but aggressive, red streaks on his face and on the scarf bound around his hand; Rehua, tough but cautious, blood on his knuckles and the knee of his jeans; and last but not least, Artifice, calm but quick, relaxed but agile, looking completely unruffled in the face of his three opponents.

Clare couldn't be certain of how long they had been fighting already, but it was clear that Shockwave, Resonance and Rehua had already taken more than a few blows. Whether they had landed any on Artifice or not wasn't obvious, but if they had it didn't seem to have affected him very much.

Artifice's mouth moved as he spoke and Shockwave, halfway across the square from him, seemed to almost spit venom in return, but neither Clare nor Linus could hear what they were saying from the distance they were at.

"Doesn't look too good, does it?" Linus looked worried. Clare was much the same.

"What was it that Fisticuffs said?" she asked. "Something like Artifice essentially being a Vigilante with a healing Ability?"

"Yeah. I think so."

Clare and Linus glanced at each other, nervous, each with the same question written across their faces. How did you beat an opponent who could heal his injuries as soon as you inflicted them and who could take away your Ability if you got too close? The whole situation seemed grossly unfair.

As they turned their gazes back to Shockwave, Resonance and Rehua, standing at scattered but equidistant points in the square around Artifice, Clare was reminded of something else that had been said to them recently – something that Resonance had told them three nights ago. What had it been?

"It's not as if we don't get along. We make a great team when need be. Maybe you'll get to see us in action some time. You might want to keep your distance though – he's not called Shockwave for nothing."

Down below, both Shockwave and Resonance moved suddenly and Clare gasped as she witnessed the truth of Resonance's words. Running forward across the square, Shockwave swung his arm back, looking as if he was gearing up to throw a punch, but instead Resonance drew close behind him and leapt; she landed precisely on Shockwave's outstretched arm and he swung forward with all his might, launching Resonance forward with an almighty roar. Resonance hurtled through the air towards Artifice and she made a wild slash at him as she came close; Artifice ducked and twisted and she overshot, tucking into a roll as she hit the ground and skidding across the ground behind him.

As Resonance hit the ground, Shockwave drew close behind Artifice as he came back up from his dodge and Artifice thrust the knife in his left hand towards him. Shockwave jumped back to avoid the blade and twisted in midair, coming back down towards Artifice with his heels; Artifice whirled back, bent low to avoid him and Shockwave landed hard on the ground where he had been, the concrete beneath his feet cracking and splitting as he touched down, deep fissures spidering out across the ground.

In one swift movement, Artifice, keeping down low, placed one hand on the ground and twisted his body, bringing up one long leg in a powerful thrusting kick that caught Shockwave in the small of his back as he straightened, knocking him forwards with an exclamation of surprise; Artifice came back up, tossing his knife into his right hand behind his back and making ready to throw it at Shockwave when Rehua sprang out of nowhere, leaping up into a kick that Artifice merely leaned back to dodge.

Artifice turned his sights on Rehua, drawing back his arm –

– "Time to go," Linus said quickly, grabbing Clare by the arm and stepping backwards. They passed through the glass balcony doors they had arrived through in the first place and reappeared at the foot of the opera house, on ground level with the square. Clare rushed forward, vanishing into the night fog –

– to throw the knife at him but suddenly there was a flurry of mist and someone seemed to come out of nowhere, tackling Rehua from behind as he straightened, and suddenly he vanished and the blade passed through nothing but thin air.

Clare and Rehua appeared in a heap a few metres away. Artifice whipped around as they spilled out of the fog and looked surprised as he realised what had happened. The soft sound of steady footsteps from behind him heralded the arrival of Linus, face set in determination, who walked into the square to stand by Clare and Rehua. Upon seeing him Artifice laughed out loud.

"So the cavalry arrives!" he said. He looked over at Shockwave and Resonance, who both looked stunned. "Not exactly the assistance you were expecting, I take it?"

Clare got to her feet, glaring at Artifice and gripping her softball bat at her side.

"Cut the trash talk," she said hotly. "Go on. I dare you to underestimate me."

Artifice held up his hands in a gesture of faux surrender that was at once placating yet infuriatingly mocking.

"I wouldn't dream of it," he replied easily. "After all, I know all about your new tricks."

Clare narrowed her eyes at him. Artifice turned to look at Linus, who kept his distance.

"Linus," he said. "You're looking well. I was actually going to pay you a visit after this."

"Thought I'd save you the trouble and come directly to you," Linus replied. He did his best to sound confident but he couldn't shake the feeling of butterflies in his gut.

Resonance snapped out of her astonishment, taking on an expression of alarm. She looked to Shockwave as he backed close to stand by her.

"You said they were with Faraday," she hissed at him. Shockwave scowled.

"I know what I said," he snapped back, his voice low. "They were when I left them. Don't ask me how because my guess is about as good as yours."

Resonance cursed.

"If she turns up that's all we'll need…"

"So what are you kids planning?" Rehua murmured to Clare and Linus. "Not that I'm not pleased to see you're alright, but…"

"Actually… we don't really have a plan." Clare grinned awkwardly. "We just thought you could do with the extra help. Were we wrong?"

Rehua looked caught between laughing and sighing. He settled for a wry smile.

"*E*. Not entirely."

"So what are you going to do now, Artifice?" Resonance called. "You're outnumbered, five to one. It's okay to throw in the towel if you want."

"Yes, I can definitely see how the addition of two amateurs gives you the extra edge you're looking for," Artifice responded drily. "But in my experience, it's not so much the numbers that count as much as what they can bring to the table." He smiled suddenly. "Wouldn't you agree?"

Shockwave opened his mouth to respond but a sudden sound came out of the darkness of the alleys to his left and made them all turn. It was a low, rumbling noise, wolfish and threatening, and it echoed off the buildings surrounding them.

It was the sound of a feral dog growling.

A large black dog with glowing amber eyes crept out of the shadow of the alleyways and came into view. Cave Canem, hackles raised and teeth bared, padded forwards into the soft white light of the square.

Everyone but Artifice froze.

"You see?" Artifice said softly. "You don't need numbers when you've got power."

The tension in the air grew suddenly so thick that it was almost palpable. Everyone stood stock still, paralysed, not wanting to take their eyes off Cave Canem.

A flicker of movement made Rehua break his gaze away and he glanced back at Artifice in time to see him with a hand at the belt around his hips, ready to draw another stiletto knife.

"*Watch out!*" Rehua shouted – and that was when all hell broke loose.

The moment Rehua cried out, the spell was broken. Artifice drew his knife and flicked it open and at the same moment Cave Canem lunged forwards with a vicious bark and pounced at Shockwave and Resonance.

Artifice threw the blade forwards and Rehua shoved Clare out of the way just in time and she began to fall, vanishing into the fog; Resonance dove to the right but Shockwave stood his ground, tensing his muscles, twisting into a forward thrusting kick that would have slammed into Cave Canem, only the black dog pushed off his outstretched foot and leapt overhead, landing behind him and darting forward to attack again.

In that instant, Clare reappeared out of the mist before Shockwave, completing her fall back into him and knocking them both back into the ground. Resonance shouted a warning and Clare uttered a shriek as she saw Cave Canem; she raised her arms to protect herself and the fog swirled in thick and fast into a shield that Cave crashed down hard on top of, claws scrabbling at its impossible surface.

Resonance ran towards them, still holding Artifice's knife; Shockwave thought fast and grabbed Clare by her waist, suddenly propelling her upwards and to the right; Cave Canem was thrown up off Clare's shield and towards Resonance in the same movement and Resonance slashed at him and the dog let out a yelp as it flew past and landed clumsily on the ground behind her. Clare tumbled across the concrete and Resonance ducked down, pulling her hastily back up again; Shockwave kipped up onto his feet and stood by them.

Cave Canem skidded around to face them, growling more furiously now than ever, a streak of glistening bloodstained fur at his side.

"We're going to have to work together," Shockwave muttered quickly. "Clare, you're going to need to act fast with us on this one."

"Okay," Clare answered, frantic, before Cave Canem gave another loud bark and leapt at them again.

After Rehua had pushed Clare out of the way, Linus immediately made his move, rushing at Artifice and swinging Mallory's tyre iron with a yell. Artifice grabbed the tyre iron in mid-swing and swept a leg out under Linus, pulling him off his feet and onto his back; Rehua ran forwards and dove straight at Artifice, his hands outstretched, and Artifice looked up, letting go of the tyre iron and raising an arm to defend himself as Rehua crashed into him, sending the two of them crashing to the concrete.

Rehua rolled away and got up in the same second as Linus did and the two of them made to attack Artifice at the same time, Linus brandishing the tyre iron again as Rehua threw a fist forward, but incredibly, as Artifice straightened up between them, he blocked the tyre iron with a forearm and caught Rehua's fist in his other hand; before either of them could react, Artifice twisted into a kick that slammed Rehua in the gut while at the same time forcing Linus' weapon back so that it struck him hard in the head.

Both of them were knocked backwards and fell heavily to the ground, Linus dazed and Rehua winded.

"You know," Artifice said, looking down at them both. "I really can't decide if going up against you two is a stupid or clever decision on your half. On the one hand, there's nothing left in you for me to take. On the other, how can you possibly hope to keep up?"

"Oh, I'll show you what I've got left in me," Rehua growled, pushing himself back to his feet. Artifice chuckled, drew another knife from his belt, then flicked it open.

"Go on then," he said, and he beckoned to Rehua.

When Clare had been a child, she'd had a nasty experience with a neighbourhood dog that had culminated with her mother having to come to her rescue, wrestling with the dog by its collar from behind. It was the most scared she'd ever been in her life, but none of that fear or adrenaline could even hope to match the sheer terror that she felt now going up against Cave Canem, who viciously and tirelessly made them dart back and forth across the square.

For every lunge that the black dog made towards them there was little that she could do but block or dodge, swinging with her softball bat where she could and using the night fog as cover or defence where an attack wasn't possible.

She took cues from Shockwave and Resonance in some of their moves, grabbing them and using her Ability when signalled, but she felt awkward and frantic compared to the two of them, who seemed so resolute and in control despite their unrelenting enemy; the two were now truly displaying their skill when it came to working as a team, wordlessly coordinating their movements and using their individual and in some ways contrasting Abilities to alternately compliment the other's style and make tactical manoeuvres together.

These were two Vigilantes skilled in their art and who knew each other well; Resonance with her light-footed movements, who knew when to move before her teammate even spoke, and Shockwave, who shattered the earth as he punched and landed from his vaults and tricks, occasionally lending Resonance strength by dealing her blows which she absorbed and turned into speed, the two of them using the fixtures in the square as launching points and barriers to place between themselves and their enemy.

As Cave Canem bounded at Shockwave and Resonance once more, Shockwave readied himself to strike again and Resonance yelled out to Clare, her hand outstretched; Clare, frenetic, dove towards her, crashing harder into her than she'd intended, the both of them falling into the fog and rematerialising several metres away in a tangled, tumbling heap on the ground. As they glanced up at each other, both of them looking dishevelled and wide-eyed, they simultaneously looked back down at Resonance's side to realise that Artifice's knife was no longer in her hand.

Rehua was usually loath to go up against weapon wielders on his own. His forte was in brute force and hand-to-hand combat, and any opponent that was armed he usually left to his teammates first. Resonance's Ability meant she could absorb almost any blow safely, save for those involving sharp edges, and Shockwave's Ability allowed him to increase his density to the point that whatever had hit him would take more damage than he himself would have.

As far as Rehua was concerned, the less hits he took, the better – sure, he was a healer, but it wasn't like he could heal instantaneously, and it didn't take experience to know that weapons could deal more damage that fists could.

So when he found himself going up against Artifice, who had a whole belt of knives fastened around his hips, Rehua mentally cursed himself for having gotten into this whole mess in the first place. The second thing he did was resign himself to the fact and focus his attention to disarming Artifice as soon as possible, and the only way to do that would be to get in at close range.

Darting in fast and getting as near as he could, Rehua proceeded to engage Artifice in a rapid-fire exchange of blows at close quarters, striking and blocking, pushing him in towards the middle of the square, little by little. At this distance it would be harder for Artifice to slash him with the knife, although a short thrust could be deadly – Rehua, however, wasn't intending on giving him that chance.

He deflected Artifice's strikes to the outside, delivering quick punches where he could – Artifice may have been a powerful Vigilante, but his energy didn't give him super speed. It was clear that he had some proficiency in close combat, perhaps capoeira judging from what Rehua had seen before, but Rehua could deal with that; after all, years of kickboxing had improved his reflexes.

Artifice came in with the knife again and Rehua struck him in the forearm with his open hand, knocking his arm away; in that split second, Rehua noticed Artifice's grip loosen on his knife ever so slightly and he seized the opportunity, delivering a blow to his wrist that knocked the blade away, sending it clattering away over the ground.

Without missing a beat, Artifice drew another knife and flicked it open but Rehua was ready, beginning another round of quick-fire blocks and strikes in which he managed to disarm Artifice once more.

Artifice reached behind himself and drew another blade, eyes narrowed, swinging a quick elbow strike at Rehua with his other arm; Rehua just barely managed to duck underneath to avoid it, but he refused to let himself be thrown off, keeping the speed of his blows and blocks fast and consistent, eventually disarming Artifice once more, then again, then one more time, sending the stilettos (*seven, eight, nine of them*) skittering away one after another over the ground.

There were three stilettos left – Rehua could see them in the slots at Artifice's right hip. This time, as Artifice thrust his weapon forward, Rehua acted almost without thinking; he twisted back and grabbed Artifice's fist, the blade biting into his hand, then seized the closed knives at his opponent's hip, tearing them from the belt and throwing them blindly, haphazardly away, before disarming him one final time, throwing Artifice bodily across the square and sending him hard back into a fire hydrant.

Artifice slammed into the iron post with enough force that it tilted back behind him, and water began swiftly gushing from the newly formed space between the hydrant and the ground.

Artifice, lying in a rapidly spreading pool of water, uttered a choking, wheezing laugh, and Rehua, hand bleeding, backed slowly away from him, trying to catch his breath and kicking the scattered knives further away as he came across them.

Linus knelt awkwardly on the ground, more or less where Artifice had knocked him back, although he had scrambled to move out of the way during Rehua's sparring match with him; he clambered upright as the edges of the water crept towards him and it swept past his shoes without pause.

Artifice slowly pushed himself to his feet, soaking wet, his hair plastered to his head and his shirt now clinging to the slender body underneath; Linus thought he could hear several sharp *crack*s as he straightened up again.

"Good show," Artifice said to Rehua, almost admiringly. "You missed one, though."

Artifice's hand darted behind his back. Rehua's eyes grew wide and he made to move, run, dodge, anything, but suddenly a flash of silver shot through the air and embedded itself into his right arm.

Rehua gave a shout of pain as he jerked backwards, tripping and falling back into the water, and Linus gasped as he saw the spray of blood; a shadow of movement made him look up and suddenly Artifice was right in front of him and he was thrusting an open-palm strike towards him –

Even three against one and working together, Cave Canem was proving frighteningly difficult to beat. Human opponents were difficult enough to battle, in Resonance's opinion, but a mad dog with the stolen energies from other Vigilantes? It was almost too much.

Even though it hadn't been her weapon, Resonance had found the knife had provided an extra edge and had helped her land a few successful hits. Both she and Shockwave were more experienced in delivering blunt force injuries, but it was hard to deal that kind of damage to a creature that moved a lot faster and a lot wilder than people did. Resonance had tried to look out for the knife after she realised she had lost it but could not find it; although, even if she had been able to spot it, Cave Canem was keeping them all too much on their toes for her to be able to retrieve it.

They resumed their back and forth battle, dodging and blocking and attacking where possible, Shockwave occasionally taking Cave Canem head-on, dealing to him blows that seemed to knock him back for a moment but from which he recovered only seconds later.

They were all starting to get tired, Resonance knew – but Shockwave kept trying. As Cave Canem started for him again, he stood his ground and roared "*Come on!*", preparing to attack again, but as the dog lunged towards him its shape suddenly changed in mid-air and suddenly it was not a dog but a person who was clawing at Shockwave's throat and eyes. With a sharp twist of his body Shockwave flung his attacker away from himself with a cry of surprise, and they tumbled away over the ground, coming to a skidding halt down on all fours.

Cavall Robinson looked up at Shockwave, hate in his eyes and blood staining his side, growling like the mad dog that he had been a second ago. Despite himself, Shockwave was taken aback. Was Cave – Cavall's – sudden transformation the employment of a battle tactic, to confuse the enemy and gain the upper hand? No – it couldn't be. It wouldn't make any sense. In his dog form he was clearly much faster, much stronger, much more powerful than he could ever be as a person. There wouldn't be any reason for him to transform in the middle of a fight. That is, unless...

"You can't control it," Shockwave breathed, stunned.

If Cavall heard, he did not answer. Giving an almighty snarl, his eyes glittering amber, he threw himself towards Shockwave, who raised his arms to defend himself, but suddenly he was facing the

black dog once more and it changed direction, leaping over Shockwave's head completely. In his surprise, Shockwave glanced around
to look for him, and it was this momentary lapse in concentration
that cost him.

Cave Canem lunged towards Shockwave and sank his teeth into
his leg.

Shockwave screamed and toppled back to the ground; the black
dog growled and forced its jaws down deeper and Shockwave's
scream increased in intensity. Resonance shouted her teammate's
name and Clare looked in horror as she saw the blood beginning to
drip from Cave Canem's teeth and the dark, wet stain appearing on
the now torn leg of Shockwave's sweats. Resonance was first to react, shouting angrily at Cave Canem, who turned his attention to
her; letting go of Shockwave's leg, he barked threateningly, blood
and spittle spraying from his jaws, and began to bound towards
them.

Resonance held out an arm to Clare and muttered *"Get ready,"*
and Clare, terrified, solidified a thick layer of mist over her softball
bat and reared it back, preparing to begin another scrap anew –

There was nothing else for it. Linus twisted quickly back to
avoid the blow and let himself fall directly into the lake beneath
him, passing through its surface to re-emerge behind Artifice by
the fire hydrant he had crashed into before.

There was a second in which Artifice did not move, as he processed Linus' sudden disappearance. Then he whirled around,
searching, before finally noticing him standing only metres away.

On his face was drawn an expression of astonishment, the likes of which Linus had not seen before, and he felt something in his chest flutter with the surprise of seeing it.

"*You–?*" Artifice began, an edge of something almost like fury in his voice. He shut his mouth and his forehead crinkled into a glower, and for the first time Linus could see that Artifice was well and truly angry.

"So you got your Ability back," he growled. "I knew I should have killed you when I had the chance. Well, no matter. I won't be making that mistake again."

There was a sharp sputtering and hissing sound, like electricity, and Linus glanced down and saw with alarm that Artifice's hands were crackling with a thin white lightning that snaked around his palms and seemed to spark and flicker. He looked back up at Artifice's face and saw that he was smiling, and somehow, although that smile seemed as charming and bewitching as ever, there was something unnerving about it too.

As Artifice began to move towards him, Linus frantically searched the area around himself for Mallory's tyre iron to defend himself with; but as he looked down, he caught his own reflection in the water beneath him, and he suddenly had a wild idea.

He glanced back up quickly and saw behind Artifice, Rehua pushing himself back up to his feet again, the knife still in his arm; he advanced on Artifice with a bellow and Artifice whirled around too late as Rehua grabbed him and hoisted him above his head.

Linus acted quickly – dropping hard onto his knees, he slammed both his hands flat down onto the surface of the water and shouted Rehua's name; Rehua locked eyes with him and then hurled Artifice towards the flooded ground beneath them with an almighty roar, and Artifice vanished into the surface of the water –

Shockwave hadn't felt in this much agony in a long time. Conflicting messages ran through his brain; the pain in his leg was sharp and focused and absolutely excruciating, but the shock of the injury was beginning to cloud his mind and he felt partially as if he were in a daze. He could see Resonance and Clare continuing to fight Cave Canem through his haze and he shook himself out of his trance, willing himself to push through the shock and stay awake and focused on the mission before him.

He put one shaking hand to his left leg and his palm came away stained with blood. Trying to fight off the feeling of nausea, he began to push himself over and up onto his hands and knees, keeping as much weight off his left leg as possible. His vision swam in and out of focus, and as he fought back the urge to collapse, his gaze fell upon Cave Canem only metres away.

All of a sudden, an uncontrollable rage welled up within Shockwave, a raging fire that began in his chest and overflowed into the rest of his body, spilling into his head, his arms, his stomach, making him see red; filling him to the brim with such fury that he let loose a wild, animal scream, the sound filling him up to his very core – suddenly he was flooding with energy and he let it fuel his Ability, drawing back his fist and driving it into the ground with the force of a meteor.

The concrete beneath Shockwave split deep, cracked deeper, the crater sinking in so far and the fractures splintering out so wide that an asteroid may as well have landed in the square; Cave

Canem yelped and scrabbled for purchase as the asphalt beneath him shattered to pieces and Clare staggered as the ground shook but Resonance merely drew herself up tall, drinking in the kinetic energy generated by Shockwave's earth-shattering punch, and she became *strong*.

Resonance grinned and reached out for Clare, yelling her name, and Clare looked at the determined look on her face and understood. She dropped her softball bat, running towards Resonance, and she leapt, arm outstretched; Resonance grabbed her by the wrist, spinning around tight, then launching Clare forwards towards Cave Canem with incredible force.

Clare drew both her hands back as she shot forwards and the fog swirled in thick and fast to form a massive hammer that she gripped tight and swung *hard* at Cave Canem, the hammer finding its target and knocking the black dog high up into the air ——

—— and Artifice came hurtling out of the high window of the Epic Theatre, falling in a fast arc, and in the same moment Cave Canem was thrown upwards and the two collided in midair; suddenly there was a *crack* and a flash of bright white lightning and somebody screamed, and before anyone could move all the lights in the square went out and there was the sound of bodies hitting the ground.

...Silence.

For a while nobody moved. No one spoke, and the only sounds to be heard were the soft rushing of water and the faint whispers of ragged breathing.

Slowly, the streetlamps came back to life again. Five figures collected themselves and looked around at each other. Resonance, bruised and battered, Clare looking much the same; Shockwave with his bloodied leg and bloodied hands. Rehua, dripping wet, pulling the knife from his arm, and Linus, looking ashen and shaking. They all studied each other, wordlessly acknowledged each other's safety, then began to gather to see what had happened.

Two bodies lay in a tangled, crumpled heap on the ground, one on top of the other. Above, Artifice, soaked to the bone and his hands smoking slightly, blood trickling down his face and the whites of his eyes showing; well and truly senseless. And pinned below, a pool of blood underneath him, a handsome, dark-haired youth with startling blue eyes, his clothes torn, his hair dishevelled and bloody gashes visible on his arms and at his side.

The true face of Cave Canem.

Cavall Robinson.

Cavall glared up at them from beneath Artifice with fierce, wild eyes, wheezing and struggling for breath. He drew back his lips and snarled at them savagely as they drew close and Resonance could see Shockwave's blood still on his teeth.

Shockwave, using Rehua for support, stared coolly down at Cavall.

"Cavall Robinson, I take it," he said calmly. "You've sure gone and caused a lot of hell for a lot of people."

Cavall didn't speak, only growling and spitting a mouthful of blood out at Shockwave's feet. Even as a human, even without his Ability, he still seemed to retain some of the feral spirit of the black dog he had been. Perhaps that black dog had echoed a hidden part of the Vigilante that had embodied him. Perhaps that part of him had been amplified by his Ability to become a part of his nature. And perhaps that nature had spilled out onto the surface to possess him — a possession that he couldn't control, but which could be kept in check with the increasing of his Vigilante energy.

"So all the bloodshed," Shockwave murmured. "This toxic compulsion for more power. It was all to buy you time."

Something in Shockwave's words seemed to reach Cavall. His growling died down in his throat, shoulders relaxing, his hands opening from the claws they had been curled into. When he spoke, his voice was low and sober.

"That's all I ever wanted."

Shockwave paused, taking in his words.

"To what end, Robinson?" he asked quietly. "Why the urge to be great — to gain so much energy? Why the need to destroy?"

Blood trickled down Cavall's chin.

"Not to destroy," he answered. "To create."

Shockwave frowned.

"…Your music." Clare murmured faintly. Cavall glanced at her.

"My music," he echoed. He turned his gaze back to Shockwave.

"I didn't want to be great," he said softly. "I just wanted to be good enough."

Shockwave didn't respond. Everyone's eyes turned to him, trying to read the aloof expression on his face with varying degrees of success. It seemed very briefly as if he were going to say or do something further, but he did nothing. Instead, he turned and began to limp slowly over to one of the benches outside the Epic, gingerly lowering himself down onto the seat with a long, rattling sigh.

Resonance continued to watch Cavall for a moment further. His eyelids fluttered as he battled briefly with unconsciousness, then finally he went slack, slipping into oblivion. Turning her attention away, Resonance began to walk over to Shockwave, the others quietly following suit.

Rehua hunkered down and inspected Shockwave's leg with a grimace.

"Doesn't look too good," he commented grimly. Shockwave only gave a half-hearted shrug.

"It'll get better," he said. Rehua undid the scarf from around his uninjured arm, trying to bite back on his pain as he did so, and began to tie it tightly around Shockwave's bloody leg just under the knee. Shockwave frowned.

"Use that on yourself." He tried to wave Rehua away but Rehua only batted his hand out of the way, pulling the ends of the scarf into a tight knot that made Shockwave grit his teeth and hiss sharply in pain. When he was done, Rehua sat down on the bench beside his teammate.

Shockwave glanced back at Artifice and Cavall Robinson, lying in an unconscious heap on the ground, and turned back to look at them all again. There were the shadows of exhaustion beginning to show on his features under the smears of dried blood streaked on his face, but he looked as serious as always. During their fight, Clare had thought that she could almost feel his aggression, radiating off him as if in waves, but now that sensation seemed to have disappeared and he just looked tired and sober – and perhaps (or so Clare thought) a little bit sad.

"This here, tonight," Shockwave began, his voice low and his tone inscrutable. "What we did here... it was a miracle. By all accounts, we shouldn't have been able to win."

"But we did," Resonance chipped in. Shockwave nodded.

"But we did," he echoed. He looked to Clare and Linus.

"Clare. Linus." He acknowledged them both. "I want to thank you for your help. I know I said otherwise, but even if our success was 90% luck, we wouldn't have been able to win tonight without you."

Rehua winked at Linus and Resonance clapped Clare on the shoulder. Linus flushed, speechless, and Clare smiled, a little flustered, not knowing quite how to reply. She looked away, embarrassed, and her gaze fell on Artifice and Cavall. Suddenly she remembered something.

"Shockwave?" The brown-haired Vigilante looked up at her and raised his eyebrows. "Can I ask you a question?"

Shockwave paused for a second, then shrugged a shoulder.

"Sure."

Clare thought for a second how to frame her words.

"Yesterday, when you were telling us why you wanted to do all this... you said you wanted to make Cave Canem... Cavall... and Artifice pay for what they had done with their lives. So just now... How come you stopped?"

Shockwave was quiet for a moment. He looked away over his

shoulder.

"To be honest…" he began. He trailed off. A sudden frown came over his features and he straightened up in his seat.

"Hang on," he said. "Who's that?"

Everyone turned around.

At the far end of the square by the opera house stood several forms, silhouetted in the thinning night fog. They started to move forwards into the square, and as they drew closer, their shapes became elucidated; five figures, three men, two women, strode towards them, four of them wearing uniform black suits and the fifth dressed in a bespoke grey three-piece suit. All of them wore dark glasses.

The four black-suited figures halted by the bodies of Artifice and Cavall and began to turn them over, and the fifth, the one in the grey three-piece, came towards them as Shockwave struggled to stand up and Rehua hastened to support him. Resonance, Clare and Linus stood to face the newcomer.

He was a tall, lean man with dark skin and strong, chiselled features, probably no older than thirty; he had silver earrings in his ears, his hair was neatly combed back off his face, and there was a small scar running through his left brow. The man took off his dark glasses and folded them, placing them neatly into the breast pocket of his bespoke suit, and Linus noticed with surprise that the man's eyes were two different colours – his right a jade green and his left an icy blue.

"What's going on here?" Shockwave demanded, and the man looked him over.

"I assume you are the ones responsible for these two?" His voice was deep, sonorous. Almost hypnotic.

"What if we are?"

The man smiled, and it seemed a pleasant smile, but there was something secretive lurking under the surface of it as well.

"Please," the man said. "Don't mistake this as a confrontation. I'm just here to thank you. That's all."

"Thank us?" The man nodded.

"We have been searching for this one for a while." He gestured over to Artifice and Cavall, now separated and lying flat on their backs. "He has proved himself to be... elusive, to say the least. But now we have him and it's thanks to you."

"And who might 'we' be?" Resonance asked, suspicious.

"Forgive me," the man chuckled. "I neglected to introduce myself. You may call me Gale. My associates and I have need of this young man that you so successfully incapacitated tonight, and because of your assistance our mission is now over."

Metres away, the black-suited men and women began to haul Artifice and Cavall up off the ground. Shockwave noticed and made to move forward but the man Gale sidestepped him and casually blocked him off.

"Please," he said gently. "Your part is over. Don't intrude any further than is necessary. You understand?" He flashed a set of brilliant white teeth at them and swiftly turned before any of them could respond, leading the black-suited men and women as they carried Artifice and Cavall away and out of the square. They were all too stunned to react and too tired to follow or fight any further, so they simply watched as the enemies they had fought so hard to beat were whisked away before them in an instant.

"Why would they need Cavall?" Linus asked quietly, perturbed. "If what I think happened actually happened, then his Ability..."

Resonance *hmm*'d, concerned.

"Maybe we've got our next mystery all ready and cut out for us. Right, Shock?"

Shockwave grunted and Rehua wordlessly persuaded him to sit back down on the bench.

"Maybe," Shockwave said. He sounded tired again. "But not now. For now I think we all need to go home and rest."

"I know I sure could do with some rest," a voice called.

Everyone became alert once more and looked up to see two familiar figures standing at the edge of the square.

Their hair tousled, black smudges of dirt on their faces and with bloodied knees, Fisticuffs and Mallory stood together, both exhausted but smiling. There was blood on the studded knuckles of Fisticuffs' gloves and her lip was split; at her side was Mallory's crowbar, a red stain on its side. Mallory's cargo pants were black as soot on the sides of her face and her elbows were grazed; the gauntlet that she'd made was missing and her right hand where it had sat was riddled with numerous small cuts.

Fisticuffs and Mallory glanced at each other and laughed. The former raised the crowbar at her side and tossed it lightly to Mallory. Mallory held up her hand and suddenly the crowbar was within her grasp, fast as lightning.

It happened so fast that it was almost as if it had been drawn to her.

Like she was a magnet.

CHAPTER THIRTEEN

THE NIGHT, ONCE MORE

The City at night could be a pretty thing.

Take this night, for instance. The way the lights from street-lamps, traffic lights and shop windows shone in the blackness gave a soft, gentle glow to the dark, a colourful reflection of the stars in the night sky above. The streets, wet from the evening rain, glimmered with the echoes of the luminescence that it lay below, and a veil of fog blanketed the ground, a diaphanous cobweb cover that softened the edges of the buildings and washed the City white.

And it was also a safe thing.

For though petty crooks and other bad sorts would occasionally roam the night, they didn't go unpunished, and as sure as there were fish in the sea, there were Vigilantes in this concrete jungle, and as long as they were present then no wrongdoing would go un-checked and the sprawling metropolis they called home remained a good place to live.

It was hard to know exactly how many Vigilantes there were in the City, but there were enough that all would be well even with-out their collective presence; and on this night, three young Vigi-lantes sat in the garage of their flat, winding down after a successful evening on patrol.

It had been three weeks now since their fight against Cave Canem and co. and in the days following, Clare, Linus and Mallory had fully recovered from the injuries they'd received in battle. A team meeting had followed in which the three of them had reflected on the events that had happened, and then unanimously agreed to return to their usual lives – which, of course, included their routines as Vigilantes.

"I think we're getting better," Clare commented. She set her softball bat down against the wall and sat down on the couch.

"Better at what, exactly?" Linus asked, settling down beside her.

"Oh, you know," Clare shrugged a shoulder. "At the whole teamwork thing. Being a Vigilante posse. You know. Who knows, we might be as good as Shockwave and Resonance and Rehua one day."

Linus laughed.

"I dunno, those three are pretty great. They've been a team for a long time."

"So we'll build up some experience!" Clare grinned. "Everyone starts somewhere, right? And we got a guy tonight, didn't we?"

Mallory, sitting at her workbench as usual, smiled.

"Only just," she replied. "We might be getting better, but we were still pretty fortunate on this one."

"Oh, come on." Clare waved her hand. "Let's give ourselves some more credit, yeah? You might call it luck, but I call it skill."

"Good thing I'm still around then, otherwise you'd just be 'luck'."

"Ooh, them's some fighting words, they are."

"What do you mean by 'still' around, Mallory?" Linus asked, curious.

"Oh." Mallory looked for a moment as if she'd said something she hadn't meant to, but then laughed at her own mistake.

"Three weeks ago," she said. "After that big fight we did together. Maddi invited me to join up with her."

"And 'Maddi' would be...?"

"Ah, shoot. You didn't just hear me say that. I meant Fisticuffs."

Clare gasped loudly and Linus bolted upright in his seat.

"Are you serious?" Clare exclaimed. "Fisticuffs? *The* Fisticuffs? Are we talking about the same person here?"

"I was surprised too." Mallory looked embarrassed, but pleased. "She said I had the makings of a great Vigilante in me though."

"Fisticuffs. Wow." Linus flopped back in the couch. "Why did you say no? You could be off on some great adventure right now."

"Are you kidding? And leave you two unchecked? I don't think so."

"Typical Mallory." Clare laughed. "Wow. Fisticuffs though. Sounds like you really made an impression. She must really like you."

"Yeah, well." Mallory seemed suddenly abashed and she looked back to her workbench, continuing to tinker with her tools. "She's a pretty great Vigilante. Definitely worth the hype and admiration."

"Well, thanks for sticking around, anyway. Now we can keep on trying to figure out for all of eternity if we only succeed because of luck or skill." Clare snapped her fingers suddenly. "Hey, let's call ourselves that!"

Linus stared.

"What? Team 'you call it luck, I call it skill'? I think that's a too much of a mouthful for a one-liner."

"Well, no, that's not quite what I meant." Clare laughed. "I meant as our Aliases or something. We still haven't chosen any yet."

"Oh yeah." Linus looked suddenly embarrassed. "Actually I've been thinking about it a little. What I what mine to be? I dunno. What do you think about 'Eidolon'?"

"Oh, nice!" Clare looked delighted. "Like a ghost or a spectre. I like it! You should go with that."

Linus grinned bashfully.

"Cheers. How about you?"

"Yeah, I've actually thought a bit about it too. And I was kidding about the luck-skill thing by the way. How about..." Clare swept an arm in the air, as if to underline her words. "'*Aurae*'!"

Linus couldn't hold back his amusement at her dramatic delivery.

"Very mysterious," he said. "And fitting. I like it."

"Darn straight you should. How about you, Mal?" Clare called over to Mallory and the girl looked up from her workbench again.

"Yeah, I decided mine a little while ago," she replied. "I think 'Forge' should just about do it."

Clare and Linus *ooh*'ed in unison.

"That's a good one," Clare said. "'Forge' sounds awesome. Really cool."

Mallory smiled.

"Thanks." And then: "Hey, want to see something else that's really cool?"

Clare and Linus glanced at each other, then looked back to Mallory, nodding eagerly.

Mallory turned back to her workbench, the corner in which sat her usual stack of metal plates. She reached out her arm towards them.

The stack of plates vibrated, then suddenly shot towards Mallory – but instead of just coming into her hand, they wrapped themselves around her forearm, plate after plate, layer after layer, around her wrist and over her palm, winding themselves around her hand into a slick metal gauntlet that flexed and moved as Mallory bent her wrist and wiggled her fingers.

Mallory glanced back at Clare and Linus. Their eyes were wide in awe and excitement, and as they regarded the gauntlet newly formed on Mallory's hand, they looked to each other and said in a single hushed whisper:

"*Cool.*"

Out in the darkness of the City, a single silhouette ran with silent footsteps to the edge of a building and perched themselves safely on the parapet. Another shape treaded over the rooftop to join then, crouching just beside their teammate on the ledge. The first figure glanced back, looked around, then pushed his hood back off his head and pulled the scarf down from his face.

"Where's Resonance?" Shockwave asked, a frown on his features.

"She was just behind us." Rehua pulled down his own scarf and turned back around to look behind them. At that moment, Resonance's silhouette appeared at the opposite edge of the building, and she pulled herself up onto the rooftop and ran over to join her teammates.

"Sorry," she muttered as she came to the ledge, tugging her own scarf down around her neck. "Caught myself on the drainpipe. Something sharp, I think."

Rehua beckoned to her, holding out his arm.

"Here," he said. Resonance wiped a streak of blood onto on her forearm and held out her right hand to reveal a gash on her palm.

Rehua took her hand in his; for a second nothing happened, but then Resonance could feel warmth as the energy flowed from her teammate through to her, healing the wound on her hand. He let go and Resonance inspected her palm to find the gash had gone, leaving behind only a thin white line. She grinned at Rehua.

"Thanks."

"You're welcome."

"Are we done?" Shockwave broke in. Resonance and Rehua both looked to him.

"Sure," Resonance responded. "Where to next?"

Shockwave pointed at the paved rooftop courtyard of the building across the way, maybe four or five metres across the alleyway below them.

"We'll keep moving south," he said. "Think you can jump that?"

"Please," Resonance scoffed. "I've been working on my precisions since before you were born."

"Is that so? I knew you were an ancient old fogey."

Rehua guffawed and Shockwave grinned as Resonance swatted him in the arm. He stood up on the parapet and bowed mockingly, making a grand sweeping gesture at the building across the way.

"Go on then," he said. "You can go first. Age before beauty, after all."

"Oh, is somebody else coming?"

Rehua's chortles turned into a roar of laughter and Shockwave straightened and dropped his hands to his sides, but he was still smiling.

"Fine then, you old bat, I'll go first. Didn't anyone ever tell you to respect your leaders?"

"Didn't anyone ever tell you to respect your elders? That's us, by the way."

"Sure, sure."

Shockwave hopped down off the ledge and walked back a few steps, pulling his scarf back up around his nose and mouth. He stared out at the building opposite, arms down at his sides and his hands spread out; for a few seconds he was silent, concentrating, but then suddenly he moved, running towards the edge. As he drew close to the ledge he jumped up, propelling himself with a powerful kick off the parapet – he soared into the air, twisted into an effortless front flip at the height of his jump, and landed on the rooftop of the next building, tucking into a smooth roll and coming back up on his feet near the centre of the courtyard. He turned back around to look at Resonance and Rehua and held out his arms in a mock-taunting gesture of invitation, shouting something that neither of them could hear.

"Show-off," Resonance uttered, a smile on her lips. She looked at Rehua. "You or me next?"

Rehua waved at the gap.

"Be my guest. Show us how it's done, 'Kinetic'."

"Oh, you two are a riot, you are."

Resonance and Rehua stepped back from the ledge, pulling their scarves back up. Resonance judged her distances. She paused for a moment, drew in a sharp breath, then launched herself forwards and jumped off the edge of the building.

Down below, in the backalleys of the City, a lone Vigilante was engaged in close combat with a trio of thugs all wielding knives. She threw a punch at one and downed another, but the third managed to dodge back, wildly swinging his knife in her direction.

As the blade came forward, the Vigilante twisted backwards to dodge and threw her leg up in a kick that knocked the blade out of the man's hand and sent it skittering away; as his eyes followed his lost weapon, she swung her foot back around again, catching him in the shoulder with her foot and sending him crashing to the ground.

The Vigilante hopped from one foot to the other, her long braid bouncing at her back, hands curled into loose fists before her. She laughed down at the men sprawled on the ground.

"You boys had enough yet?" she taunted. "Or have you still got it in you for some more?"

A shadow of movement above made her look up. At the edge of the rooftop of the building to her left, an indistinct somebody hopped down from the parapet and stepped back out of view. Seconds later, the same silhouette reappeared again, leaping off the brink of the building, flipping in midair, then vanishing over the edge of the apartment block to her right. Following them, another figure, smaller, launched themselves off the ledge and into the air, and only a split second after that another, bigger shape followed, the two of them disappearing and landing – presumably – safely on the rooftop they were aiming for.

The Vigilante grinned up at the sky. She knew exactly who that had been.

She looked back down to see her opponents had staggered back to their feet again and the third had picked up his knife. Her eyes crinkled in amusement and she pulled one foot back behind her and clenched her leather-gloved fists.

"Looks like this party's getting crazy," she said, and she sounded pleased.

The men lurched towards her.

"Let's *rock*!" Fisticuffs crowed, and threw her fist forward with a roar.

EPILOGUE

In a hidden location far away from the stretch of the City, a young man opened his eyes to find himself lying on a single-mattress bed in a square and windowless room.

It was a big room, maybe five by six metres. The walls and floor were made up of large white panels that reflected the harsh fluorescent light off their every surface and made him squint. Save for the bed he was lying on, the only other objects in the room were a rectangular aluminium table in the middle of the floor, set out with one chair on either side, and a domed security camera in the corner of the high ceiling.

He sat up and swung his legs over the side of the bed. An uncomfortable scratching against his skin made him look down at himself. He was dressed in what appeared to be medical scrubs, nondescript, made of starchy white cotton and as plain and white as the room he was in. His feet were bare, he noticed, and his arms and legs seemed to have been scrubbed clean, though he thought he could see the telltale yellow marks of healing bruises here and there. There was a cotton wad under a piece of tape stuck to the crook of his elbow, and faded brown lines swirling over his right hand and forearm.

The sound of a click made him look up, and across the floor from him a hidden door swung open from the panels in the wall and a stranger stepped into the room.

He was a tall, lean man with dark skin and strong, chiselled features, probably no older than thirty. He wore a well-cut grey three-piece suit, pristine black loafers, and dark shades over his eyes. He had silver earrings in his ears, his hair was neatly combed back off his face, and there was a small scar running through his left brow. Against the stark white panelling of the room, he stood out like a dark swan in a snowstorm, elegance and all. He carried himself straight and upright, exuding an aura of authority, his hands clasped behind his back.

"Shaan Mehra," the tall man said, and his voice was deep and sonorous.

Shaan stood up from the bed and the floor was cold beneath his feet. The man smiled, charming yet mysterious, and beckoned to him with a finger.

"Come," he said, and he gestured to the table. "Sit."

The tall man in the grey suit sat down straight-backed in a chair and Shaan, not knowing what else to do, came and sat opposite him. The man took off his dark glasses and folded them, placing them neatly into the breast pocket of his suit, and Shaan could see that his eyes were two different colours – his right a jade green and his left an icy blue.

The man folded his hands neatly on the table before him.

"I'm sure you must have a lot of questions," he said, and Shaan thought he could hear a trace of an accent in his words. He considered his answer carefully.

"You could say that," he eventually replied, his voice calm and collected. The man's smile seemed to widen.

"Things like, 'where am I', 'how long have I been here'... 'who are you' and 'how do you know who I am', correct?"

Shaan paused then nodded stiffly, and the tall man chuckled.

"It is to be expected," he said. "Well, Shaan Mehra. At present you are in a secret facility in a location I am not at liberty to reveal the name of. You have been here three weeks, and we collected you immediately following a skirmish you had in the City with several other individuals. As for how we know your name... well. Let's just say we've been searching for you for a while now."

"And who might 'we' be?"

"Of course. My apologies. You may call me Gale. I am a representative of a small collective of extraordinary individuals, much like yourself. We call ourselves the Pantheon. My colleagues and I came to learn of you and your... *unique*... capabilities... and we hoped that we might be able to acquire your willing cooperation to assist us in our work."

"Sorry," Shaan replied coolly. "But I already have a job."

"Ah, yes. As a manager for a young musician, correct? Cavall Robinson, was it?"

A thought suddenly occurred to Shaan. If he was here, then where were his friends? Where were Faye and Anton? And more importantly, where was Cavall?

His realisation must have shown on his face, for the man Gale smiled at him.

"Relax," he said, soothing yet taunting in the same breath. "Your friends are here too, and they are safe... for now."

Shaan narrowed his eyes at him.

"What do you want from me?" he asked, and he sounded cold. The man Gale held up his hands in a placating gesture.

"Nothing much," he replied. "Just that you listen. A moment of your time, if you will. If you decline, I will respect your decision. We will let you go and you may return safely to your home. But I cannot guarantee that you will ever see your associates again."

"And the alternative?"

"You cooperate with us. Work with us for a time. And then you may be reunited with your friends."

"Forgive me if I sound ungrateful, but that's not much of a choice."

"It's the only one we'll offer you."

Shaan looked to his hands, gripped tightly together in his lap. His knuckles were white and he felt sick. He hated not being in control of a situation, he really did – and this was so goddamn cliché. He wanted so badly to say no, even if just for his pride – but what other choice did he have? He swallowed hard and looked back up, staring the man Gale in his mismatched blue and green eyes.

"Alright then," he said quietly, and he felt cold inside. "I accept."

The man Gale flashed a set of brilliant white teeth at him in a grin.

"Good," he replied. He held out a hand to Shaan.

"Shaan Mehra. Welcome to the Pantheon."

fin.

ABOUT THE AUTHOR

Michelle Kan is an independent filmmaker/videographer and writer based in Wellington, New Zealand. *No More Heroes* is her debut novel and was initially written during her first National Novel Writing Month in 2014.

Michelle is passionate about the arts, exploring her cultural heritage through her creative output, and is a lover of graphic novels, video games, action/martial arts films and parkour/movement disciplines – all profound influences which helped her shape the world and characters of *No More Heroes*.

Michelle can be found at http://facebook.com/fishandswallow

CPSIA information can be obtained
at www.ICGtesting.com
Printed in the USA
LVHW011601170119
604290LV00018B/950